D0780123

The Witness of St. Ansgar's

The Witness of St. Ansgar's

A NOVEL

Francis W. Nielsen

Steerforth Press
Hanover, New Hampshire

Library of Congress Cataloging-in-Publication Data

Nielsen, Francis, 1920–1990.
The witness of St. Ansgar's : a novel / Francis Nielsen. — 1st. ed.
p. cm.
ISBN-13: 978-1-58642-100-7 (alk. paper)
ISBN-10: 1-58642-100-X (alk. paper)
1. New York (N.Y.) – History — 1898–1951 — Fiction. 2. Manhattan (New York, N.Y.) — Fiction. 3. Acolytes — Fiction. 4. Franciscan friars — Fiction. 5. Monastic and religious life — Fiction. 6. Working class — Fiction. 7. Catholic fiction. gsafd I. Title.

PS3564.I3494W58 2006
813'.54–dc22
2005029899

FIRST EDITION

To Will

Contents

♦1♦

Friar Benigno

Joseph Zoller, rechristened Friar Benigno, was honored on the sixtieth anniversary of his admission into the order.

The high altar was an island of flowers, candles, and opulent hangings. The side aisles were draped with strands of colored lights, the center aisle canopied with banners, and all the walls and arches festooned with swags of bunting. It was high pageantry. The interior of St. Ansgar's shimmered, enchanted by the full blaze of lights.

The sanctuary was packed with visiting clergy and religious in their distinctive garb: Dominicans, Benedictines, Passionists, Carmelites, Jesuits, Franciscans, Paulists, Augustinians, and one lone boy in plain cassock and white surplice.

Three priests in golden vestments stood at the high altar, swinging censers in short arcs, puffs of the sweet-smelling incense rising; from overhead the tremendous peal of five great bells rang in staggered harmony.

Not a seat to be had, every pew was packed, the congregation moving as one, standing, sitting, kneeling, one great unified mass. All those voices, the swell of the organ, combining into a hymn of exultation.

Mario's senses reeled, he was made drunk by the ritual, the panoply, the mystery.

Who was Joseph Zoller who came to be called Friar Benigno? In time Mario would be expected to say, to bear witness, but not then, not yet.

Friar Nicodemus, that most illustrious among the friars, a Roman scholar, an august preacher, was in the pulpit, extolling Benigno's virtues, his years of service. Every Dutchie in the congregation agreed with the words of praise uttered by the roly-poly preacher. He was "their" Benigno, theirs! Baumer the baker, Moltke the butcher, Samuessen the undertaker, Wolfram the organist, Hans the sexton, Mario the boy, everybody on that banner day knew Benigno.

Mario watched him in the midst of his crowded sanctuary. He was seated on a wooden folding chair. Benigno refused to sit on one of the plush, red-velvet-cushioned side chairs used for such solemn occasions. He was dressed in his habit and he wore his skullcap to protect his bald head from the draft which swept across the sanctuary. His stubby beard rested against his tunic, his face was grave, his strong, thickset body appeared tense. He was putting up with this fuss. It was not his idea, but the order insisted upon making it a jubilee. Mario knew he was squirming.

And yet it was appropriate. All the pomp and ceremony, honoring Benigno, because in a very real sense Benigno was the embodiment of St. Ansgar's. Some of the more argumentative Dutchie parishioners would have it that Benigno *was* St. Ansgar's church.

It was this kind of braying, ignorant talk which would get Benigno's goat.

"Ah, they're noodleheads. You never know what they got in their heads. Such nonsense! When you hear them say such things, Mario, you close your ears."

"But you did see them building the church, Brother."

"Oh, ja. I see them put it up. But lots of the people at that time see it, too. In them days there are no buildings around where the church is being put up. It is a field. They have goats eating the grass. There is a spring where the people come with their jugs to get the soft water.

"They cart in the blocks of stone in long, flat wagons, sometimes three teams of horses pull the loads on account of they is so heavy. The blocks is all marked. The masons with their hammers, how they ring when they hit the stones, they are like fliers they are so high up in scaffolding. Ja, I see them build St. Ansgar's."

One time Benigno took Mario outside, to the east wall of the church, to show him the buttresses. You couldn't see them from the street anymore because a large commercial building had been shoehorned in next to the church on that side.

"Everything have a beginning, Mario. You, and though I am so old you don't maybe believe it, I have a beginning once, too, so naturally St. Ansgar's have a beginning. Everything, everything, except God."

Benigno was born halfway along the block from the church, he could look from a hallway window and watch the walls of the church rise course after course. He could hear those echoing hammer blows, the shouts of the workmen, the hiss of the steam derricks swinging up the stones.

"But the church it was not built by the order. Oh, no, not on your tintype. It ain't built for Dutchies. We ain't got the money. Nah. It was built for the rich people, ja. Rich people live on Stanley Street in them days. You see, them rich people they never think one day the Dutchies is going to come off the boats and settle here. But by the time the church is up, it's a different story . . . the Dutchies have come!

"The rich people is all upset to see so many Dutchies getting dumped on the West Side. They don't want to be with them greenhorns. They don't want their kids playing with us who can't speak no English. They don't want their daughters and sisters to get married to Dutchie men. Ach, I tell you, it was a fix they was in. Here they have this beautiful new church, just finish, so new the paint still smell, and the Dutchies take it over. Ja, the Dutchies see a church, they come to it. But the rich people they skedaddle. They move out of the neighborhood, move uptown where it is ritzy and no Dutchie have come. Ja, after they have flown the coop, it get to be a very ticklish sitooation. What they going to do with this new church? The Dutchies can't pay for it, they is too poor. So what happen, the bishop of the diocese transfer the church to the order, a bunch of Bavarian friars. It be rededicated to St. Ansgar, and that be how it all start. And if it had not happen that way, well, maybe I never become a friar. Maybe I grow up to follow my father's trade which was cigar maker.

"My mother and father have come from Passau, just like your grandmother and grandfather. How come they settle here? This is where the boat stops and unloads! And after the first boatload, then the rest follows. They stick together like in the Old Country. Today it is hard to believe how bad it was back then. Ja, tough days. That was the time after the Civil War. There was riots, people hating one another, food was something to get . . . daily bread. I remember my mother and father worrying about how they feed us. My uncle Emil who live with us, he come on some rotten potatoes which he bring home. By jingo neddies, you think he have found gold."

Mario would listen to these memories spellbound. Benigno was talking of days which somehow only seemed out of a history book. Those events actually had happened! Mario was astonished.

"Ja, one time, and I never forget this. My mother and father, my uncle Emil, and my sisters, we get all dressed up on a weekday, because there's no work that partickler day. I was very young, very. I am on Uncle Emil's shoulders. We go to Tenth Avenue. At that time there is a railroad station down there. The trains come in to there from all over the country. They change the steam engines there. This day I talk about, we find the place filled with the people. They stand on the platform, on the street, on the tracks. And they are so quiet, so quiet, Mario. They got their hats off, and many of the people have tears running down their face, but they are so quiet. I whisper into Uncle Emil's ear what is wrong. Why are the people the way they are. I never forget what he say . . . never.

"The President Lincoln's body is in that train!

"Ja, his body was being taken home. I see the casket in the railroad car, a flag is over it, the people lining the tracks. I never forget that sight. It is so awful quiet, just the steam engine it pant . . . Ja, it pant like it been running hard . . . ja . . . ja . . ."

Mario's eyes filled with tears, so moved was he by the description of the funeral train.

"I remember when your grandmother and grandfather comes to this country. I remember your father and mother getting married. I put the chrysanthemums on the altar for their marriage ceremony. Ja, I have even talk to your mother the day she come to be blessed because she is carrying you . . . ja. I tell you something else. You have cried all through your christening. Ja, all the way through, like you don't approve of it."

Mario asked how it was Benigno had become a friar.

"I am not the best kid in the world, I tell you. I have an awful, terrible temper! And I do a lot of fighting with the fists. I get into very much trouble. My father is pretty much disgusted with me. And I don't go to church. I smoke. And I curse. One day, after I have been up to my old tricks, my father grab me and shake me up. He is boiling mad. He drag me upstairs, make me take a bath, make me put on my suit, and he strong-arm me to St. Ansgar's. I don't have no idea what he's up to.

"Well, anyways, it happens that a mission is being given by a very famous preacher, Friar Polycarp. He could have been a Dominican he is such a talker. The mission is being given for wife beaters, drunks, crooks, and as my father says to me: 'For good-for-nothing kids like you, Joseph Zoller!'"

Benigno smiled: "I wasn't very old at the time and I'm the only young one with all of them older people in the pews and I think they all looking at me. I tell you, when that Friar Polycarp look down from the pulpit, he seem to be right on top of you, he is one big fella. I get the feeling those black eyes of his is seeing right down inside of me. I tell you, Mario, he scare the lights out of me. He have a great big black beard, and his eyebrows is like brushes, and his voice is like thunder. Whew, he is something.

"He start in on St. Francis. Telling how wild he was when he was a kid, run around a lot, raise Cain. He was a kind of a good-for-nothing kid, rich too. God fill him with the idea of being the poorest of the poor, the servant of the minores, the poor little folk. St. Francis takes off his rich clothes, he gives them away to the poor, he goes to the lepers and tend them. I remember how Friar Polycarp draw himself up, he is tremendous, and he cry: 'St. Francis he don't move uptown like the rich people. He don't beat the women. He don't drink until he is drunk like a pig. He don't rob and steal and crook.'

"I tell you, Mario, inside I am shaking like a leaf, that fella he have a hand around my heart . . .

"Anyways, he goes on, and tells how St. Francis dressed in rags goes before Pope Innocent to get him to okay an order set up to serve the minores. The pope have a dream the walls of the Lateran palace is crumbling and that a beggar man comes along and holds up the wall. And lo and behold, by jingo neddies, along comes St. Francis in rags, just like the beggar in the dream the pope have. So the pope tells him to go ahead and start the order."

Benigno paused, took off his glasses, and said thoughtfully: "Ah, Mario, it have one heck of a wallop for me what this friar is saying. I don't know what it is that is happening then. It just strike me that this St. Francis is some fella, wonderful. He have found the worm in his path. He bend down and pick him up and move him out of the way so he not be trampled on. I feel this something inside of me, something I never have felt before, it fill me, Mario. It fill me with a wanting . . . ja, a wanting.

"My mother and father, they don't believe me, when I say I am going to become a friar. But I go and see Friar Polycarp. He make the arrangements. When I first start I think I become a priest but I got not the head for study, but I do have good hands, and I love the flowers, so I decide to become a brother. St. Francis, you know, never become a priest. He always remain a brother. I enter the order in 1872." Benigno put on his glasses, looked at Mario, and said with a straight face: "It have almost cured me of my bad temper . . . almost."

"You never wanted to leave, huh, Brother?"

"Well, I wouldn't say that . . . no, I wouldn't. When I first get out there at the motherhouse, we is in the wilds. There's no houses for miles, no streetlights, no nothing, just the wind. They give me a pair of sandals which is made like boards, and they put a scythe in my hand. I never have use one before. And then we cut oats, miles and miles of oats, with a hot, itchy woolen habit on. Ach, I'm in agony, my hands is all blistered, my feet rubbed raw, my body, every muscle sending me telegrams, and then they get me up at two o'clock in the morning . . . ja, they get me up from sleeping on a plank. It was no bed of roses to be a friar. I learn that. And nobody but the masters talks. And I get so lonely. I tell you it get so bad, I start talking to the birds . . . ja, I talk to the birds, to the pigs, to the horses . . . ja, my temper, it get pretty good and flatten out. I even run away once I am so unhappy . . .

"But a most peculiar thing, I am more unhappy away . . . this wanting I feel make me go back." Benigno paused, glanced at Mario, and murmured: "I still have the wanting. To this day. Ja, so after a while I learn to accept and live according to the Rule. The plank I sleep on at night grows softer, my sandals break in, the habit don't itch me no more, and my beard grow, and I make my solemn profession, I get my cowl, and I am a one hundred percent member of the Order Minores, a friar. And you know what happen after all of this? They ship me right back to where I come from, to Stanley Street, to St. Ansgar's where I am assigned as sacristan, can you imagine?"

Benigno laughed. "Ja, they could have sent me to a dozen other places in the country but right back here I come. And I tell you, I know it was going to happen. St. Ansgar's is never out of my mind. You should see what happen when I come back. My mother and father, my uncle Emil, they keep their distance, they can't believe that the fella with the beard and brown habit is their boy Joseph Zoller, that good-for-nothing, that one with the terrible temper. Oh, ja, ja, it's a funny thing how things happen, Mario.

"Look, I show you something . . ." Benigno searched inside his tunic pocket. He brought out a set of wooden rosary beads with a flat wooden crucifix. They looked worn from regular telling. "You see, the Dutchies have these made for me in Passau. They give them to me when I am here ten years. They make up their mind slowly, it take them ten years to accept me as sacristan. Look at it."

Mario took the rosary beads and examined them. The wood felt soft to his touch.

"Look at the back of the cross, Mario."

Mario read: "Joseph Zoller, Passau."

Mario returned the rosary.

"Ja, they all gone now. My family, so many of the old-timers. All gone . . . but you are here, Mario. You. And one day, I give you my beads."

The jubilee service continued. Friar Nicodemus in his Bavarian-inflected English was detailing Friar Benigno's years of service, his enrichment of St. Ansgar's . . .

Mario's thoughts drifted away. Somehow it seemed appointed that he should become Brother Benigno's helper. He pestered and pestered his mother to become an altar boy. She took him to see Brother Benigno. Mario could tell from her tone when talking to Benigno she was proud of her son, and making an offering of him. She'd lost all of her other children, Mario was all she had.

Benigno taught him his Latin, rehearsed him in the service ritual, and after a while Mario found himself running every day to St. Ansgar's. It was not to pray, to meditate, it was to be there, be there near Benigno . . . yes, to be there, a need, to catch the light, the colors of the stained-glass panels, the airy shafts slanting from the clerestory, and the great hush walling out the noise of the throbbing city. Yes, Mario ran to be there.

And one day Brother Benigno came to him as Mario knelt at the communion rail. Benigno looked into the boy's large, brown eyes. He said: "Come, Mario. I need a helper. You will be my helper. Ja, my helper." He touched Mario's head with his hand. "You wait for me."

Benigno changed into his civvies, a square black jacket coat, baggy black pants, and soft leather shoes. Together they marched down Stanley Street to where Mario lived.

Mario's father was at the sink in his undershirt, washing away the day's grime from his arms and elbows, the supper was cooking on the gas stove, the gas chandelier was lighted, the shadow of the fixture cast on the ceiling.

"Mario, where've you been? You're so late. Ah, Brother Benigno, come in."

"Ah, Lena, I come to explain. It be my fault Mario is late. I have keep him back. I want him for my helper."

"Get a chair, Mario. Have a glass of wine, Brother."

Mario's father dried himself, peeling away with his fingers one stubborn fleck of paint. He was a scene painter.

"I tell you why I come. I want you to tell me it's okay if Mario come and be my helper, after school and on Saturdays. I pay him."

Mario watched his mother's face light up. Already she had him fully robed, his chasuble hanging stiffly on his frame, bending over his mother, giving her his first priestly blessing. But his father, who was less visionary, turned to his son and asked: "What about it, Mario?"

Mario's face burned as he looked from one to the other, joyfully.

And so it was settled.

Mario came to learn many things; most of all he came to know Friar Benigno. He watched him, studied him, imitated him, loved him. Benigno was many men rolled into one: a brute for work, stubborn, impatient, purposeful, gruff, down to earth, a marvelous craftsman, irascible with a fierce temper, submissive, compassionate, tender, a man who never betrayed his inner life, a man who sat hunched, his cowl on his head, in one of the oaken stalls in the friary choir, his eyes closed in prayer.

Mario learned the never-ending succession of days in the church calendar, the old being reborn into the oncoming. He learned the pervasive sadness of Good Friday, the muffled air of even the city traffic on that day, the solemn changing of the friars of the Tenebrae service and the Lamentations of Jeremiah, and then the dawn of

Holy Saturday, the bells ringing joyfully, churning the air with the announcement of Christ's rising. And all the details of renewal, the blessing of the enormous Paschal candle, the striking of the flint to spark new fire, the consecration of the freshly drawn oil, the consecration of the vats of water: death and entombment, followed by resurrection and new life. All eternally repeating, and each time renewing the juices of the spirit.

Yes, Mario learned, his senses drenched by the unfolding process. And Mario recognized that not only was he affected by these times and seasons, but Benigno was, too. Yes, the old man loved the pageantry, the ritual, the tradition, loved it with an almost childlike devotion. Benigno would spare no pains, work impossible hours, to create the Good Friday sepulchre, that scene of darkness and despair. And when the night changed to the day of Holy Saturday, the entombment diorama would be bathed in dazzling light, a stone rolled from the entrance, an angel seated nearby, announcing HE IS RISEN.

But it was the season of Advent which brought out Benigno's greatest achievement. His Christmas diorama was famous the length and breadth of the West Side. For Benigno it was not just a crèche, a representation, for him it was a spiritual expression throbbing with actuality. When Mario was a small boy, his mother used to take him to St. Ansgar's to look upon the wonder of Christ's birthplace. And now Mario was on the inside, a party to the making of the scene.

At the start of Advent a side altar would be curtained off, hiding it from the public view. And then the work would begin. Every free hour, and far into the night, Benigno would construct his Christmas diorama. Bales of fresh moss, cork bark from Portugal, a painted background of the bare hills of Jerusalem (painted by Mario's father), hundreds of hand-carved wooden figures from Bavaria, and each strictly to scale. Yes, it was in this manner Mario learned of perspective.

Slowly, day by day, the transformation was wrought. Cork became stone and rocky outcroppings, moss became the earth and grass and arid pasture, the wooden platforms became the underlying topography of the Holy Land, all assembled, and peopled with the carved figures, to create a majestic drama. Shepherds with crooks on distant slopes, sheep, goats, asses, all in size and scale. Gradually the spectacle unfolded, a hillside in that distant time, in that faraway land, was filled by nomads, shepherds, beasts, and a sky pinpointed by stars, with that one great star hanging in the east. The slopes fell away to a pasture where a spring bubbled up under the rocks (the plash of water could be heard in the quiet church). And in the foreground the tumbledown stable, the tilting roof, the lighted windows of the adjacent inn, and front view of the manger, the animals, the ox chewing its cud, the asses with their ears erect, and then the principals: Joseph, Mary, and the Christ child. For a brief interval, if there was belief in the viewer, he could rise above the turmoil of Stanley Street and be subsumed in the timelessness of Bethlehem.

And that was the purpose of the Christmas display. Benigno explained the origin to Mario.

"St. Francis sets up the first Christmas scene. It was his idea. You see the people of Assisi was very poor and downtrodden, these were the little people, the minores. So Francis he make the crèche to fill them with hope, so they lift up their eyes and heart. But Francis he use real animals, in a real stable, and under the open sky. St. Francis want people to have hope, to have joy in their heart. Man have got to have hope and joy in his heart. St. Francis believe that . . . Ja, he know without hope and joy in the heart, man have no understanding of God!"

Benigno spent himself at this time of year. He never complained of his stiff and aching joints, his fatigue, his spells of dizziness. This was his small connection with St. Francis, an offering to hope and joy. And when the curtain was removed before the solemn high mass at midnight of Christmas, Benigno would stand at the back of the church, his face gray with weariness, his legs paining him so badly he clutched the pew backs to support himself, and he'd appraise his work. He'd say to Mario if he was satisfied: "Ja, so, Mario. Bethlehem in Judea, where a miracle have happened!"

Then the doors of the church would be unlocked, the Dutchies young and old would stream in, approach the Nativity scene, their eyes would take in the wonder, and perhaps for a moment what St. Francis strove for would come to pass: hope and joy in man's heart.

All these aspects of the man who sat in the sanctuary being honored on this his anniversary went through Mario's mind.

And when the ceremony was over, after the congratulations of the clergy and the religious, and after the Dutchies had surrounded him, "their" Benigno, after Mario had snuffed all those dozens of candles, Benigno tiredly came into the quiet of the second sacristy, that workplace. Mario had poured a glass of the sacramental wine for him.

Benigno sat at his desk, removed his skullcap, and groaned: "Ah, such a fuss. I tell you, not for a million dollars I ever go through such a business again." He sipped his wine. "By jingo neddies . . . I tell you, I am wore out, Mario. I be glad when tomorrow comes so we can go back to work."

When Mario pushed open one of the large street doors of the church, he found a knot of Dutchies still gathered at the bottom of the steps, men in their cluster, women in theirs. They were all chattering about what they had participated in.

Moltke the butcher: "There should be some kind of sign put up."

Baumer the baker: "How you gonna hang a sign on the street."

Samuessen the undertaker: "Put up a brass plate on the house where Benigno was born!"

Professor Wolfram the organist: "Maybe we should get in touch with Tammany Hall, they do something, huh?"

Samuessen: "Don't waste your time. They know we vote for them anyways."

Hans the sexton: "Something should be done. Someday maybe der Benigno be made a saint."

And then Mrs. Baumer, a substantial woman, opinionated and very forward, butted in: "You all talk nonsense. All of you. What we need a sign for. We all know Brother Benigno. The neighborhood knows him. The cops know him. The politicians know him. Everybody knows him. Is all these people going up in smoke that Brother Benigno be forgot? You foolish men, always foolish, stupid. We got children. They will forget Benigno? Never. We will remember Benigno . . . and our kids, too. He don't need no signs or the brass plate . . ."

Her voice was loud; it cowed the Dutchie men. Mario thought she made sense.

He saw them standing with the sunlight splashing down around them. He saw the large buildings rising up solidly on either side of the street. He saw the flash of the river. He heard the whistles of the locomotives in the freight yards. Yes, if all should pass away, Friar Benigno would endure. After all, what is memory for, if not to bear witness? Mario walked home with a quiet sense of fulfillment.

♣2♣

The Burglar Alarm

Friar Benigno knew most things about St. Ansgar's church, and what he didn't know he sensed. Sometimes Mario thought the walls, aisles, arches, statues, stained-glass windows, pews, nave were extensions of the old man, nerve endings of his. It was astonishing how he could detect the slightest alteration in the atmosphere of the church: he'd cock his head, his eyes would become intent, his whole body would tense.

"There's something going on," he'd growl, and go charging out into the church.

Benigno taught Mario that a church is a natural gathering place for a wide range of humanity, some pious, some curious, some sleepy, some homeless, some crooked, some drunk, some eccentric.

The eccentrics vexed Brother Benigno no end. He forced down his impatience, he tried to be tolerant of their peculiarities, but he never quite managed to ignore them. And he reproved himself for not showing true Franciscan compassion for these odd numbers of humanity.

There were those whose religiosity showed itself in most unusual ways. Some planted themselves in front of a particular statue and argued with the plaster saint, others would throw themselves bodily across the Pietà and weep uncontrollably, still others would travel from shrine to grotto to side altar and go through an astonishing series of movements, as if they were mechanized and timed: they'd whirl about six times to the right, then six times to the left, pause, take several dancelike steps, and throw their heads back to stare up into the high vault of the nave. This would happen day in and day out without variance. Then there were the "pawers:" Benigno called them that because they couldn't control their hands from stroking, caressing, rubbing, massaging all the religious objects in reach. Many times this obsession with touch wore away a statue's toe or staff or arm, or turned the Virgin Mary's blue cape into a thing of ugly off-white plaster. The kissers were a sub-branch of the pawers; they lipped every saint, crucifix, sacred picture.

And then there were the bathers. They'd anchor themselves by a holy water stoup and compulsively splash themselves — eyes, mouth, ears, chin — and in the course of it get the floor wet and slippery. In another category, this one quite large, were the genuflectors, individuals whose right knees seemed loosely hinged, forever bending; they couldn't go two paces forward without genuflecting. Every conceivable type of manic behavior seemed to be liberated inside of quite ordinary-appearing people once they set foot in church.

Benigno would patiently or nearly patiently watch these practitioners go through their antics, sighing audibly, sighing rather than growling. But at night such refinement didn't work. You couldn't be subtle. Benigno could not close the church at the end of the day without becoming militant. He had to stand over them, rattling his keys, growling, while he herded them toward the foyer. And they were very adroit, tricky, they'd conceal themselves in the grotto for the Madonna, yes, hide there so they could spend the night in the dark, locked church.

Yes, the grotto, or the confession boxes, or even up in the pulpit. Benigno had an established routine for flushing them out: every single night he'd search every nook and cranny, organ loft, foyer closet; it took an hour at least to make sure one of the eccentrics hadn't settled for the night. And all the while Benigno would be muttering: "Nuts . . . nuts, they be nuts!"

Another class altogether were the drifters who used the church for a flophouse, many of whom were "smoked." Smoke was a lethal drink available in all kinds of stores in those days. It ranged in price from the five-cent half-pint to the quart bottle at thirty cents; this contained enough smoke to knock out half a dozen men (or women, no sex differentiation among the imbibers). Benigno would say: "Two drinks of smoke and the fella is knocked out of his mind. It got the wallop of a mule." Certainly the alleyways, sidewalks, halls, stoops, even gutters were littered with smokers overcome by the potent liquor. Many of them sought church pews in which to collapse. The smokers gave Benigno more trouble than the nuts.

There were certain difficulties involved in picking out the smokers, distinguishing them from the sincere worshipers. After all, the church was in semi-darkness when services weren't going on, and the smokers had attained a high level of dissimulation. They aped marvelously the attitude of rapt adoration: head bent, eyes closed, body still, lips moving. For all of their stupefaction, they had developed tactics. But so had Friar Benigno. He had developed the "wideawake" to combat the smokers. The wideawake consisted of a bamboo pole, much like a fishing rod only incredibly long, to which was affixed at the end a feather duster. Benigno could stand in an aisle and reach anyone sitting in a pew. When he located a questionable figure in a pew, the wideawake would be manipulated, the feathers of a duster gently brushing the worshiper. Benigno would pause for a response; if it was not forthcoming, he would be in the pew like a shot, grab the smoker under the arms and haul him outside, where he'd prop him on the sidewalk. Of course the system wasn't infallible. Sometimes he would happen upon a perfectly innocent worshiper who for some reason or another would be caught up in prayer and not respond to the wideawake. That resulted in some mortification . . . and explanation. Yes, the smokers, the bums, gave Benigno a good bit of trouble. But as he explained to Mario: "You got to do something. Otherwise they turn St. Ansgar's into a Bowery flophouse."

Of course there were occasions when Benigno came upon someone in the pews, someone destitute, someone fallen into a hungry stupor. This kind of occurrence was handled very differently. Benigno always found some way of providing help for those in want. And he'd explain to Mario: "These people, the poor, they are the minores, they got to have something in their bellies, and a roof over they heads."

The nuts, the smokers, the bums, all part of Benigno's daily routine. And sometimes Benigno might be amused and laugh as he told Mario about some particularly artful bum or nut, but there was one bunch against whom he waged war to the death: the crooks! They disturbed Benigno's sleep. He'd leave his cell in the middle of the night and come down into the church to make sure it had not been sacked. The church was very vulnerable with all the coin boxes scattered about for donations. There was a box before every statue, shrine, grotto, candle stand, literature rack. Here Benigno really rose to the challenge. He was a first-class mechanic. He studied up on concealed hinges, unforceable locks, impregnable metal. He refashioned every donation and poor box in the church. You'd have needed dynamite to open one of Benigno's improved coin boxes. But the subject of crooks was never far from Benigno's mind. He was always mulling over preventive measures, precautions.

Benigno was often critical of the laxity of other churches that seemed to disregard common safeguards. He'd say: "What you expect. They don't do nothin'. The crook feels invited in to swipe the stuff." So when a burglary was reported at St. Fergus's or St. Carmine's, Benigno would shrug. "Don't tell me about it. What can you expect, ja? They is churches who have a lay sacristan. He get paid, it's a job. He go home at night. You think he gonna worry about what happen when he be home sleepin'? Nonsense!"

Those were nighttime depredations. But when the news came out of the daring daytime despoiling of the Irish church, Benigno was roused to wrath. A crook had entered the sanctuary, climbed up on the main altar, and stolen the monstrance that was on display before the tabernacle.

Benigno stormed, his words being choked off abruptly by his fury: "Sacrilege! That's evil . . . that is stealing God Himself. That the worst I ever hear of! Blasphemy . . . oh, that ruffian . . . that Antichrist. I would . . . I would . . ."

Benigno was not himself after the dreadful crime. Mario would find him in the second sacristy brooding and occasionally muttering, one of his cheap, rank cigars burned out in his hand. Once in a while he'd fling out a phrase: "Judas . . . Judas who would do such a thing . . . selling the sacred host for a little gold . . ." Mario knew the old friar would come up with something.

And he did. Benigno knew exactly what had to be done. The Altar Boy Society of St. Ansgar's, which had been founded by Benigno fifty-five years before, was a reservoir of ready help, a regular network of influence. Those boys, now men, many of whom occupied positions of considerable prominence, were always willing to do their best for Benigno. One of them, now a lieutenant in the detective bureau, Valentine Spatz, urged Benigno to arm himself. That was the only thing these dirty crooks respected, a gun and somebody who could use it. A friar with a gun? Friar Athenasius, grooming his long, full beard with his fingers, was flabbergasted at Benigno's request to purchase a revolver. Benigno explained the matter, got Valentine Spatz in to bolster his case, and poor Friar Athenasius reluctantly agreed. But, but, only as a trial. "Ja, until we see what happen, Benigno, ja. So soon as you come to shoot that gun, ach . . . ach . . ."

Word was gotten around. Friar Benigno had a revolver. Now let some ruffian try swiping something from St. Ansgar's. Not only that bit of information was circulated but the additional, and perhaps more convincing item: Benigno had arranged with Captain Bernard Malloy of the local precinct house to use the pistol range in their basement. Oh, yes, Benigno was not a man to do things by halves. In time he could use a .32 police regulation revolver with the best of them. Actually Captain Malloy told him if he were a cop, he'd qualify as a sharpshooter!

Benigno said to Mario, contentedly, "So, Mario. So. We have take care of it . . . ," and he showed Mario the gun. And he also showed him the cartridges that he had in his tunic. He kept the weapon unloaded, but the ammunition was near to hand! "So, Mario. So!"

All was well, security was established, and Benigno could now concentrate on his regular chores. And then, out of the blue, the whole fabric of security was blasted, and blasted by Mrs. Neider.

Ulrica Neider lived at 531 Stanley Street, second floor front. She was a small, arthritis-ridden woman in her late fifties whose face was as netted as a screen, which made her look even older. It was painful to see her walk, so swollen were her joints. All of her children but one had been early casualties. The single survivor, Gus, had grown up with an itch to rub Stanley Street's face in the dirt. The proud Dutchies simply shrugged off Gus, saying he was no better than his father and he was absolutely no good, and both of them were a disgrace to their Dutchie heritage!

Gus's first attempt to show Stanley Street got him hauled before the juvenile authorities. His second got him four years up the river, and his third got him nine years. This last trip up the Hudson seemed to affect Gus. When he was released on probation, he looked old and worn, and his face was so wan, the neighborhood nicknamed him Cheesie, a name that stuck. But Mrs. Neider had never lost faith in her only living child and was overjoyed to have him home at last; her only fear was that it might be of short duration, her Gustav's track record for being out not being too good. It was a nagging fear; Ulrica needed her son to love. She fussed over him, waited on him hand and foot. You might have gotten the idea that Gus was a king in exile rather than a convicted felon.

Everybody on the block was sorry for Mrs. Neider. Life had been a grim experience for her. Her husband, Otto, had been an ostler for the Sunny Brook Dairy, a man who spent twenty years of intense boozing and beating — he beat his wife, his children, and the stable full of horses under his charge — and who in turn was beaten by the flailing hooves of a terrified horse. Otto, who was boozed up at the time and injured by the attack, mistook an open elevator shaft for a doorway. And so he fell downward to his end. Some of the Dutchies said, out of the hearing of the grieving widow, downward was the proper direction for Otto, one he was destined for all his life.

In a very real sense, this was the nadir of Ulrica Neider's life. Poor woman was overwhelmed by disaster and despair. Her husband dead, four children dead, and her son Gustav up the river. She prowled those four front rooms, groaning with her hurt, her arms around herself to still the pain she felt, the heartbreak!

And then, perhaps because the company attorney indicated a potential lawsuit, the elevator shaft gate being open, the Sunny Brook Dairy gave Mrs. Neider a job, cleaning up the offices at the end of the day. It was her lifeline. Every day, six days a week, you could see old Ulrica hobble up the block on her way to the yellow brick dairy company's building for her nightly chores. This was her life, this and going to St. Ansgar's for her devotions, until Cheesie was sprung.

Of course nobody on the block believed for a second that Cheesie would see spring on Stanley Street. He'd see it back up along those stony banks of the Hudson from his cell. But Ulrica had faith, and she was happy, happy. She said her boy had changed. She said her boy — aged forty-three — was sick and broken. He'd learned his lesson. He was home for good. He was home all right. You rarely saw him. Once in a while he'd creep out of the hallway at night and stand on the sidewalk in the darkness. He looked like a scarecrow, his clothes hanging on him, his lips moving, talking to himself. He did appear sick, broken in spirit, frightened of his shadow. Every now and again Mario caught sight of him, holding on to the wall of the tenement and staring intently toward the river where the fog came up in great puffs.

No matter that her son lived off her meager earnings, that her son was more like a zombie than a man, that he lay around the house all day making glass paintings (learned in prison). Ulrica's life had meaning. You'd see her at the first mass of the day, see her at the five fifteen afternoon service, you'd see her at the communion rail praying, her watery eyes resting on the tabernacle, her coal-scuttle hat askew on her head. Benigno would say to Mario: "Ulrica is a good soul. It be her faith. The kind of life she have had, it be her faith that keeps her going."

Mrs. Neider was "making" a novena for the holy cross. Friar Polycarp Guenther, an eloquent, frequently emotional preacher, was conducting the novena. St. Ansgar's had a relic of the true cross. Once Mario had had a chance to look at it close up, inside its gold-plated reliquary. It was a speck, a speck resembling nothing so much as a splinter, the kind you'd have taken from your finger. But it was an authenticated if almost microscopic bit of the timber upon which Christ had been crucified. Friar Polycarp had dwelled upon the miraculous power of the relic; there was no limit to what it might bring to pass for those who had faith. "Illness, despair, peace, salvation, hope restored, the sinner rescued . . . remember Dismas, the thief, crucified beside Christ . . . he was raised to glory with Jesus . . ."

Ulrica Neider was caught up, stunned by the tide of fervor aroused by the friar's flood of eloquence.

At the end of the service, the congregation breaking up, Mario was dousing the candles. He saw, from the corner of his eye, Mrs. Neider open the gates of the altar rail on a side aisle, cross the sanctuary, and go to the altar where the reliquary had been laid temporarily by Benigno before it was returned to its place inside the sacristy. Right before his eyes, Mrs. Neider swept up the relic case, stuffed it into her pocket, and with a movement so swift on those arthritic limbs of hers she was beating her way down the side aisle on her way out of the church. Mario couldn't believe what he'd witnessed. Benigno had come out of the sacristy and went to the altar to return the relic to the sacristy safe. He was dumbfounded. It was gone.

"Mario . . . Mario . . . what have happened to the holy cross relic? Where it get to?"

Mario told him what he'd seen. He related it as if he had dreamed it. And Benigno with that hair-trigger temper of his let out a fierce growl, lifted up the skirts of his habit, and took off in pursuit of Ulrica. Mario could hear the slap of Benigno's bare feet against his sandals until the sound disappeared behind the swinging main doors. Mario could imagine the brown-habited old man, racing along the sidewalk in a towering rage, chasing after the crippled Ulrica. Yes, and overtaking her, grabbing her, his gun out, and marching her to the police station, having her arrested and sent up the river. Yes, Ulrica sent up the river. Oh, Mario was miserable, dreading what was to happen to the poor old woman. He found himself praying, praying for Ulrica.

About half an hour later a much-winded Benigno returned, the relic carefully enclosed in one of his large bandanna handkerchiefs. He was trying to catch his breath. He gasped out: "That foolish old woman. That crazy bug. She have took that relic . . ."

"You got it back, though, Brother."

"What you think I find her doing with the relic? She is rubbing the relic all over that good-for-nothing son of hers, Cheesie. Ja, she's wiping him with the true cross like he is a piece of furniture she is polishing. Now I have see everything. Ach, for cryin' out loud. This is too much . . . ," Benigno panted.

Mario asked fearfully: "You took her to the police station, Brother?"

"Police station, Mario?"

"Have her locked up?"

"Locked up . . . ?" Benigno understood then what the boy was getting at. His eyes behind those oval-shaped lenses grew very solemn, thoughtful. He said, measuring out his words as if he was thinking of something else as he talked: "No . . . no, Mario. She is a poor soul . . . a little cracked in the head . . ." Benigno's words trailed off. He sat, holding his head, as if it were very heavy indeed. Suddenly he looked at Mario, and with a rush of energy: "My God, Mario . . . here I have take steps against the crooks . . . and Ulrica, from this church, she have by your leave cross the sanctuary and swipe the relic . . . no crook have to do it . . . any nut can do it . . . by jingo neddies, I got to figger the whole thing all over again . . . the whole thing!"

The fruit of Brother Benigno's thinking was the famous St. Ansgar's burglar alarm system.

Sheets of copper, coils of wire, switches, connections, bells, gongs were delivered to the second sacristy. And a schematic drawing was wheedled out of another of the ex-altar-boys who was now an electrical engineer. Benigno's tools were scattered all over the second sacristy, and the whine of copper sheeting being sawed set every tooth in the friary on edge for days. It was the wiring which was the biggest part of the job. Friar Athenasius, the bland superior, hung around the second sacristy, fascinated by the project. Benigno explained to his superior exactly what was being done.

"You see, Father. The wires go to the plate, the plate is hidden; when it is touched, the alarm goes off. There is plates bunked away in the whole church, the statues, the confessionals, the pulpit, the organ loft, the altar, every place that can be burgled there is a plate."

Athenasius stared uncomprehendingly, his fingers stroking his full beard: "Oh, ja, Brother? Ja . . . that is something."

And it was something! It was a marvel of design, and a tribute to Benigno's gifts as a mechanic. He worked like a Trojan and Mario did, too. Mario learned to connect up wires to bells and gongs, to alarm boxes, to splice, to switch. In a few weeks there were squares of copper sheeting located strategically all over the church, and the whole system controlled from a new switch box placed directly above the huge box which controlled the whole church's lighting. And the real, ultimate flourish was Benigno's stroke of genius. He had gotten the whole vast network tied in to the station house switchboard. Yes, it was fed into Captain Bernard Malloy's headquarters.

Benigno was a throwback to the golden days of the church, the days of Julius the Second. There were alarm bells in the kitchen, the refectory, in the wine cellar, the altar boys' dressing room, and under Benigno's pallet in his cell was an enormous gong, no chance of his not hearing it when it was activated! And Benigno knew another former altar boy who was now an executive of a protective agency; he had him come in and check out the system.

After weeks of labor, Benigno unlocked the new switchboard, activated the circuits, thrust out his stubby beard, and said grimly:

"Ja, Mario, now let them try something. We got all the bases covered, crooks, nuts, bums, smokers . . . we got it covered one hundred percent!"

Of course there were some bugs to be worked out, but not necessarily in the system. For example, one night through some fluke one of the nuts managed to secrete himself and get locked in the church. At some point during the night he climbed into the pulpit and preached a sermon to the empty pews. During his sermon his hand came down on the pulpit rail, which set off the burglar alarm. Friars bounded from their cells, Benigno came charging into the church pistol in hand, and police pounded at the center doors of the church ready for action. It all ended with the erstwhile preacher being carted off to Bellevue for examination.

Father Athenasius wondered if such nightly alarms were likely to be frequent.

Brother Benigno reported gleefully to Mario next day: "By jingo neddies, Mario, our system it works. It works beautiful, just like we figger."

Yes, it worked. There were a few more episodes of accidental tripping of the alarm, but soon everybody in the parish learned to step nimbly and to keep his hands to himself. It even had the effect of inhibiting the antics of the nuts.

A dozen times a day Benigno would stare proudly at the new switch box. Now he was in complete charge of the security of St. Ansgar's. He set the alarm with the same persistent thoroughness he brought to everything he touched. He had the key that opened and closed the switch box, he and the superior, nobody else. No crook in his right mind was going to take a chance on challenging Benigno's masterpiece. Yes, word got out: don't try and knock over St. Ansgar's. And after a time, the alarm system became just another part of the day-to-day routine. But every now and again, Mario would catch a glint in Benigno's eyes, a glint Mario interpreted as: *By jingo neddies, how I wish one of them fellas try, try just once to swipe something here . . .*

◆

The Very Reverend Nicodemus Grosheibach, a short roly-poly friar with a luxuriant beard and a habit which showed grains of snuff, his great vice, was to receive a great honor. From Rome had come word Nicodemus was to be named a doctor of the church. Nicodemus and Benigno were both about the same age, but Benigno spent his time humbly as a sacristan at St. Ansgar's, while Nicodemus had spent several terms as the provincial general of the worldwide order, stationed in the Holy City. Yes, Nicodemus had held the highest office possible for a friar. Now in the declining years of his life he chose to spend his days at St. Ansgar's in semi-retirement. But he was in great demand as a confessor, a very special confessor, a confessor to the high dignitaries of the church, bishops and cardinals and monsignori. Nicodemus was a merry old man; Mario often found it hard to believe such a good-natured old man was so eminent. Benigno said he held a bishop's rank and that's how it was he was called the Very Reverend Friar Nicodemus. There was nothing Nicodemus enjoyed more than a good scatological joke (Friar Vicar had a special store of those). You could hear him laughing over one of them half a block away. Professor Wolfram, the organist, said to Mario that in this way Nicodemus was like Mozart who also relished earthiness; it was a south German characteristic, so said Professor Wolfram. Often Nicodemus would wander into the second sacristy to observe Benigno and Mario at work. He'd take a few pinches of snuff, sneeze, and then watch in admiration as Benigno brazed or welded or threaded pipe. He would marvel at Benigno's ability with tools. The two old men would then start talking together in Bavarian, forgetting all about Mario.

Now Nicodemus was to be honored, the pope was sending a delegate to represent him, two bishops were to attend, and the solemn high mass would be celebrated by a Dominican, a Benedictine, and the father provincial of the Capuchins; religious from all over the country would be present to show their esteem for Nicodemus. Friar Athenasius informed Benigno of the augustness of the event, and Benigno informed Mario.

Everything was laid out, inspected, planned to the smallest detail. The heavy golden vestments, the gorgeously worked missal, the jeweled chalice, the brocaded tabernacle drape. How they worked, scrubbing down the marble altar, dressing it with starched linens, polishing the sacred vessels, selecting the fat, huge yellow beeswax candles, decorating the gradines and back altar with vases of flame-colored gladioli.

And then the finishing touch: Benigno and Mario assembled the bishop's throne. Length by length they joined together the polished brass rails, the thick red carpet was laid, then the seat itself, a heavy, plush red chair overhung by a fringed canopy. It was every inch a royal throne.

Mario knew Benigno was bursting with pride. He would show his beloved St. Ansgar's to the world. He, Benigno Zoller, the neighborhood boy, would show his church in its magnificence. Father Athenasius, standing in the sanctuary looking at the splendor created by Benigno, was moved. He said: "Ah, my goodness, Benigno . . . what you have done . . . Ah, Himmel . . ."

Benigno patted Mario on the head, smiling, making sure Mario shared in the praise.

"You go home now, Mario. Get a good sleep. Tomorrow we be busy as bees with all the big shots. All them extra masses to be said, the friary it be packed with visitors. You get here early. We got a pile of work. You have done good, Mario!"

The next morning lived up to Benigno's forecast. What with robing priests, lighting candles, starting the censers, arranging the cruets of wine and water, putting more chairs in the sanctuary, the sacristy was like Grand Central Station at rush hour. Mario hardly saw Benigno; each of them had his hands full. Priests and prelates, abbots came and went in the sacristy. It was dazzling and distracting. Mario found himself checking off on his fingers last-minute details. Meanwhile out of the corner of his eye, amid all the chaos, Mario saw the cause of it all: Nicodemus, talking calmly to the scarlet-clothed papal delegate.

At last the three priests were vested, the altar boys paired off, the censers smoking, the visiting clergy lined up; the bells began ringing, the organ swelled, the choir sang, and Mario's surplice was tugged. Benigno said fiercely: "You put out the cruets, Mario?"

Yes, of course he had. But Mario was so flustered he went out into the sanctuary, to the gospel side, to double-check. Yes, the two small flasks of wine and water were in place. But no way of telling Benigno now, everything was in progress. The whole ceremony, lights, music, vestments, the shimmering altar, ritual, panoply, went off in Mario's imagination like a Roman candle. And inside, his head silhouetted against the small glass panel in the sacristy door, was Benigno looking out, probably standing on his tiptoes.

The father provincial was in great voice: *"Exaudi quaesumus Domine, supplicum preces, et devoto tibi pectore . . ."* The choir outdid itself. The altar boys were models of precise movement, and the bishop sat upon his throne with crozier and mitre. St. Ansgar's throbbed with emotion. It was a day never to be forgotten at the Dutchie church, or in the neighborhood.

And then the bishop, magnificent in his scarlet regalia, rose, supported on either side by attendant clergy, placed a jeweled slipper before him and planted it solidly on a small carpet, setting off the wildest cacophony of bells and gongs, which drowned out organ, choir, celebrants, and stupefied the bishop, the papal delegate, and petrified the congregation. Mario was thunderstruck. Benigno had forgotten to deactivate the system. And suddenly the discord ceased and an awful silence came in its wake. Slowly, almost tentatively, the ceremony resumed. Yes, the introit was nicely started and the choir lifted its voice, at which point the rear center doors swung open and a squad of policemen, guns drawn, rushed into the church, Captain Bernard Malloy at their head.

But the church had survived greater threats. And in time, the ceremony proceeded without further interruption, though it was said the bishop was very uncertain in his movements after he'd put his foot in the wrong place that one time. And the Very Reverend Nicodemus Grosheibach was invested as a doctor of the church.

◆

Yes, the Very Reverend Dr. Nicodemus was raised and the Venerable Benigno Zoller was crushed. Everyone was gone, the splendor put away, the flowers wilted, and in the gloom of the second sacristy Mario saw Benigno seated at his desk, holding his head in his hands. He was inconsolable. Mario hardly knew what he should do, he wanted so to tell him it was all right.

And then Mario heard the slap of soles against sandals; someone was coming. Yes, in the dim light, Mario saw Dr. Nicodemus, the roly-poly friar, looking about in the dusky second sacristy. He didn't see Mario but he did spy Benigno at his desk. The new doctor of the church grabbed an empty candle crate and plunked it down next to Benigno. And this is what Mario heard him say softly in Bavarian:

"Listen to me, Joe"—it was the first time Mario ever heard Benigno called by his baptismal name—"it was nothing. Nothing at all. The bishop he understand how many crooks they is around stealing from the churches . . . yes, Joe, yes. He is going to ask you how you make such a great system to defeat the crooks . . . listen to me, Joe. I could tell you some of the things that go wrong at St. Peter's in Rome. Yes, I could tell you some stories about that . . . things I have experienced when I was there as provincial general . . . let me get you a glass of wine . . . I want you to forget what happen."

Benigno lifted his head and Mario shrank into his corner.

Mario doubted that Benigno ever completely recovered from his humiliation. But the friars, though they must've chuckled in private, were outwardly trying their best to soften Benigno's anguish. Even Athenasius, who might have had cause to be critical about the fiasco, said reflectively, "We take out the bells and gongs . . . you get rid of the gun, ja, Benigno. I think you have proved your point . . . no crook bother St. Ansgar's with you here . . . ja, Benigno?"

And so the famous protective device was dismantled, the pistol surrendered to Captain Bernard Malloy. And later, Benigno said to

Mario, and gruffly: "You see how stupid an old man can be, Mario? How his pride, his smartness have get punish? I ain't no policeman. I ain't no rich man . . . I forget how St. Francis handle the crook. He say 'Hey, brother crook, what I got you want. I give it to you . . .' Not like Joseph Zoller who gets a gun and builds the burglar system . . . no . . . Joseph Zoller's pride get him where he belong . . . back, back to be a friar."

One fact which no one but Mario seemed conscious of: Cheesie Neider never went back to prison. He got a job as an unloader at the Sunny Brook Dairy, just like his father before him. He lived with his mother, went on with his glass paintings, and came to church with her on Sundays. Mario never wanted to point out this fact to Benigno because it might have reopened old wounds, but Mario was convinced there was somehow a connection between Cheesie's regeneration, the relic of the holy cross, and the burglar alarm system.

✦3✦

The Rule

Those cigars that Friar Benigno smoked, small, torpedo-shaped, cheap, and with a tendency to give off showers of sparks unexpectedly, were very much like the man himself.

"My father was a cigar maker. I can tell a good cigar by just holding it between my fingers, or by the faber — color — or by the sniff. But it don't be right that I should smoke the expensive cigars."

Mario was never quite sure if this wasn't a backhanded criticism of those friars who would gather in the common room on the second floor of the friary and light up those silky panatelas. Their bouquet, the blue smoke, would come drifting down the stairs and in blue clouds ride the drafts.

Mario would see Benigno lift his head, his nostrils moving. He'd say: "Sumatra tobacco. Somebody must have give it to him. It ain't cheap!"

In that case, in the instance of someone giving a present, was it all right for a friar to smoke and enjoy a superb cigar?

Well, it was and it wasn't. It was a ticklish proposition. Benigno would frown, stick out his beard, and turn to stare out the window. "After all, we took the vows. They be the backbone of our lives." Then he'd make a three-hundred-sixty-degree turn. "Ach, there can't be no harm for a fella to smoke a scrumptious cigar he have been given."

Mario realized there was a lot involved, more than the propriety of a friar smoking a fancy cigar. Benigno was troubled, uneasy, by what he viewed as a growing tendency to compromise the fundamental commitment of the friars. And yet the old man realized he might be hopelessly behind the times. He'd argue with Mario (though really with himself because Mario would have no position on the matter):

"I ain't no doctor of canon law. What I know about such things, ja? After all we ain't Trappists!"

It was not Benigno's nature to shilly-shally. He'd say: "If you going to make a mistake, by jingo neddies, make a good one so everybody can see it be a hundred percent mistake." But in this area of consistency with the three vows of poverty, chastity, and obedience Benigno was ordinarily dogmatic. Mario knew the old man was more and more concerned with the slackening (or the appearance of it) shown through the changes which had seeped into the order.

Once Benigno, to give Mario a treat, took him to a museum where a special exhibit of Spanish religious paintings was being shown. A Murillo canvas depicting a friar bemused, staring out upon a mystical landscape, greatly excited Benigno. He pointed to the figure's sandaled feet. "Ach, Mario, look! That fella Murillo he know his business. He really have study what happen to the sandals from a friar wearing them. See how he show how pushed in the inside of the sandal be. See, see, the bulge there. Ja, that's made from the ball of the foot, where you come down with your weight. You make that hollow in the leather. I show you when we go back to St. Ansgar's . . . now that fellow Murillo he knows his business."

What was behind Benigno's excitement? A confirmation of what he knew? And what was that, an order of friars who had an unchanging commitment to a way of life? Or was it something else, deeper, more subtle? Was it the subterranean current of age swiftly flowing away, so Benigno's landmarks were dimming, his connections loosening? Some major shift was taking place within Benigno; Mario didn't know, but he sensed the alteration. Was it inevitable, the contrast of his time with the present, always a gulf between what was and what is? Was that it, separation? Mario would catch those old gray eyes turned inward, bemused, considering some hidden preoccupation. At those times Mario would feel cold, cut off, and become uneasy with foreboding.

Then Benigno would snap out of it, come to some kind of accommodation with his struggles. After all, if the heads of the order were perfectly satisfied with the way things were going, who was he to criticize. After all, he was supposed to be obedient, live up to his vocation as a humble lay brother. He had his own soul to save.

Mario would see Benigno sizing up a young friar's thin-soled, soft-strapped sandals, made as if to cradle the foot, made to order. What a far cry from his own thick two-strap harness-leather affairs, with soles like boards, cobbled and recobbled until they at last fell apart from use.

And it was the same easing up when it came to the beards. Without realizing it, Benigno would express his concern to Mario: "We ain't supposed to use the razor. That's how come we have beards. So what do they do today? They use the clippers . . ." He'd stare at Mario and shake his head. "We get to be like Chicago lawyers . . . use the loopholes. We bargain with the Rule. Ja, we bargain. Take the habits today. Look at mine. Rough, thick, it take a beating, it suppose to last a long time. It is meant to be worked in. We suppose to be workers. Look at the habits they have today, can you work in them? Not on your tintype. They too fancy, too soft . . . even the cincture . . . St. Francis grab a piece of rope, ja, any old piece of rope to tie around his belly to keep his rags together . . . see mine is a old piece of wash line . . . but these young fellas . . . they have these fluffy strings, pieces of embroidery . . . ah, Mario, it's like we are actors today, wearing the costumes. Often I wonder what have happen to the Rule?" Benigno would lift his shoulders, make a face of disgust, and let the subject drop.

Mario used to puzzle over the Rule. It had a profound meaning, he was sure of that, but he lacked a real understanding of that meaning. When the right moment came he asked Benigno.

"The Rule is the law laid down by St. Francis. It be the thing that all friars be ruled by. St. Francis take it to Pope Innocent and get him to give his okay. It be our rules for our way of life as friar minores. It not supposed to make our life easy. It expect us to make sacrifices to live according to the Rule. Then there comes the time when some fella come into the order and try to fool around with the Rule. They bend it here and there. Like they know more about things than St. Francis. They going to bring it up to date! Oh, ja? They just be trying to make things easy. It make me sick to see how they fiddle with what St. Francis have put together."

The Rule. Mario puzzled over it. Was it capable of different interpretations, some more ascetic, some less? And was Benigno's view of the Rule the current one? Or was his more a matter of his aging? Frequently Mario would catch the young friars looking at the old man as if he was to be humored, respected, but still a museum piece. Certainly there was more than a slight difference between a friar like Benigno and some of the newer ones.

For example, Mario could tell which friar was approaching by his particular scent. Yes, by the smell of cloves, lavender, pine, patchouli, lime. And they paid much attention to their hair: very few wore tonsures, unless they were naturally balding up on top. Yes, they were regularly barbered, so they appeared neat and trim. With Benigno, it was altogether different. Every couple of months he'd grab the shears used for clipping the flower stems, sit at his desk, and say: "Time for the shearing, Mario."

That matter of the Rule. It was really never too far out of Mario's mind. Mario would see Benigno watching how the barbered, fragrant young priests would come out of their vestments, hurriedly, carelessly tumble them on the robing table, and rush into the choir to say their post-mass prayers and then chase off to the kitchen to get their breakfast. Benigno would stare after them. Those vestments, their care, preservation, were a sacred duty for Benigno. He knew the history of each chasuble. He handled them with reverence. They were carefully aired after each use, examined for wear, and then carefully laid away in the special wide, shallow drawers of the robing table, a layer of white linen between the folds.

Once Benigno said so quietly Mario thought he was talking to himself: "I have help vest and divest cardinals, bishops, monsignori, provincials, and they never have been in such a hurry as these fellas be in today. They don't tear off the chasuble, the amice, the stole, crumple up the alb like they're late, they gotta catch a train . . ." Benigno would mutter: "The Rule. Ja," sighing: "The Rule!"

In the sacristy proper, what was called the first sacristy to distinguish it from the second sacristy where all the drudgery was performed, everything had its allotted place. Chalices, ciboria, monstrances, patens, copes, dalmatics, chasubles, albs, amices, altar linens, it was a room of dazzling cleanliness, an atmosphere of holiness, if you will, since it was here every service was prepared for. There was a lingering fragrance of burned-out incense from the thuribles, hanging from their stands, and the sharp odor of wine, and the sense of starched linens and opulent gold thread, rich brocades. The albs were kept in two tall, deep cupboards, each draped from its own hanger. When Mario first started as Benigno's helper he was too short to reach the bar the albs hung from. He no longer needed a stool for that; he had grown taller.

The alb, that long, nightgown-like white garment over which is draped all the other vesture for the saying of the mass, as with everything else in the friary, belonged to the order. The friars put on whatever alb was laid out for them. The same way with chalices, common property of the order; even though they might have been gifts, once they came into the friary there was no such thing as private ownership, personal. And this was part of the Rule. Again Mario came up against that ubiquitous guide and code. It was in regard to albs that Mario found out at last the significance of the Rule: when Friar Balthasar arrived at St. Ansgar's, assigned to the friary, he brought along with him albs, personal albs. Benigno bristled!

Friar Balthasar was a slight, erect man with what Mario called a Near Eastern face. Why Near Eastern? Mario once had seen a copy of Sir Walter Scott's *The Saracen*, which had a colored picture of the protagonist which was the spitting image of Balthasar: dark-skinned, curved nose, trim, short beard, long mustache that blended into his beard. He walked very quietly in his sandals, an air of mystery about him, and he had a glimmer in his eye which Mario took to mean he had some private joke. He was not a popular friar at St. Ansgar's; all you had to do was take a look at his confessional on Saturdays: nobody was lined up waiting for his ministrations. And the other friars seemed to keep their distance from him. But despite his appearance Balthasar was as much a Dutchie as anybody else in the area, his name being Gottfried Schelegel. He came from a farm family, one which operated in Nebraska; his parents were still alive and farming. It was his mother who painstakingly made those albs for him. They were beautiful. The cotton used was of the finest quality; all Mario had to do was to run his hands over the fabric to recognize its costliness, hold it to light to catch the silky sheen. There were everyday albs and two albs for high holy days. The latter were so opulent, diaphanous, with elaborate lace appliqués, Mario had his heart in his mouth when he handled them, lest he hurt them in some way. But Benigno would growl: "Put them in the cupboard. Why you handle them like eggs? They just albs!"

No doubt as to Benigno's position on Friar Balthasar's personal albs. Still, Mario would see Benigno putting out Balthasar's albs for his use only. Mario couldn't quite get the hang of that. It couldn't be Benigno was afraid of him. Benigno wasn't afraid of anybody . . . but no, that wasn't true, Mario knew, Benigno was afraid of somebody: Benigno himself, his temper, his pride, his impulsiveness. Benigno was afraid of not being humble in keeping with his vocation. Was that why Benigno automatically placed Balthasar's alb on the robing counter each time the friar's name appeared on the mass assignments?

Mario made no bones about his own reaction to Balthasar: the friar scared the daylights out of him. There was that about the Saracen which made it perfectly plain he wouldn't tolerate error or interference, or welcome friendly overtures from anyone! Most friars were open and friendly, quick to kid around, joke, laugh, easy to get along with, companionable with each other, but not Balthasar. He was reserved, aloof, very much a loner. Maybe it was because of that farm in Nebraska; Mario had an idea Nebraska was in the same class as the Antarctic, total wasteland. No, Mario ducked as soon as he could when Balthasar came in sight. He didn't like that critical look in Balthasar's eyes.

Everything in a friary is organized, fitted to schedule, prepared for. Take the mass assignments. Friar Vicar would come into the sacristy the evening before with the next day's mass schedule. Each friar would be assigned a mass, either in the church or in one of the many chapels within the friary. The masses in the church would commence at five in the morning, and the last one would be celebrated at twelve fifteen to accommodate the lunchgoers. Benigno would prepare the first three mass vestments before he retired for the night. Everything would be laid out in the proper order for robing: amice, alb, stole, chasuble. All the priest had to do in the morning was to look at which stack of vestments had his name on it. But ordinarily Benigno was in the sacristy so there'd be no mix-up. Benigno taught Mario the routine and in time Mario became adept at it.

One Saturday morning, Mario was in the first sacristy pouring wine from the gallon jug into the cruets. Benigno had gone down to the kitchen for his cup of coffee and crust of French bread. Mario heard nothing and yet he knew someone had come into the sacristy. He looked behind him and there was Friar Balthasar. Mario was startled and spilled some wine. He quickly wiped it up and stammered out: "G-g-g-good m-m-morning, Father."

The priest nodded, put his breviary on a table, and said quietly: "I've exchanged masses with Friar Urbain." He followed Mario with his eyes as the boy washed his hands so he might assist the priest in robing. Mario knew he was being watched. And when he stood ready to help in the vesting, his face was red with embarrassment as he said: "Brother Benigno's in the kitchen, Father Balthasar."

Balthasar gave one of his secret smiles and stepped to the robing counter, prayed quietly for a moment, then kissed the string of the amice and draped it over his head. The vesting had started. Mario's hands were cold, why was he so nervous, he knew what to do. The priest slipped the alb over his head, Mario shook out the folds, passed him the cincture, helped lift the chasuble over Balthasar's head, and then Mario's heart stopped. Balthasar said he'd swapped masses with Urbain. He was wearing a community alb . . . not one of his own! Mario was struck dumb. The priest gave no sign. Mario's face was burning. Mario rang the bell for the altar boys, who came tramping up the stairs from their room. The priest swept his chalice from the ledge, took a dip of holy water, and then gave Mario one Saracen look before he followed the altar boys out into the sanctuary. That look, it said: *You'll never make that mistake again, will you!*

Benigno came in wiping the coffee and crumbs from his white beard and mustache. He automatically went to the small glass panel in the sacristy door and peered out, standing on his toes. He turned around. "Hey, Mario, that ain't Urbain out there. That's Balthasar who says the mass."

Mario held his head down as he explained the switch. He went on, almost crying: "I didn't remember to put out Father Balthasar's special alb. I forgot to do it, Brother . . ."

Those gray eyes sparked. Out came one of those horny hands; it rested on Mario's head. "Oh, ja, Mario. Okay, come, we got flowers to fix." And it was said as if Benigno had something completely different on his mind, something of much greater importance.

Mario fretted over the incident, dreading what would take place when the mass was over and Balthasar came back to the sacristy. He lifted out the peonies from the long carton, passed them up on the worktable. Benigno separated them, examined them, graded them. Mario started to say: "I didn't mean . . ."

Benigno cut him short. "Schnell, schnell, we got the flowers to fix. We ain't got all day."

Mario saw the old man's jawbone firm.

Benigno had each friar timed down to the minute. He knew exactly how long it took each one to say the kind of mass which was assigned, high, low, solemn, requiem. There were the slowpokes, the average, the swift, and the speed demons. Balthasar held the undisputed crown for speed. He held the record for saying the fastest low mass in the history of St. Ansgar's. The altar boys were hard-pressed to keep up with him. Balthasar's Latin came out of him with the clatter of a machine gun. Balthasar once or twice had complained about the altar boys' slowness of response. They should be awake when they served at the mass. Benigno muttered in Mario's hearing: "Ja, and you ain't supposed to be going to no fire neither!"

When Benigno abruptly put down his pruning clippers and suddenly left, Mario knew Balthasar was about to come in from the sanctuary. Mario wanted to hide, stop his ears. He knew Balthasar would let Benigno know of his displeasure. Yes, in that secret insinuating way Balthasar would get back at Benigno, humiliate him. Mario was not brave, his imagination made that impossible, but he was not thinking of himself just then. He quickly followed Benigno to the first sacristy. He got there just in time to see the priest sweep inside, the altar boys duck down the stairs to the safety of their quarters. Balthasar swung the chalice upon the ledge of the vesting table and began to remove his vestments. The sacristy suddenly seemed to shrink and grow airless.

With his most Saracen smile, Balthasar said in silky tones: "This is not my alb, Friar Benigno."

Benigno proceeded with helping in the disrobing. Mario's heart skipped a beat. And then with lowered head, Benigno said humbly: "Ja, Father Balthasar."

Now they were getting to it.

Still smiling, Balthasar now looked at Mario with his dark, keen eyes. "Are all my albs being laundered?"

Benigno's voice was unfamiliar, it was so docile. Only his jawbone locked into a knot, his temper was there, but the words were soft and without provocation: "No, Father, your albs is all here."

"I should think my albs would be recognizable to you" — he darted a swift glance toward Mario — "by this time."

"Ja, that is so, Father."

Mario stood, blushing.

The priest stepped out of the house alb, walked over to where he'd left his breviary, picked it up, and said: "I'm sure next time you'll remember to put out my alb."

"Ja, Father."

Balthasar's nose seemed very curved as he smiled some more at Mario. "Thank you, Mario."

It was a rebuke. It stung. And that soft tread disappeared into the friary.

Benigno was extra busy with the vestments the priest had taken off. Mario saw him swallowing, swallowing his humiliation, it was too much for Mario, that acceptance: "Oh, Brother Benigno, I'm so sorry, so sorry, it was all my fault."

Benigno turned on him, his eyes blazing, his voice harsh: "Don't you say nothing to me. You hear? You got nothing to be sorry for. That fella he got everything to be sorry for! Ja, and someday he know it . . . someday, ja, someday."

"But I knew it wasn't his alb."

"Mario . . . you don't know what you talk about. Go to the cupboard. Now bring out one of Balthasar's albs. Go ahead."

It took Mario no time to get out one of those splendid bits of sewn cotton.

"Take it over to the window. Hold it up in the daylight. That is Friar Balthasar's alb?"

"Yes, Brother, one of them, an everyday one."

"How you know that, my Mario?"

Mario was puzzled: "I know it, Brother. The cloth, the cotton fringe on the sleeves and skirt."

"Is that what it tell you?"

Mario stared into Benigno's gray eyes. He said lamely: "I just know it, Brother."

"Is there something, a tape, a label which say Friar Balthasar, some mark, some writing? Go ahead, look. Find it."

Mario examined the alb, checked the seams, the collar, sleeves, the skirt, the armpits.

"You find something, ja, Mario?"

Mario did find something, a little tongue of cotton tape on the inside of a shoulder.

"What that tag say, Mario?"

"St. Ansgar's Friary."

"What? It don't say Friar Balthasar?"

"No, Brother."

"No. No. *No!* Okay, you put it back in the cupboard. On the hanger. *It don't belong to him. It don't belong to anybody but the order!* He don't own anything. I don't own anything. That is the *Rule*. The Rule." Benigno's face was red with passion: "We don't own nothing. Poverty means when you be without anything. That is the *Rule*. That is the vow he takes, the vow I take, the vow the father provincial take. Balthasar owns nothing, so I don't want to hear you be sorry for something what ain't. You understand what I telling you? That fella should be ashame of himself. Ashame. He the one who should be sorry. He should be on his knees, grateful he can say the mass, grateful he have an alb to put on. He should be filled with joy to have the habit on his back. St. Francis was joyful when he be covered with rags, ja, rags. He have no alb, no fancy sandals, no fancy cincture . . . he be joyful he can have nothing but his God. That is the Rule . . . the Rule. We don't own nothing!"

There was a sequel to the episode and a further explication of the Rule. It was a matter which was hushed up; not many in the parish had an inkling of what happened, and ordinarily Mario wouldn't have known it, but in this specific instance Benigno wanted to share it with him. He felt it was the boy's due.

"Father Balthasar have gone."

"Transferred, huh, Brother?"

Without flinching, looking directly into Mario's eyes: "He have run away with a woman!"

"Run away? With a woman?"

"Ja, you have seen her in the church. Der zaftig one. The widow of that politician, the one with the big floppy hats . . . you seen her in the church . . ."

Mario knew from the description what woman Benigno was talking about. He had seen her making the stations of the cross in the dusky church. She'd look about as she prayed. A big woman, stately, with very red splotches on her cheeks, rouge, and always dressed fit to kill. She'd once stopped him and asked him how she could get a priest for confession. He pointed out the bell to push. As it turned out, Friar Balthasar happened to be the one on duty that day! Mario'd forgotten all about it; it had happened months before.

"With her . . . he's run away?"

"I just tell you that. But you say nothing. We don't wash dirty clothes in public. I tell you because I want you to know."

Mario found it very hard to believe. He kept brooding over it, trying to figure it out. That trim, erect, swarthy friar with his secret ways, soft walking, like a cat, with his near-cruel manner, running off with a woman.

Mario wondered: "What about his vows, Brother?"

"Ja, what about them?"

"Oh, a priest, breaking his vows . . . running away with that lady . . ." Mario's words slipped out, filled with dread, as if at any moment a thunderbolt might shoot down from the sky.

Some of the sternness left Benigno's face. "It have happen before. Sure, it have happen to other friars before. Just because you take the vows . . . solemn vows, it don't mean that's the whole job. Ah, no, Mario, that just the beginning. You have to learn to be strong. To grow as a man. To have in your heart the Rule. Ja, the Rule in your heart. The temptation is always there, it only when you fight against the temptation you get strong. But it be tough . . . but St. Francis never said it be easy. It ain't easy no matter what you do . . . not even when you ain't friar it's easy . . ."

Benigno and Mario looked at each other. The old man's face softened.

He said wistfully: "You know, Mario, you got to feel sorry for that fella Balthasar. He think he going to be happy, just because he don't have to follow the Rule no more, but they is all kinds of Rules, you know, all kinds . . . you wait, maybe someday, just someday . . ."

Mario hadn't any sense of what someday might bring. But he certainly had a better grasp of what the Rule was, one he never forgot. Neither did he forget Friar Balthasar, the Saracen.

♣4♣

The Ianucci Funeral

Val and Auggie Samuessen, two of the undertaker's sons, pounced on Mario when he entered the foyer from the street. In a frenzy to get rid of their news, they both talked at the same time:

"Beau was dead."

"Bumped off."

"Stuffed in a crate."

"In an empty lot on Thirtieth Street."

"Had on silk underwear."

"Rings on his fingers."

"Blood smearing him."

"Mess."

Beau dead? Right away that peculiar equipment inside of Mario which gathered impressions, scenes, smells, stories, fears, memories, that often made his life wretched, set off a train of feelings. Beau was called variously: Eye-Eye, Snot-rags, Georgie Faye, Bandylegs, Italo Ianucci.

The Ianuccis lived in four rooms, ground floor front at 541 Stanley Street, smell of garlic, oregano, sweet basil, and tomatoes. Mother, Father, Sister, Beau. All short, olive complexions, intense black eyes, showing their teeth when they talked, using their hands. Beau bumped off? The only Italian family on that block of solid Dutchies. Live by the gun die by the gun. Beau was a racketeer? Numbers runner? Bootlegger? Gunsel? When Beau smiled you saw gold edging his teeth. He stood out on the block. He didn't fit. Neither did his family. Italians. Sour hard bread, acrid smell of his father's cigars. Outsiders. Went to St. Carmine's church, Italian church.

Used to pitch for the Dutchie hardball team. Sore loser. Argue with the umpire, yell at the opposition, bawl out his teammates, aim his fastball at a batter's head, slam his glove on the ground. Guys were scared of him. Go crazy when he fought. His eyes would get a glassy look, his fists and arms and legs were all moving at once, in a whirl, like a dust storm. A terrible, awful fighter, kick, bite, claw, his nose running. Beau was dead. Could they straighten out his bandy legs?

Val and Auggie told Mario: nobody wanted to bury him. Nobody. Under any name! St. Fergus's said he wasn't Irish for all that he was called Georgie Faye. St. Carmine's wouldn't touch him even though he was born Italo Ianucci. His body was in the basement of their undertaking establishment. Nobody wanted to give him a funeral mass!

Val and Auggie got right next to Mario. They whispered. Their poppa got a secret telephone call, a very tough voice on the other end of the wire. Get the Ianuccis, take them over to the morgue and claim the body. Take care of all the formalities. Don't worry about the expense, everything'll be paid for. Just make sure that Eye-Eye got a classy funeral, solemn mass, three priests, and all the fixings. They were depending on Samuessen to take care of everything. And he better because they knew where he lived, they knew he had a wife and children. They were depending on him.

Mario's forehead felt cold, it was wet with sweat; he swallowed all of the details in great, raw gulps. Why did it knock him for such a loop? Death was such an awful, black-hooded figure. It blanketed Mario's mind. Was he the only one on Stanley Street who was hounded by the specter of Death, the only one who was unnerved by it? Val and Auggie weren't paralyzed by it. Maybe they even got a kick out of it. What things they saw in their father's basement as he plied his trade. Mario had once tried to look down into that big room from the small basement window. He'd lost his courage and run away and had bad dreams for a week. Mario couldn't get himself to look at the face of the dead, even though Stanley Street believed that it was not the dead you had to worry about — it was the living who could hurt you.

Beau was dead and Mario was terrified. Where was his faith? His belief in God? Death was the beginning, not the end. What kind of a Dutchie kid was he to be so frightened? He should get used to Death. It roamed Stanley Street like a landlord. Drunks stiff in alleys, bodies thrown from speeding limousines, cops shooting guys in freight yards, longshoremen using their bailing hooks on scabs, Mario should be used to Death, it was familiar; Stanley Street was its stalking ground. Bandy-legged Beau was dead. Never again would Mario see him running wildly away from the freight yards, clutching a carton of silks, the railroad bulls on his heels, Beau ducking into a hallway, Mario watching, the bulls with their guns out, flying by: "Kid, you see a bandy-legged guy run by?" And Mario shaking his head, his face a blank.

Beau was dead, no call for the guys to chip in and buy him a big blue cotton bandanna to use on his nose. "Disgustin' to see that snot runnin' down your nose. Use a handkerchief." Beau told them what they could do with their Goddamned Dutchie wisenheimer handkerchief and put up his fists. "Bunch of friggin' Hunyaks, talkin' a billy-goat language."

Val and Auggie pulled Mario toward the center doors of the church. They edged one open to show Mario what was taking place before the gates in the communion rail. Their poppa had brought over the Ianuccis to appeal to Brother Benigno. Benigno was the single most important friar stationed at St. Ansgar's. If he could be persuaded, then everything else would follow.

The interior of the church was dim, the sanctuary light flickering, the back altar looking blanched. Benigno stood, his beard on his chest, two veiled women in black on their knees in front of him, a gnarled old man standing to one side looking around aimlessly, and Samuessen with his gray undertaker's suit rubbing his hands together nervously. The church was so quiet you could hear the sputter of candles hissing out their flames on the votive stands. And then the single cry: "Please, please, Your Excellency, please to bury my Italo who have been killed. For the mercy of the wounded body of Jesus Christ and His Blessed Mother, bury my son so he not burn in Hell."

Mario watched Benigno bend over, his arms outstretched, clasp Mrs. Ianucci, and lift her to her feet. He could not hear what Benigno said to her but he could feel the power of Benigno's compassion in raising her. Mario was struck by that. Mario saw Benigno lead both women across the sanctuary toward the sacristy door, while Samuessen tried to get the gnarled old man's attention. Mr. Ianucci had been injured in the freight yards, he'd been struck by a rail being hoisted from a flatcar, he'd never been the same since. Before he'd always been a happy little man, humming and smiling as he walked along the block at the end of his day's work. The kids used to tease him then, singing: "Where-a you work-a John? The Delaware an' Lackawan'? What-you do-a all-a day? I work-a work-a, away." And Mr. Ianucci would grin broadly, he never resented it. He must have enjoyed the singing. He was the only one Beau seemed afraid of. Mr. Ianucci used to whale the tar out of Beau when he got in trouble. He'd use that broad leather belt that held up his pants. But not anymore; Mr. Ianucci's days of connection with life were gone. Angie, his daughter, would take him out and sit him on a chair in front of their flat when the weather was bright, and the old man would stay there staring around him, like a watchman in a trance. Mario saw Samuessen finally get him to go along with him after the others.

Mario heard the slap of Benigno's sandals against his bare soles. His face was solemn. The friar caught sight of Mario standing near the sinks. "Ah, so, Mario." He came close to him, looking at his eyes. "Why you are so pale? You not eat for lunch, huh?"

Something passed from Benigno to Mario in that exchange of looks. Mario said softly: "Beau is dead, Brother."

"Ja, Beau be dead." Benigno kept watching Mario.

"St. Carmine's won't give him a funeral?"

Benigno pulled out a candle crate and sat Mario down.

"They refuse. Why don't you eat lunch? You get sick if you don't eat."

"St. Fergus won't do it, either."

"No. Why you so upset?"

"We going to have the funeral here?"

"Ja, we have the mass. How you know all about it?"

"Val and Auggie Samuessen told me . . ."

"Ah, so." And then Benigno saw the chalky whiteness on Mario's face. "Put your head between your knees, Mario. Come, put your head down. I be right back."

Mario felt the dizziness, the hum in his ears, the sense that he was slipping out from himself. Benigno came back, passed a small bottle in front of Mario's nose. The ammonia fumes seemed to leap into Mario's brain, straightening him up.

"Why you so upset, Mario?" Benigno put a hand on Mario's head. "Now you listen to me. The man be dead. Whatever he have done in his life our Lord know all about it."

Mario's head cleared, whether from the ammonia or the presence of Benigno's hand on his head, he didn't know.

"They're Italians, Brother."

"Ja, so was St. Francis. And Jesus Christ was a Jew. What that got to do with it? Those churches should not have refuse him a requiem. It be God's job to judge us when we die. We are friars. St. Francis wash the lepers. He pick up the worm so that it not be stepped on. He give his clothes to the poor. He tame the wolf. He comfort the sorrowing. We say the mass for Beau."

"Yes, Brother."

"St. Francis never deny, he never turn away. He not worry about what the law says. Beau leave a mother and a father and a sister. There not be so many rules that God forget to be merciful." And then: "Go down to the kitchen and tell Friar Didicus I want him to fix you up a cup of hot tea and give you some bread. You go down there. I don't want you to be sick. Go ahead."

Mario finished his work for the day and went along a side aisle toward the rear of the church. Hans the sexton spied him and made a gun out of his thumb and forefinger. Mario saw the imaginary gun jerk as Hans approached, a grin on his face.

"I haf shoot you, Mario. Just like the Beau." The fumes of Old Overholt came off Hans's breath. "Why we haf to bury this fella?" He frowned. "Why don't the St. Carmine's do the job?"

"They refuse."

"Ach! I know that. But why we got to do it? He was no good. He was der crook. Why we should do the dirty work? It ain't right." Hans shook his head.

Professor Wolfram was coming down the curving steps from the choir loft as Mario came through the foyer. Wolfram beckoned to him.

"Hey, Mario, is this true?"

"Yes, Professor."

"Gott in Himmel, we have a solemn requiem for this gangster. Why we got to do it? He don't belong to St. Ansgar's. His people don't come here. Why don't they handle it at the other churches, huh? Their Italian funerals is terrible affairs. Ja, they scream and yell. They throw themselves on the coffin. Such carryings-on you never have see." Wolfram scowled.

"He was no good, Mario. Hundred percent no good. I don't like it. Any fella got so many names! Irish name, French name, Italian name. Why they change their names these gangsters, huh? Because they is ashamed! I tell you I don't play no Giuseppe Verdi. No, sir, I don't do it. I refuse. The choir won't like to sing for no Italian gangster. And I don't blame them. Samuessen must have got plenty of gelt for this job. He get the body and then he dump it on us. It ain't right, Mario. You wait, this gives us plenty of trouble."

Baumer was standing out in front of his bakery, his apron flapping in the wind. He was staring down the block where one of Samuessen's assistants was fastening crêpe in the Ianucci hallway. He reached out and grabbed Mario.

"Mario! What the devil we doin'? How we come off to bury Beau? He was a rotten kid. He steal buns and rolls from me when he is just a little schizzer. He stand on the sidewalk across the street and he call me a dumb Dutchie. Ja, ja, ja, he always stealing or insulting us. Why should we bury him? Why should we get into it? All them gangsters will come to St. Ansgar's. Ja, they will!"

"They'll come to the mass?"

"Naturally. First they shoot him, then they go to the funeral, then they take care of all the expenses. I don't think we should get mixed up in this kind of business."

Mario glanced uneasily down the street, the tenements on either side darkening in the dusk, the cobblestones glistening from the river damp, the wind rattling the garbage cans on the sidewalk. How often he'd seen the bandy-legged figure of Beau under a lamppost, all alone on the deserted block. Mario's mind was haunted by Baumer's suggestion that all the gangsters would attend the funeral mass.

Baumer had more to say: "Listen, Mario. I know what I'm talking about. It's the way these things work. Mark my words. They'll be a whole bunch of guys with scars, all dolled up in black suits, black ties, their black hair plastered down, their fingernails so polished you think they never touch anything dirty in their lives. Oh, ja, Mario, they be there at St. Ansgar's." Baumer leaned over confidentially: "Not only the big shots be there. But the one. Ja, the one who have pulled the trigger. The guy who have bumped off the Beau. The one who have kissed him, like Judas . . . the kiss of death. Oh, ja, ja, he be there in one of the pews, and he look as holy as St. Joseph. That what is going to be in our church . . . in our St. Ansgar's."

The whole scene flowered in Mario's mind: the kiss, the killer, Beau in his coffin, the chanting of the Dies Irae, the lugubrious chords of the organ . . . Mario broke away from Baumer and began to run, a litany inside of himself intoning: *Death, death, death, death*. He averted his eyes, he didn't want to see that crêpe of white flowers perched on the hallway doorjamb, didn't want to see those shuttered windows on the ground-floor front flat, didn't want to smell the odor of tomatoes, basil, oregano, garlic, didn't want to imagine Beau suddenly stepping from that hallway, smiling secretly, all dressed up in a blue pin-striped suit, gray homburg hat, and shoes with highish heels to make him taller. And Beau grabbing him: "Hey, Mario. Commere. You're gonna be a priest, huh, huh? That's good. You stick to it. Hear me?"

Mario was running hard, with his mouth open, the cold river wind hitting his stomach, making him nauseous. Halfway down the block he had to stop under a lamppost. He thought he was going to throw up. His forehead was clammy, his stomach churning. Mario was sick.

"Psssssst . . . sssssssuuuuuuussssss, Mario." It came from a dark hallway. The kids must have shot out the light with their BB guns. Mario was so frightened he forgot being sick. And then he made out the derby hat that stuck on top of the pumpkin-like head. It was Adolph Obermuhl. Adolph had a crush on Angie Ianucci. It had not prospered. Adolph was not all there in his upper story. It was thought at one time he and Angie had something going. Angie wore a red sash around her dark dress as a kind of sign that she was conscious of Adolph's attentions. Angie was never like the Dutchie girls, who palled together, laughing and kidding, gossiped on the block, and had some life of their own. Not Angie. She could always be seen in the front room of that ground-floor flat, kneeling before a statue of the Blessed Mother, praying, a small blue votive candle flickering in front of her. She was kept at home. Italian girls were like that. Adolph would stand across the street, keeping up a vigil, hoping that Angie would look from her window and see him. The whole thing was good for a laugh on the block. Pumpkin-head Adolph and the little Ginnie girl. It was a joke. But Beau didn't see the joke. No. No, he didn't. He warned Adolph. Told him to make himself scarce. Lay off his sister or else. But maybe because Adolph was too dumb or stubborn he didn't get the message. And as a result, he caught a terrific beating one night. He never squealed, never said who did it. After that, Angie took off the red sash from around her dress, and now pulled down the shade in the front room. The Dutchies never forgave Beau for hurting Adolph.

"Hey, Mario, somethin', huh? They brought him home. Samuessen delivered him. Bronze casket. Closed. Ain't gonna be opened. Can't see Beau. Won't lift the lid. He's all in pieces. Like chopped meat. Yeah . . . yeah, they used a tommy gun on him."

Mario leaned his head against the cold metal of the lamppost shaft. Adolph was grieving. He said sorrowfully: "Like why they have to kill him, huh? Whatever he done . . . why they have to chop him up? You can hear his mother takin' on . . . hear her cryin' and screamin'. He was her son, you know? And Angie, she's all busted up . . . everythin's on her shoulders now . . . you goin' over an' pay your respects?"

"I got to get home, Adolph."

"Not gonna go, huh? You'll serve at the funeral mass, though, huh, Mario . . . you'll do that, huh?"

"Yes. Solemn requiem . . . three priests . . . nine o'clock."

"That's good Mario. Like for Angie's sake. I'm goin' over . . . like I wan' her to know . . . I'm by her side . . . you know . . ."

Bronze coffin, chopped meat, tommy gun, Mario knew unless he made the effort and broke away Adolph would go through the whole thing all over again.

"I got to go, Adolph."

"Oh, sure, Mario. Me too. I gotta go to Angie . . . terrible things happen in this world, huh, Mario . . ."

Mario ran, his stomach churned, and then he saw his mother standing in front of her doorway, she had a shawl over her head, and stood listening to Big Ned Swayne the cop, who had his nightstick in one hand.

Big Ned was talking. He had very thick lips for an Irishman, and he'd been drinking. He shot a bleary glance at Mario as he came up.

"I sent Beau up the first time. He was no bigger than Mario then. Ah, he wus rotten from the word go, Lena. I warned him and warned him. I even went to his mother, poor soul. I felt sorry for her. I don't know if she could tell what I was sayin', her bein' a foreigner. He had the goods right on him. What could I do but run him in. Ah, them beady eyes of his. I thought he might learn his lesson. Bring him to his senses . . . he was a terrible kid."

Suddenly Big Ned interrupted himself. He sniffed the air. The west wind carried the fumes of cooking hops; one of the illicit breweries was making up its nightly batch of beer. And Big Ned, who'd had many a payoff from those brewers, said: "I'll tell you somethin', Lena. Beau was tied up with them guys, too . . . them beer barons . . ."

Mario's mother brought the conversation to a close: "All I know is his poor mother is heartbroken. Whatever the son was his mother's heartbroken." She turned to her son: "You're late, Mario. Go on up and eat your supper. I left it out for you. I'm goin' up to the wake."

Big Ned twitched his nightstick several times. "I'll walk along with you, Lena. Might just as well pay my respects, too . . . good night, Mario . . . you stick to the church . . . ah, they'll be a big turnout from the precinct. Yes, the captain will turn out a squad or so. Be heavy traffic at St. Ansgar's. Besides, we like them gangsters to know we're there, looking them over."

It rang in Mario's ears. Beau was in the beer business, too, and every cop in the neighborhood was on the take. Not only Big Ned. They all lined up every Friday to get their weekly payoff. Mario went up the stairs, the gas jets flaring into tongues on each landing. Beau had once given him a new baseball glove. Maybe he'd stolen it? Or maybe he'd never forgotten the time Mario kept his mouth shut when the railroad bulls were after him. But Beau was dead, locked in his bronze coffin, soldered shut. His mother and Big Ned would stand in the living room banked in floral wreaths and smelling of candles and no doubt a friar was there chanting the rosary. What had happened to Beau's guardian angel? Everybody had a guardian angel!

Mario couldn't eat his supper. He jumped into bed and pulled the covers over his head. He lay there trying to make his mind a blank. A scuffling in the wall, the rats beginning their nightly races. He shivered, all the fragments of the day racing through his consciousness: the telephone call, the silk underwear, the morgue, the kiss, sealed bronze coffin, chopped meat, Mrs. Ianucci's cry, Angie draped in mourning, Mr. Ianucci staring around vacantly. And Beau, his bandy legs moving like pistons, Beau racing, his chest heaving, his eyes darting like a terrorized horse. Mario got up in a rush, tore out to the toilet in the hall, and threw up. He was sick, panting and heaving.

And then he thought of Brother Benigno, the old friar, who wasn't afraid of death. Slowly, wretchedly, Mario crawled back to bed, keeping the covers over his head, afraid to look out, afraid he might find a hooded figure standing there.

Friars Athenasius, Vicar, and Urbain, three priests, all vested in black, stood in the rear awaiting the casket. The altar was hung with black trappings, with fat orange candles burning, and vases of St. Joseph lilies stood out starkly against the somber background. The church was packed with Dutchies and strangers. And the bass bell tolled: *Beau . . . Beau . . . Beau . . .* The organ rumbled underneath. Mario waited with the priests, the other altar boys stood two by two. The censer gave out lazy wisps of sweet-smelling smoke. Outside on the street dozens of policemen were on duty. Slowly the casket came up the church steps, six swarthy-faced men bearing it on their shoulders. They came to a halt before the three waiting, facing priests. Father Athenasius the celebrant began to intone prayers for the dead, he incensed the coffin, Mario passed the aspergillum to the subdeacon who passed it to the deacon who passed it to the celebrant who flicked holy water on the bronze coffin. In an instant the church rang with the full-voiced choir and the great swell of the organ.

Mario gaped in astonishment. Behind Mrs. Ianucci bent with her grief, behind Mr. Ianucci staring about aimlessly, behind Angie in her weeds, were two lines of scar-faced men, black-suited, black ties, their hair plastered down, and the polish of their manicured fingernails gleaming in the light! The gangsters! Mario swiftly averted his eyes, he didn't want to look them over; suppose his glance happened to land on the killer?

Up the aisle the cortege moved, the casket coming to rest below the sanctuary steps, the priests and altar boys moving into the sanctuary, starting the mass. Mario could see Brother Benigno's head silhouetted against the window in the sacristy door. Mario's heart thumped while the ceremony proceeded, the liturgy chanted, the choir responding antiphonally, the ritual movements taking place. And all the while, in the midst of the terrifying power of the Dies Irae, where Professor Wolfram put the organ through its most dramatic passion, Mario was waiting for that killer to bound from the pew, rush to the altar, and cry out: *I killed Beau. I killed him. I kissed him and then killed him.* Nothing happened, except Mario became more and more involved in his private drama, that of waiting, expecting, imagining. Nothing. Not even during the stupendous, the overwhelming roar of "Tuba mirum spargens sonum" — *The last loud trumpet's spreading tone shall through the place of tombs be blown; the written book shall be outspread and all that it contains be read to try the living and the dead.* Surely the killer would shriek out his guilt at that? Nothing . . . nothing, except for some coughs in the church, and Mrs. Ianucci's wail. Nothing.

"Quid sum miser tunc dicturus?" — What shall my guilty conscience plead? And who for me will intercede, when even saints forgiveness need?

Nothing. Nothing, except Mario seeing Beau running along the street, Beau running, the mucus oozing from his nose. Beau standing by the gutter fire, all alone in the darkness, his father having just beaten him with that thick leather belt. Beau not crying, his face expressionless, staring into the last crumbling embers of the fire.

"Et latronem exaudisti" — and take the thief to thine embrace.

Beau no good, rotten kid, vicious, cruel, dirty fighter, surrounded by the infuriated older Dutchie boys. They were sick of his bullying, his filthy tongue, they were going to give him a lesson. Beau's eyes glazed, Mario watching from outside the group: "C'mon, c'mon, you friggin' Dutchie bastards. You got shit in your blood. C'mon." They knocked him down and picked him up and knocked him down again. Beau never yelled, never cried, the blood running from his mouth. The big Dutchie kids were scared. They'd hurt him bad? They wanted to help him up: "Keep your friggin' hands off . . . shit in your blood, yellow bastards." And off he went like a licked animal, off he went down by the docks alone, licking his wounds. Beau was no good, absolutely worthless. Everybody knew it . . . except his mother, his sister, and possibly his father. Beau was dead and all those scar-faced men had plotted his killing, and one of them had done the slaying!

The music, the ritual, the mouth-filling Latin, that august panoply of death, made Mario's head reel. All light had fled from the world and Mario was cold with hopelessness.

"Suscipe, Domine, preces nostras pro anima famuli . . ." — Receive our prayers, oh Lord, on behalf of the soul of thy servant Italo that, if it is still soiled by any earthly stains . . . they may be wiped out . . .

The cortege, slow-paced and ponderous, moved down the center aisle, the casket once again borne aloft by the six swarthy, scar-faced men with polished fingernails, all to the accompaniment of the Chopin Funeral March. Mario felt himself marching leadenly toward the fires of Hell. They couldn't get old Mr. Ianucci from his pew. Angie was talking to him in Italian, trying to get him into the procession. All those scar-faced men, ringing Mrs. Ianucci, like so many surrogate sons, supporting her, their expressions doleful. And at the rear in his professional black suit was Samuessen, a look of compassionate sorrow on his face. In the foyer, Friar Athenasius chanted the De Profundis, flicked the aspergillum, the drops of holy water stippling the metal casket, Mrs. Ianucci threw herself at the casket: "Italo!" That one single cry, cutting through the organ, the choir, the church. The scar-faced men removed her gently. The bell tolled: *Beau. Beau. Beau. Beau.*

And outside the cops held up the traffic.

The altar was stripped of its black hangings, the orange candles replaced by white ones, the censers emptied, the altar linen changed, and the church quiet, only a few lights burning along the nave, and sunshine coming into the side aisles from the stained-glass windows.

Hans was in the second sacristy giving a report to Brother Benigno.

"They haf twelfe open coaches of flowers. Twelfe. An' there gotta be more cops den I ever see eefen in the St. Patrick parade . . . an' the cops on hosses. Jees, whatta bisness it is, Brudder. You dink it wus a great man instead of Beau . . . Beau who wass a good-for-nothing gangster . . . Ach . . . Brudder . . . make you sick."

Mario was numb, sitting by Brother Benigno's desk.

When Hans left, Brother Benigno came over to him. He sat down next to him. "Ja, Mario?"

Mario said tonelessly, confessing: "I'm afraid to die, Brother."

"Ja. I know, Mario." Benigno put an arm around the boy. "I am afraid to fall. You be afraid to fall?"

Mario looked into Benigno's gray eyes. "To fall, Brother? No, I'm not."

"You see?" Benigno smiled. "I not be afraid to die but to fall I am very afraid. Sometime it will come you will not be afraid to die but you then be afraid of something else. We have the fear in us. And we have the God who help us."

Benigno looked at Mario, put his arms around him. He knew what Mario was going through. He said: "We say the mass for the Beau because we all be men, and all men must die, but all men have open to them the mercy of our Lord. Oh, ja, even the Beau, who was a bowlegged little gangster. The mass it ease the pain for his mother and father and sister. And . . . and it make our Dutchie people remember to be merciful . . . ja, be merciful, because they got to die someday also . . . be merciful. Ja, Mario, not the killing, not the punishment, not the hating, not the being scared, but mercy, mercy. We got to depend on the mercy of God . . . Ja, Mario . . ."

Mario let his head rest against Brother Benigno's tunic.

♦5♦

Friar Alain

People let down their guard when they're in church, particularly in off hours, hours when there's no service, when the light patters down from the clerestory, the pews are relatively empty, and the whole interior is held in quietness: Mario took all of this in.

Often he was struck by the air of surrender which he saw on those faces deep in prayer. Such absorption seemed to suggest that there was indeed a Presence to be invoked. And sometimes this impression became so powerful it made Mario look about him, expecting God to have assumed substance and be very near, waiting to be discovered.

Mario learned to recognize as familiars many of those quiet worshipers at St. Ansgar's. Nearly always they had favorite locations which they slipped into each time. Often when he was at work in the church, he'd have a glimpse of one of them entering. That he knew them only by sight, never spoke to them, never saw them except in these off hours, didn't prevent Mario from inventing lives for them. He gave them occupations, relationships, homes, characteristics, experiences, all imagined.

But there was one figure among this anonymous band who stood out sharply, put Mario's imagination in check. He was young, always wearing the same dark suit, and at first glance so ordinary looking as to escape notice. He arrived punctually, like clockwork. Took up his same place, the bend in the communion rail, and from this angle he would kneel motionless, staring at the high altar. He remained exactly forty-five minutes (Mario timed him) and then departed. The first few times Mario blinked, the young man suddenly was gone, vanished, as if he'd never been. Yes, he became very much an object of speculation for Mario.

Chances were no one paid the slightest attention to this shadowy young worshiper except Mario, who waited for his arrival. In he came, found his place at the communion rail, knelt down, his arms at his sides, his back straight, his head cocked slightly to one side, his eyes closed, and tears would run down his face. Tears! He was utterly still. This statue-like absorption gave Mario the notion the young man had parked his body there and stolen off. Sounded crazy to Mario but that's exactly the way it seemed. So completely rapt in his devotions, carried away, Mario would kick his scrub pail or drop his cake of hard soap to get a rise out of him. Nothing. No sign of being there. He was away.

And those tears. Mario was quick to sense sorrow. Stanley Street provided plenty of experience with sorrow. Those tears did not seem to be an expression of sorrow. And yet, what are tears for? There they were coursing down that immobile face. It puzzled the life out of Mario. At last he mentioned it to Brother Benigno.

Benigno knew whom he meant right away. Mario had a notion Benigno wanted to dismiss the matter. Benigno looked out the sacristy window into the church, looked right at the place the young man ordinarily occupied.

"That fella by the rail? Ja, he's a convert. Friar Vicar have instruct him and take him in to the church. He work over in the train station. Ticket seller. He comes here every day on his lunch hour."

Couldn't have much time to eat, considering he spent three-quarters of an hour every day kneeling at the communion rail, Mario figured.

Benigno added: "Comes from Canada somewheres. You can tell he don't come from this country . . . I think he be French."

Ah, French! Not Dutchie, French! Mario asked tentatively: "Why is he always crying, Brother?"

Benigno looked at Mario. And then he crinkled up his eyes, smiled: "He be a ticket seller, that fella. If you work with the public all the time, for crying out loud, you cry, too."

Mario understood at once. There was something here Benigno did not want to get into, perhaps he was puzzled, too.

◆

Not so long after, Mario was flabbergasted to see the mysterious young man wearing the habit, seated at the long table in the kitchen.

"How come he's wearing the habit, Brother?"

"He becomes a third-order brother!"

"What about his job in the train station?"

Benigno growled: "I guess he have to give it up!"

"Just like that."

"Mario . . ." Benigno interrupted himself, took a breath, and then said in measured tones: "It have happened that way. Anybody can become a member of the third order of St. Francis. He set it up for lay people who want to live the holy life. This fella he want to do that, I guess. He come here to try it out, see if he like it. He have taken no vows. He just make simple promises, nothing bind him in. If he find he don't like it, he leave. Take a look when you see him. You going to see his habit ain't got no cowl, and he don't have no beard, and no tonsure . . ." And then with a closing growl: "I answer your questions!"

Mario persisted: "He came in here to live the holy life. Huh! Maybe something went wrong out there for him, huh, Brother?"

"Ach, Mario, the questions you always has." Benigno caught the brooding look in the boy's large brown eyes. "All right. Sit down."

The two of them sat in the second sacristy.

"Sometimes a fella can't take the world no more. He want to get away from it. It happen with plenty of people. They get sick and disgusted with all the nonsense out in the world." Benigno balled his hand around his beard: "And sometimes, too, something else happen. Something happen inside a man. He wake up to something calling inside him . . . telling him what he should do . . . where he must go . . . ja, Mario?"

"Yes, Brother." Then in a moment: "What's he going to do here?"

"He work as door porter."

"Yeah. What's his name, Brother?"

"He keeps his own name on account of he ain't professed. If he stick it out and join the order, take binding vows, then he get a name because he have a new life. For now he keep his own name, Alain. That be what he get baptized with. Friar Alain. Now for jingo neddies' sake, you can't have no more questions. We go to work!"

Now that Alain was a member of the community, Mario saw him frequently. He took to greeting him by name. And Friar Alain returned the greeting. Brother Benigno was right. Alain certainly talked with an accent. But he was hardly a talker. He seemed to keep very much to himself, doing his work answering the door and attending devotions. Mario watched him intently, he was still very much of a mystery. A man who had a secret life, one who lived in another world.

Separating the first and second sacristy was the choir, a small chapel used by the community of friars for devotions. Other than for very special uses, the public was not allowed in the choir. It was here the friars chanted the office, or litanies, or special ritual observances. It was a good-sized place with a vaulted wooden ceiling with a single stained-glass window at the end away from the altar. Three sides of the chapel were taken up with dark oaken stalls, and a dado of embossed paneling covered the walls. The choir was a twilight place, visited at all hours of the day by the religious who'd tuck themselves away in their stalls and meditate. Sometimes Mario would be startled by a friar suddenly leaving his stall; so shadowy and quiet was the choir, you never knew anyone was there.

It was in the choir, in the rear back corner, Mario looked to find Friar Alain. He seemed to have been assigned that spot. He'd be there when he was not on duty answering the door. In the duskiness of the choir Mario would see Alain take up that distinctive statue-like pose he'd first seen in church; and again he'd see the tears welling up in his eyes. Yes, even in the dark, Mario could catch the glisten of those tears. Alain would stay there for hours! What a puzzle he was.

◆

The best way to learn anything about a newcomer to the community was to observe how the other friars treated him. Usually you could catch them relaxing in the common room on the second floor of the friary, reading the newspapers, or shooting pool, or even playing pinochle, or just shooting the breeze. This didn't work with Alain because he'd never go to the common room, he didn't mingle. The friars seemed just as puzzled about their fellow religious as Mario. Was it because he was French and they without exception Dutchies? The only one who seemed to have an inside track was Vicar, but then, he was the priest who had converted Alain and brought him into the friary and spoke French as well.

Once, and only once, Mario witnessed another side to Friar Alain. Friar Urbain had been a newspaperman before he joined the order; he was a man with a terrific sense of humor. He got Alain to laugh. It was an astonishing sight. Alain clapped his hands together with glee; his face opened and shone with joy. What had Urbain done? He had sung, with an odd nasality, a French Canadian song about the effect of pea soup on the stomach; an earthy song.

Yes, Alain was a puzzle to Benigno as well. Mario caught his old friend studying the young man. Benigno never tried to hide his feelings, nothing underhanded or covert in his scrutiny. Benigno didn't stare, rather his eyes simply took things in without making for offense; it was a kind of invitation, Benigno wanted to share with you. But it fell flat in Alain's case; he was distant. And Benigno was flummoxed by it.

The maintenance of the choir was a touch-and-go operation simply because it was used at all hours by the friars for their private devotions. Many times Benigno strained just waiting for the last friar to clear out of his stall so he and Mario could get in and do their housekeeping. They'd have the small vacuum cleaner, the wood polish, the rags, the scrub pails, everything at the ready. Once they got into the choir, all the lights burning, the friars would steer clear of the chapel until they finished. But it was the getting in there. Benigno would wait impatiently, flicking his feather duster, staring at an occupied stall, itching to get started. The old man would parade back and forth between the two sacristies, clapping his bare soles against his sandals in a special way that telegraphed his impatience, letting the praying friar know he was holding up Benigno's work, and it was time for him to cut short his devotions.

None of this worked with Friar Alain. His protracted meditation in the choir was more like a takeover than a visit. It was an occupation. Mario couldn't understand Benigno's tolerance; it was completely out of character. It was Mario who became impatient, wanting to get on with the cleanup of the choir.

"What you in such a hurry about, Mario? We get the choir clean. The work ain't going to run away. We take care of it. Don't you be so impatient . . . you too young to get that habit . . ."

Mario certainly had plenty to think about, and most of it concerned Alain. How had he managed to make Benigno patient? The old man was making allowances for the young friar; absolutely unheard of. Mario couldn't remember a time when Benigno had tempered his forceful management of duties for anyone else. Then, slowly, Mario got the sense Benigno knew something about Alain. Yes, he knew something no one else knew. What it was, Mario hadn't the ghost of an idea. But he was convinced it was something of great importance.

They were burning off dried wax from the bronze candle tips. The wax hissed and sputtered and dripped as Mario passed the tips across the gas jet. He said: "He doesn't talk much, huh, Brother?"

Benigno wiped off the tips passed to him by Mario: "Who you mean?"

Mario knew that Alain was in the choir at that moment, so he lowered his voice: "Friar Alain."

"He talk."

Boldly: "I never hear him say anything, Brother."

Benigno caught a hot tip, burnished it with his rag, and said teasingly: "Next time he talk, I'll get you, so you can hear. No need to worry about talk. We got plenty who make up for him. Some of the friars never stop talking . . ."

After a while:

"Does he have a family, Brother?"

Benigno chuckled: "Ah, my Mario. He got to have a family . . . at some time, else how did he get born? Stands to reason he have to have a momma and poppa."

"But nobody ever comes to see him . . ."

A dab of hot wax had hit the tabletop and quickly solidified. Benigno methodically lifted it from the surface with his knife blade. He said tenderly: "You know, Mario, some people be very private, it don't mean nothing big, it just the way they be. I tell you, I'm sure that God know everything that have got to be known about Alain."

Benigno wasn't chiding Mario, nor was he cutting him off; it was his way of imposing a moratorium on the subject, and Mario understood it.

But the moratorium covered only so much; it didn't extend to Mario's observation or his conjectures. No, it was a matter he could not keep from his mind. Every time he crossed the choir, his glance automatically strayed toward the corner stall. There would be Alain, in that struck attitude, like a figure cast in metal. And Mario had the oddest sensation, something prickled along his spine, that there was someone with Alain. But there was no one else in the shadowy chapel, no one. Mario was certain of it, his glance had taken in every stall, all vacant. Odd. Still he could not shake the sense of someone else with Alain. This intuition he kept to himself; he held back his impulse to mention it to Brother Benigno.

They were locking the church. For some reason, the nuts were out in force: the whirlers, the genuflectors, the holy water sprinklers, the statue strokers, the cross kissers, the communion rail clutchers. They had to be herded from the church. Benigno rattled his ring of keys, muttering, growling. At last in a combined flanking movement,

Mario from one aisle, Benigno from the other, the last, inveterate holy water splasher was squeezed out into the night air.

Benigno said irritably: "I don't know what get into them some nights." He cast a dissatisfied glance at the empty church. "Come on, Mario. Tonight, we look extra. One of them maybe have hid himself."

They separated, combed the various places of concealment, confessionals, pews, statues, pulpit, grotto, side altars, organ loft. Mario could hear the clap of Benigno's bare feet in his sandals coming from the narthex. Suddenly Mario froze. He stared transfixed at the statue of St. Francis. Mario had passed it and repassed it hundreds of times, dusted it, repaired it, washed it, it was part of his familiar world, but at that moment he saw the figure in its brown habit, the closed eyes, tears, painted tears, welling from the corner of the eyes, the arms limply on the side, the head slightly cocked . . .

Brother Benigno called from the foyer: "Mario . . ." And then again: "Mario . . . why you don't say something . . . you have found one?"

And then impatiently the old man came charging from the rear, came along the side aisle, his beard thrust out. He saw the fixed expression on the boy's face, his stiff body. "What's the matter? What happen?"

Mario pointed stiffly. "Friar Alain."

Benigno caught the power of the emotion which charged through the boy, and in an instant the old man became as solicitous as the Samaritan. He said softly: "Mario . . . Mario. I don't know what you thinking . . . but lots of people copy what they see . . . they try to put on what they see . . . they try to take after a saint . . . that all it is, Mario."

Benigno looked into Mario's face, the wonder-struck expression in his eyes.

"Mario, you have let this thing work on you. It is nothing . . . nothing. Come. Come now. We go inside, the church is empty, all the nuts has gone home for the night. Come . . . come away." Benigno put an arm around Mario's shoulder and they walked together back into the sacristy. Benigno sat him down in his chair, got him a small eyeglass full of sacramental wine, and watched the boy drink it. "You be feeling better soon. Now, Mario . . . I want you to forget all about what you have think . . ." Benigno stared hard into the boy's face. "Ja, Mario, ja?"

But Mario could not forget! Imagination or no imagination! Over and over again he would stand before the statue of St. Francis when the rays of sunlight poured down in slanting conduits, raising sparkles of dust. There was not the slightest doubt, Friar Alain had modeled his attitude, his devotional posture upon that of St. Francis. But what was so peculiar about that? Brother Benigno had been right, many people aped the saints. What was so strange that Alain should? Mario didn't know. But as his eyes carefully strayed over the plaster cast representation, the marks of the stigmata glowing ruby red against the pale flesh, Mario could not shed his feeling of deep disquiet.

And Benigno had not forgotten, either. He kept an eye on Mario. The old man knew all about the way people would have miracles bouncing around as if they were Ping-Pong balls. Stanley Street was as gullible in this respect as the most primitive village, Dutchies though they were. Yes, he could recall the time when it was reported that the Blessed Mother's face and figure appeared on the outside wall of a warehouse, an apparition at least forty-five feet square. Every Dutchie, even those bedridden, went down along the docks, in the icy air, night after night, to see the materialization that never came. For weeks and months after that, when asked by the old parishioners about the "miracle" Benigno replied: "Some drunk have said he see Her. With that rotgut inside of him, and what it do to his head, he could have seen anything."

Yes, Benigno knew all about the purported miracles, and he went out of his way to explain to Mario how most of these happenings could be traced back to simple, understandable phenomena: indigestion, booze, guilt, fear, imagination, excitement, sickness in the head. "People's always looking into the sky to see the signs. Be better if they keep their eyes on the ground so they can see where they be going! They always expecting the Lord to be putting on a magic show for them, like He's a magician. They want a miracle, this way they don't have to do nothing themselves. You see, Mario, people want the miracle because they don't have no belief in faith . . . I tell you, seeing miracles all the time it could tear apart the church."

After a while Mario came to look upon the matter more reasonably. He could understand the connection between the French Canadian friar and the Poverello in much simpler terms, emulation. Yes, that was the word one of the friars had used in a sermon: emulation. Trying to resemble, model ourselves on a saint. Yes, Mario, what with Benigno's commonsense outlook and his own less heightened view, came to accept Friar Alain and his ways for what they were.

And then it happened!

Mario heard the thud. It came from the choir. It was an unusual sound. He rushed from the sacristy. He searched about the dark choir, his eyes finally resting up in the corner, rear. And then he saw, sprawled on the waxed tile floor, in front of the oaken stall, Friar Alain. Mario ran to find Brother Benigno. The old man came hurrying behind Mario and went to the fallen Alain. He touched him. He said to Mario calmly, too calmly: "Mario, the friar have fainted. Go get Father Athenasius. Don't . . . run . . . walk . . . slowly."

That afternoon, Benigno in his chair at his desk and Mario on an empty candle crate, the old man explained: "He fainted. He have been fasting. So what happen when you don't eat? The fire go out on account of it don't get no fuel. Your body is burning up food to keep going. When you don't stoke it . . . well, it go out, whssst. It quit on you." He looked at Mario intently, holding the eye contact. "That's all . . . what have happen to Friar Alain . . . that's all . . . you understand, Mario?"

In a few weeks Mario had only to cast a glance to the corner stall in the rear to see Friar Alain in his customary place in his customary attitude. And once when he met the young man coming from his devotions, the latter smiled at him. Smiled! Though what struck Mario at the time was the fact that he'd seen Alain's eyes for the first time, what a turned-in look they had! Yes, Mario realized again, what a trouble his imagination was to him. Good thing Brother Benigno was around to pump sense into him.

And then when everything seemed settled, Mario began to notice how the other friars began to regard Alain, keeping their distance as it were. He'd even catch Benigno giving Alain quizzical looks. There seemed to be a kind of brooding expectancy that pervaded the friary, and it seemed to focus about Alain. Once again Mario's imagination worked overtime. He wanted to speak to Brother Benigno about what he was feeling, this atmosphere, but he kept it to himself. But Benigno knew Mario.

"You see, Mario, Alain is a young man. He is a convert. He is trying out the religious life. He want to push himself. He want to be holy so bad. He want to show God he have a vocation. It happen to us when we first enter the religious life. We want to try so hard . . . to be the hermit, to live like the saints. We push ourselves. It stand to reason, when you try too hard, sometimes it make you dizzy."

Friar Alain was removed from his duty as door porter. Mario heard no explanation for it. Benigno seemed to shy away from the matter. And twice, quite by accident, Mario had a glimpse of Friar Vicar talking to Alain, the latter standing submissively before the deputy superior. Later, Mario saw Benigno scrutinizing Alain, and the old man's face seemed shot through with suffering.

No, it wasn't Mario's imagination. Something was going on.

"The church have to be on guard against the wild stories. You know, you let something get around in a parish, the whole thing can blow up. The church have to be very careful." That's what Benigno said.

Ah, was that the reason they'd removed Alain from his job as door porter? To keep him away from the public? Out of the sight of prying eyes and loose tongues? Of course, Mario saw it at once. Suppose, just suppose one of those nuts got a look at those tears streaming from his eyes, or suppose he suddenly pitched over again. Wow! The parish would go crazy! That was it. Mario understood now. The friars dreaded more than anything else the slightest hint of the supernatural, the miraculous. Yes, they were afraid of what it might give rise to. Why, every biddy in the parish would come running for a scrap of Friar Alain's habit, his nail parings, hair trimmings, anything that would give them some little bit of him they could use to heal their ills. Yes, Stanley Street would take the friar and rub him over its multitudinous ills and be raised, healed. Mario understood: acts which contradict the scheme of things are unwelcome! Especially in the church.

And all this time, Friar Alain led his quiet unobtrusive existence, spending almost all of his time in the choir, hidden away. Mario could almost combine the walls, the stained-glass window, the stalls, the shadows, with Friar Alain, he was so much a part of the whole. Yes, it was a most peculiar period in the life of the friary.

What took place occurred in a blinding instant! In the choir, in that dim and quiet retreat, against the dark luster of those oaken stalls and the colored tones of the rose window. They both heard the fall.

Mario arrived first, Benigno coming next. Alain on his back, his face contorted, his breath coming in great gasps, blood spreading on the tessellated floor. Mario saw the swellings on his bare insteps, like open mouths, the gashes on his palms, and the dark stain slowly discoloring the side of his habit. Benigno held Alain in his arms. He whispered: "Get Friar Athenasius, Mario. And you go and stay in the altar boys' room. Don't come back in here."

It seemed to take place in another place, another time, if . . . if it took place at all. Yes, that was the way Mario looked at it. Did it take place?

When Mario returned that afternoon, everything was quiet, peaceful, he could hear the ticking of the sacristy clock, the fluttery sound of candles. He looked for Brother Benigno. He saw him kneeling in the choir, his cowl drawn up over his head. Mario tiptoed across the choir to the second sacristy. But Benigno must have caught sight of him. He followed Mario into the second sacristy. He looked at Mario with an expression of deep concern in his watery eyes.

He said gravely: "I want to tell you a story. Sit down. You listen very carefully. When St. Francis is alive, there was a boy friar. Maybe he was very much like you with big brown eyes. And this boy he love St. Francis very much. He love him so much he always want to be with him. He want to see St. Francis at prayer. Now, St. Francis lots of time he wake up in the night and steal away to a clearing, all by himself, alone, to pray. So what this boy does? He tie a cord to St. Francis's robe so that when St. Francis he wake up, the cord pull at the boy, and he wake up, too. Now the boy does this. And he fall asleep on the ground next to St. Francis. When St. Francis wakes up, he discover the cord the boy friar have tied to his habit. Very quietly he untie the cord and he go off to say his prayers alone. The boy he wakes up and find St. Francis gone. So he gets up and he go look for him. He find him in the clearing, praying. But St. Francis have company with him in the clearing on account of the boy hear him talking. When he sneak closer, he sees this great light in the clearing. Great light. And there he see Jesus Christ, His Mother, and John the Baptist, and St. Francis. It is too powerful for the boy to see this vision and he fall over in a faint, like he is lifeless. St. Francis after the vision stumble over the boy in the darkness. He pick him up and carry him in his arms like Christ carry the lamb. Slowly the boy come back to life. He not sure what happen. St. Francis command him. Now, St. Francis never command nobody, so you can see when he do it must be very important. He say to the boy: he is never to tell nobody what he the boy has seen as long as St. Francis live."

Without warning, Mario began to cry. Benigno pulled Mario's head against the tunic of his habit. He whispered to him: "I not be St. Francis. And I can't command you. But my Mario, please don't talk about what you think you have see today. You must be like the boy friar . . ."

And Mario never spoke of what he had seen.

But he often thought of Friar Alain when he passed the statue of St. Francis in the side aisle.

6

Chaldean Furnaces and Assyrian Mire

In the first place they were always The Irish, and in the second Ohmigod Eileen was the most hauntingly beautiful girl on the whole of the West Side, and in the third, Himself, as O'Dell was called by everybody in the neighborhood, was a terrible man.

Mario never saw O'Dell set foot inside St. Ansgar's, which was not so strange; as a matter of fact O'Dell never set foot inside St. Fergus's, which *was* strange because it was The Irish church. Brother Benigno said what was strangest was that O'Dell could set his foot down at all considering his ordinary condition.

O'Dell was visible enough. Mario would see him staggering down the block, right in the middle of Stanley Street, cars and trucks honking at him, but there he'd be stumbling along the cobblestones, his eyes abrawl, his fists raised. Like a gladiator staring at the stands, O'Dell would look from left to right at the Dutchie matrons who leaned out of their tenement flats and he'd shout: "Take in your heads you spawn of Chaldean furnaces and Assyrian mire!" Nobody knew what that meant, but the women vanished from their windows, their cheeks burning with shame and humiliation, with some conviction their morals had been traduced.

O'Dell was always stewed, his eyes always bloodshot like those of a crazed horse. Sometimes Mario would spy him wobbling along the docks, yelling at the freighters tied up, raising his arms toward the littered filth of the North River: "Oh, Western Ocean, body of water which bulks between me and the Land of Heart's Desire." Often his mood would change abruptly and he would begin to sob, tearing at his one and only suit, and weave precariously on the string-piece of a pier, staring at the dirty river water, looking as if he might pitch headfirst into the murky depths of that great Western Ocean. Brother Benigno said O'Dell was an unhappy man, a man who yearned for his homeland. Most of the Dutchies wished whatever it was he yearned for would come and carry him away from Stanley Street.

Ohmigod explained to everyone that Himself was not an average man. He was a poet, an occupation until then unknown on Stanley Street. What kind of poetry did he compose? It was the kind which concerned itself very much with the "farces": life, death, beauty, decay, longing, the spirit, and the mystical soul of Ireland. Mario never read any of O'Dell's poetry. Ohmigod Eileen said it was published in a small magazine down in the Village (Greenwich). Mario would like to have read it, once at least anyway. Brother Benigno said he was better off for not having read it (O'Dell was anti-clerical, fulminated against the church, called it a horse-leech embedded in the flanks of mankind).

Ohmigod was a neighborhood boast, a delight, cherished on account of her ravishing loveliness. When Ohmigod walked along the sidewalk, the redbrick tenement walls to one side, every eye on the block automatically zeroed in on her. Her skin, her hair, the light in her eyes, the way she held her head, her walk, her lips like juicy fruit, just to see her brought a gasp to all those Dutchie observers. Mario thought it was in this way she'd gotten her name. You know, she was so arresting looking, it seemed quite natural one would say, getting a look at her: "Oh, my God!" But that was not it, Brother Benigno said. Instead he said she got the name simply because she prefaced every remark with "Oh, my God!" Also it was the neighborhood's way of distinguishing her from her mother, who was called by an equally pious nickname. Benigno told Mario to ask his mother about it. Lena said to her son: "Her mother was called Jesus, Mary, and Joseph Malloy. Anything she said always included that and Eileen was embarrassed by it. Seemed sinful to her, so she used something nicer like Oh, my God."

It was a letdown for Mario. He would much rather it had been Eileen's gorgeousness which had gotten her the name. But however she got her handle Stanley Street stuck up for her, even though she was one of The Irish, which went to show (as far as Mario was concerned) the Dutchies were not indifferent to natural beauty; so powerful was its influence on them it even overcame entrenched prejudices.

Mario's mother was a great champion of Eileen. She prided herself on not being "small." Lena was ready to do battle in Ohmigod's behalf when some narrow-minded critic would condemn Eileen for having "taken up" (this being the cover for living with someone outside the bonds of matrimony), keeping house with O'Dell at 527, first floor rear. But Lena's support did not extend to O'Dell's moodiness, his tendency to pummel Eileen when the "farces" overcame him. At such times Mario and his father would sit quietly at the supper table while Lena would glare at them, raising her voice as she said: "That shrimp. That Harp! I wish he'd raise his hand to me. Ohhhhhoho, I wish he'd do it just once! That'd be the last time he'd lift his arm against a woman! The bastard!"

It was true about O'Dell's hands getting away from him. Occasionally Mario would see Eileen wearing sunglasses on a rainy day, or a scarf covering one side of her face. A can had fallen off a shelf and hit her in the eye (she'd say) or she had a terrible gumboil (she'd say). No one believed her, and everyone on the block would place another black mark against O'Dell's account. But Ohmigod never said a word of complaint, nor did they ever hear her cry out when O'Dell knocked her around. There was a good bit of knocking women around on Stanley Street, particularly on the hot steamy nights of summer when their screams and moans would linger in the humid atmosphere.

Brother Benigno would raise and shake his fist. "What kind of man it take to punch and kick his wife . . . the mother of his children? Huh? What kind of man that be? I tell you I fix their wagon if I catch them . . ." Benigno would thrust out his beard, his eyes blazing.

Special novenas were conducted for the purpose of curbing wife abuse. The most exceptional preachers among the friars would use their powers of eloquence to bring home to the men what they were doing. But it was to no avail since it was only the women who would attend the services. They'd sit there in the pews weeping. Benigno would say in frustration: "Ach, what the point is of bringing tears into their eyes? They already have cried when they get socked." And then Benigno would show his provincialism: "It don't be the Dutchie men who knocked around their women, it be the Irishers. Don't do no good to preach here at St. Ansgar's. Why don't they do it at St. Fergus's?"

In Ohmigod's case it really didn't matter, she attended neither church and O'Dell would have drubbed her for going, period. But Mario's mother could remember the time when she and Ohmigod would go, arm in arm, to the evening services at St. Ansgar's. "Oh, the laughs we had. And what wonderful preachers they had back then. Eileen and I had good times. We'd take the ferry at Twenty-third Street and go across the river to Hoboken. Out in the middle of the river there'd always be a breeze of a summer night. And there'd be musicians on the boat, an accordion player, a fiddler, and a tambourine player. Yeah, Eileen was just a kid then . . . I was like her big sister. How beautiful she was even then. Yes, Eileen used to go to St. Ansgar's before she was trapped by that son of a bitch O'Dell!"

Mario might have been a little in love with Ohmigod, though the difference in their ages was considerable. He had an unforgettable vision of her coming down Stanley Street, her two arms clutching bags of groceries, her cheeks reddened by the crisp wind from the river, her hair blowing about, her eyes sparkling, and a laugh on her lips. She'd beat by as if lighted up inside by some magic radiance. She'd yell out, "Hello, Mario . . . how's your mother?"

It was funny that such a peach as Ohmigod had no sense of her own staggering good looks. She had no sense of what such a beauty demanded. It was a kind of blindness. And it had to be the deep-down reason for her tying up with such a louse as O'Dell. Yes, it could only be because Eileen didn't recognize her own splendor. She could have had any man, even one of the biggest of the Irish bootleggers. To throw in her lot with a man like O'Dell, always soused, combative, small and ugly, acid dripping from his lips . . .

He'd plant himself off the curb, his hat in his hand, like a Roman in the forum, and address himself to any head showing from a tenement window. There was a floweriness to his invective: "You're a gathering of ants. Your souls rusted with industry. Your eyes are cash registers. Your hearts filled with sand. Your parents were dung beetles. You're hag-ridden by respectability, by the church, by your own runty minds. Oh, you're a pack of cemetery worms." Things would come hurling down from the windows. O'Dell would clap his hat on his head and begin to dance about, using his fists like a boxer. "Spawn . . . spawn of Chaldean furnaces and Assyrian mire." Bags of garbage would come pelting down . . . O'Dell would make an obscene gesture with his middle finger.

Oh, yes, the account against O'Dell was very lengthy. He had spared no one with his scathing tongue. His belligerence was entirely democratic: cops, storekeepers, friars, children, other bums, ward heelers, landlords, anybody. Mario guessed O'Dell had some kind of unquenchable hate inside of him. And he wondered if O'Dell let loose in hopes of getting a terrible beating. He asked Brother Benigno if such a thing was possible.

Benigno put an arm around Mario's shoulder: "Ja, my Mario, you know something. That be exactly the case with O'Dell. He be begging to have some fella knock his block off, to bust in his head. I see that kind of thing before. You see, the O'Dell he be sick. He have got the con. Ja, the con make a man like a firecracker, he go off all the time."

The "con." Of course! O'Dell was doomed all right. Mario had seen other consumptives at St. Ansgar's praying, seeking remission from their sentence. And Mario understood the disease was well named consumption for he had seen it consuming its victims, their flesh from their bodies, reducing them to scarecrows with great hollows in their flushed cheeks and eyes that burned like expiring suns. That was what ticked away inside of O'Dell. Did Ohmigod know? Did the neighborhood know?

But then who could be compassionate when that crocodile tongue began to wag, when his offenses were toted up? O'Dell was the curse of the West Side. If the Dutchies knew he was dying they would have brought him a shroud so he'd hurry the process along! Imagine such a flannel mouth, sponger, drunk, woman beater, freeloader, brawler dying! Yes, dying!

He never brought a dollar home. Eileen paid for everything. She worked over in a five-and-ten on Herald Square. She was in charge of the cosmetics counter; with her looks, the glow of her skin, it couldn't have been otherwise. Women flocked to buy that which only nature could provide. But the cosmetics department flourished under Ohmigod's charge. Lipstick, eye shadow, powder, and secret ointments and emollients, but nothing in the way of art or magic could change O'Dell. As Mario once heard an old Dutchie say, but discreetly so that Eileen might not hear: "Chust the same, Ohmigod is The Irish. O'Dell is The Irish. The Irish goes wid The Irish."

Infatuation! Romance! Eileen adored him. And he — though he walloped her — always, however loaded, stumbled his way back to 527. Some of the adolescent Dutchie girls, feeling the first licks of the secret life, were thrilled by the passion of the relationship. It was wild and savage, so unlike Dutchie passion.

One spring evening, the air like wine, Ohmigod dropped over to Mario's flat for a visit. And like old times, Mario's mother and Eileen knelt at the front-room window and looked down on the street. There they were, elbows on the sill, chattering, laughing, passing remarks, recalling their good times from other years, and all the while taking in what was going on along the block.

Mario and his father were in the front room, sitting at the table, his father sipping a glass of wine, Mario trying to do his homework, the gas mantle throwing an orange glow. The western sun threw a great shaft of light along the block from river to river. Once in a while Mario would see his father casting a glance at the pair of rumps shoved back into the room while Lena and Ohmigod talked as if there were no tomorrow and today were everything, talked for the sheer joy of talking together at the window in the glorious light and wonderful air; oh, the world was young and everything was possible and no one would ever die.

Suddenly and without preamble, the idyll was destroyed. From below rose the hoarse flannel-mouthed demand. "Where's me supper, you rip!"

Mario was astonished when he caught sight of Eileen's face as she turned back into the room. Joy! Joy! It sprang to her face like a tiger pouncing on prey. Joy! Incredible. His mother was astonished at the reaction as well. She tried to detain Ohmigod. And O'Dell down on the curb, just itching for a shouting match, shouted: "Today. Now. In the twentieth century, Eileen Malloy. Do you hear me?"

Mario's mother couldn't keep herself from boiling over. She poked her head out of the window and shot down three floors below: "She'd have to be dead not to hear you."

"I'm talking to my woman, woman. Eileen Malloy, you're away from home. Could you not be there for me after a long day's toil?"

Mario's mother was mumbling something.

"You're a shame to me, Eileen Malloy . . . as your mother must've been a shame to your poor father" — old Mr. Malloy had bent his elbow, too — "and that would have been something, your father being shanty Irish. And all your relatives no better than fleas on a dead horse."

O'Dell was cranking himself up, and what was amazing to Mario, Eileen, instead of quaking, was rapturous, as if she were being wooed by some honey-voiced prince from across the sea. It was Mario's mother who was boiling. But she was a Dutchie and that made the difference.

"Will you get down here, you worthless seed of worthless parents? Your brothers" — Ohmigod hadn't any — "were mangy goats, and your father's sweat dried on your mother's belly. And you were begotten of horse droppings and cat piss. Oh, come down, shake your big ass. Goddamnit, this is Himself calling to you."

Mario's father got to his feet. He was there to soft-pedal Lena, whose fuse was burning rapidly toward the charge of powder.

Then with a roar: "You scumbag . . . you scumbag!"

Now of all the terrible epithets, the one that was most awful on Stanley Street, the one that would launch armies, had just been uttered by O'Dell. Perhaps it was because everybody pictured what it meant: scumbag, the lewd, passion-spent condom so often seen bobbing like a pale worm in the dirty water of the river. It was a battle cry.

And Lena shoved herself out the window and let rip: "You no-good, lousy son of a bitch! You dirty, rotten, freeloading, rag-picking bastard! Worthless shit! Get away from my door or I'll wipe the street up with you, you gutter rat . . ."

"Lena . . . Lena . . . ," but Mario's father couldn't stem the tide.

She whirled on him. "You can stand here and let your wife be insulted by that Irish son of a bitch?"

Immediately the front room was tight. One of those sudden explosions which were always occurring on Stanley Street. Ohmigod stood, her face suddenly drained of color, a hostage, a very Helen of Troy trying to understand how her presence had set off such a row.

From the sidewalk: "Ah, is that the voice of broken glass? Do I recognize the tongue of the fishwife? Is it you, Lena? I should have known soon as me back was turned you'd get your hooks into my Eileen, poison her against me. Send her down to me, you poison-tongued smut. Do you hear?"

Mario's mother reached a hand behind her, feeling for the pots of begonias and sweet onions which stood on the end table. Her hand had eyes and clutched one of the flowerpots and in one continuous sweeping arc, the pot swished out the window and shattered on the stones below, not a foot away from where O'Dell stood.

"Is it a fight you want you hellpot? You've picked the right one this time. I'm not afraid of you, Lena. I'll take care of your hash . . . fight . . ."

Mario's heart began pounding inside of him disagreeably, what had happened so swiftly, so sharply, to make the mood of violence seem inevitable? They went out on the landing, Mario, Eileen, Lena, and Mario's father. Coming up the stairs, from landing to landing, they heard the tramp of O'Dell's feet. It was all crazy. Everything was twisted out of shape. Eileen trying to get away from his mother, the gas jet flickering, the downward line of the banister rail, the heavy breaths of the ascending O'Dell, and the fiery taunts from his mother planted on the top of the staircase: "Keep coming, O'Dell. Just show your filthy head, you son of a bitch. Just bring it up and I'll bust it open for you . . . keep coming."

And then Mario's father moved. He grabbed his wife and thrust her from the head of the stairway, got Eileen out of the way, and glanced toward Mario to see he was out of the line of skirmish. Then: "You be quiet, Lena." And she was.

Mario's father called down: "Mr. O'Dell. No need to come up. Mr. O'Dell, no need for all the upset."

Mario could see in the subdued light of the hall the scarlet face of O'Dell showing through the banisters on the lower treads of the last flight of stairs. He was winded so badly he could hardly get his words out.

"There's . . . no . . . stopping me now . . . no . . . holding . . . me . . . off . . . you . . . won't stop . . . me . . . you . . . paint . . . pot . . ." — Mario's father was a scene painter — "I'll . . . show . . . you . . . how . . . to . . . make . . . that . . . viperous . . . tongued . . . woman . . ."

Mario's mother made a lunge toward the stairway but was pushed back against the wall by his father. Eileen stood next to Mario biting her knuckles and making funny soft sounds.

"Mr. O'Dell, it's all a misunderstanding . . ."

"It is . . ." He was breathing stertoriously. "It is . . . you've mis . . . understood . . . your man . . . I'm Brendan . . . Michael . . . O'Dell . . . come . . . to settle . . . the score."

It was so swift, such a clean movement, so effortlessly executed: Mario's father in one powerful, unbroken sweep lifted O'Dell from the steps, over the banister rail, and pinned him against the wall. Mario heard the trumpeting air go out of him, plastered as he was like a poster against the wainscoting. Eileen was screaming out: "Please,

please, don't hit him! Leave go of him! Oh my God, don't hit him! Please, please, he don't know what he's sayin' half the time!"

Mario's father hadn't struck him. He'd just stopped him and pasted him against the wall. And when he pulled his hand away O'Dell slid down the wall to the floor, collapsed like a folding ruler, his head drooped forward, and Eileen was on her knees, her arms sheltering him.

And banging up the stairs, those size twelve regulation police issue, and the bellow: "Cut it out! No more! Cut it out! Lay off! It's the law. Do you hear?"

It had an odd, unreal ring to it. Everything was hushed, except for Ohmigod's cooing. It was even odder to suddenly see the great, red oxlike face of Big Ned Swayne the cop looming up in the hallway, puffing and blowing out his cheeks.

"Will somebody tell me what's going on?"

Mario's father said calmly: "Good evening, Ned."

The cop glanced around at the scene, the gas jet flames billowing in the wind. He put down his nightstick, got down on one knee. "O'Dell! I should have known. I swear I heard the noise all the way down on the docks. I thought for sure somebody was being butchered . . . what the hell's happened?"

"Mr. O'Dell had a spell," explained Mario's father.

"A spell?" He checked it with Eileen.

"Oh, yes, Ned . . . he's took bad . . ."

Ned clicked his tongue. One could almost read his mind at that moment, wishing perhaps that O'Dell might be "took" for good . . . "I'll ring for the ambulance."

"No . . . no, Ned. If I can just get him home to 527 . . . all he needs is to get home . . ."

"Yes, I can see that. Well, come on, we'll get him there. A spell, you say?"

Mario's family stood watching. Mario saw the big cop's neck bulging out of his tight tunic collar as he hoisted O'Dell erect. He was like a doll, all the sawdust emptied out. Yes, it was a spectacle, the footsteps going down the stairs, labored, scraping, the heavy breathing, and Eileen looking back sadly at the three of them on the landing. And they remained standing even after the front door slammed shut on the ground floor. Mario noticed his mother's face; she seemed like a sleepwalker.

Much later that night Mario from his bed heard his mother crying. Heard his father soothing her. It had started out as such a lovely evening, the light, the smell of the air, and now there was just an ache.

From that evening onward O'Dell seemed a mere imitation of himself. Mario puzzled over it. Was it the disgrace of his performance or the natural progress of the con? But the Dutchies kept their distance from O'Dell. They didn't trust him. As Mrs. Schroter said: "He got the tricks of a backyard cat!" But Mario's mother made chicken broth for him. She reported back: "He's bad . . . skin and bones."

The ambulance from New York Hospital came several times in the nights that followed. O'Dell was hemorrhaging. But stricken as he was, the poet would not go to the hospital. He muttered something about the "farces." And he did rally to the point where he got out on the sidewalk, but the stuffing was gone out of him, he couldn't manage even one insult.

Ohmigod missed work for days at a time. She had to wait on him hand and foot. He'd punch her sometimes. You'd see the marks on her arms and neck. Eileen grew thin and pale. And once in a very great while you'd hear something like the old bite in O'Dell's voice but an echo really, an echo.

One night, at twilight, Mario'd just come home from St. Ansgar's, Eileen stood down in front of the door and called up: "Lena . . . Lena . . . Oh my God, Lennnnnaaaaaa. He's been taken . . . send Mario for a priest . . . Leeeennna . . ."

Mario never forgot that cry of desolation.

They sent Friar Callistus. He'd been a football player and wrestler. He was a mountain of a man. But it was a tribute to O'Dell. Here he was practically wrapped in his shroud and they were taking no chances, they sent their most muscular friar. What a reputation O'Dell had on Stanley Street.

O'Dell went to his Land of Heart's Desire that night when the steam rose from the river. He was laid out in Kinsella's undertaking establishment on Tenth Avenue. All the Irish used Kinsella's, the Dutchies used only Samuessen's. And there he was in his casket, rosary beads clasped in his clean hands. Yes, out of respect for Ohmigod the Dutchies went to that alien place and said a prayer for O'Dell's soul. But Mario noticed they kept well away from the coffin, some lingering fear it might all be a trick, and O'Dell would rise up and revile them. O'Dell was buried from St. Fergus's.

"Ah, ja. It's only right. After all, O'Dell he was The Irisher of The Irish." And Brother Benigno said it without malice.

Ohmigod spent a lot of time at Mario's flat. She took O'Dell's passing very hard. Nobody really understood the depth of her sorrow. Baumer the baker scratched his head: "The block be so quiet now O'Dell is gone. She don't get beat up no more. No black-and-blue spots. What's wrong with that girl? Why she broken up?"

Mario's mother said time was a healer. At first. And then she changed her tune slightly and said Eileen had to make an effort. And then impatiently: "Eileen, you gotta get ahold of yourself. He's been dead a year!"

But Ohmigod didn't mend. It got so bad they removed her from the cosmetics counter, transferred her to goldfish, turtles, and canaries. You see, her glowing loveliness had vanished . . . gone! Mario would see her kneeling at the communion rail, a black shawl over her head, telling her beads for O'Dell's soul.

Brother Benigno said: "See, Mario, it don't make no difference. She have love him. He could hurt her, walk all over her . . . but she have love him. The feelin's is everything . . . the brain be okay but in such matter like this . . . the feelin's is everythin'."

And some of the guys on the street, standing around the gutter fire of a winter night, forgetting what Ohmigod had once looked like, would see her coming down the block, murmuring to herself, dressed in mourning, they'd say: "Oh, Jesus, here she comes. She looks like the last rose of summer!"

Even at home some subtle change had taken place in the relationship. Mario's mother had stood by Eileen through her tribulation. Yes, Lena listened to Eileen spouting off about what a great man O'Dell was, that someday his poetry would be recognized. Yes, Lena was long suffering but . . . but . . . it was something Mario's father said which put a damper on the closeness with Eileen.

He said it dreamily: "I wish I'd painted Ohmigod in her prime. Oh, how I wish I had."

Mario caught the look his mother shot at his father. He couldn't figure it out. All he sensed was that something critical had happened. Whether his mother mistook what his father meant by *prime*, taking it to mean posing in the nude for him, showing all of her glorious curves . . . whatever, a coldness developed between Lena and Ohmigod, one which never thawed.

But Mario knew what his father meant.

At night, when he leaned his head against the cold windowpane, a ferryboat tooting on the river, he felt it was terrible there should be no record of Ohmigod's haunting loveliness. Stanley Street had not much beauty to boast of. What a pity that Ohmigod's had vanished without a trace.

♣7♣

Friar Vicar

A sure sign of Friar Vicar's popularity was the lines of penitents waiting patiently on either side of his confessional on a Saturday afternoon. By all odds the numbers that queued up made him champion confessor.

Somehow this observation was tainted with a suggestion of dispraise in Mario's mind: Vicar was an easy confessor! That got around like the news of any bargain on Stanley Street. Lots of things got around about Friar Vicar. It puzzled Mario that it should bother him personally. It didn't bother him that Brother Benigno was lauded to the skies. Benigno was a pious man. Benigno would be made a saint. Benigno was the keystone of St. Ansgar's parish. Benigno was the glory of the West Side! This vaulting praise didn't in the least grate on Mario. Whatever was said of Benigno, Mario would magnify ten times. But when it came to Friar Vicar, Mario dug in his heels like a balky mule. Why was this? And was Mario missing something simply because of some ignorant bias?

Friar Vicar was second in command. He'd been first mate of the friary of St. Ansgar's for twenty years. He was tall and stooped, nearly bald, his skin sometimes had a yellowish cast. He had a potato nose, a nasal voice, and a pigeon-toed walk. Plus . . . plus a pervasive rumor of Vicar suffering from a lingering but mortal ailment: long term, at least twenty years. It affected the Dutchies deeply, made them revere Friar Vicar, that courageous man.

Vicar knew everybody, the high, the low, cops, crooks, politicians, bootleggers, chorus girls, loafers, boxers, ladies of easy virtue from the strip along Twenty-ninth Street. How had he built such a wide and diverse following? Mario figured it was done by way of the confessional box, and the sympathy he excited because he was stricken by this mysterious, incurable malady.

His enormous popularity could be gauged by the concern voiced by his followers every four years when the Meeting of Chapter convened. The Meeting of Chapter was the convention of top-ranking friars who gathered quadrennially in Wisconsin to manage the affairs of the order. It was at this assembly that a new provincial was elected, new superiors appointed, and friars reassigned or shifted to the various churches in the Province of St. Ludger. It was a model of ecclesiastical administration which would have excited the admiration of any top-flight corporation, it was so efficiently conducted.

Among the friars themselves this meeting was called the quadrennial raffle. Among the parishioners, it was no joking matter, because for them it might mean the transfer of a favorite friar to some other city far away. And like the hint of spring on Stanley Street, every four years the tension grew as the day of Chapter neared. And never was this mounting tautness so acute as when the name of Friar Vicar came up as a likely transferee. Gloom, anxiety, resentment, and incipient rebellion became part of the atmosphere. How could they do such a thing to St. Ansgar's? That Vicar had been stationed there for twenty years, had survived five of the Meetings of Chapter without being disturbed meant nothing. It was like a rumor of the end of the world, daily everything became more dire. Mario would often be stopped in the church by a tearful old biddy, rosary beads in her hands, lamenting the loss of Friar Vicar. Where did this information come from? How could she know he was going? It irked Benigno; he often growled: "The Chapter ain't even be held yet! The father provincial haven't even got a list made up yet. I don't know where they get this nonsense in their heads . . . ja, these people . . . phew, sometimes . . ."

But the jitters really set in and had mostly to do with Friar Vicar; oh, there might be some passing fear as to Brother Benigno's transfer, but he'd been there fifty-six years, it seemed unlikely they'd move him at this late date . . . but Vicar, ah, one could never be sure. It was incredible, the kinds and types who would stop Mario: sleek, pinkie-ringed, manicured-fingernailed men, women wearing very tight, tight dresses, slit on the sides, and smelling like bunches of flowers, and old, poor people, all with the same note of solicitous inquiry. "Is Vicar going?" Or the militant: "My God, how can they do it . . . huh?" And this sentiment uttered while looking at the confessional assigned to Friar Vicar.

Even Hans the stone-age sexton would get less oafish and, with a most lugubrious finality, moan: "Ihr geht. Ach, Jesus, Mary, und Josef. . . und der odder saints . . . ihr geht." And Hans would click his tongue against his false teeth, the alcohol coming off his breath knocking you over if you got too close. It was a most extraordinary display of collective anxiety and despair. How did it get about? How?

Why, from Friar Vicar. Yes, from Vicar himself. Mario discovered the fact on his own. Mario was so quiet, so unobtrusive in his work about the church that he became a witness to many things. People just forgot he was around. So it was he learned it was Friar Vicar who put up those kites of information about himself. Of course he never ran out those snippets of news directly, straightforward. No, never something you could quote, attribute, pin on. No. It was managed with broken sentences, sighs, looks, pauses, looking toward Heaven, weary shrug of those stooped shoulders, smile of despair. Perhaps his most telling, affecting, and staggering suggestion of his impermanence was when he'd light a cigarette (Benigno said he smoked so much he was like a chimney). He'd hold the match in his hand, letting it burn out slowly and die. And then he'd smile philosophically. It would devastate the onlooker.

Mario once heard Friar Urbain, the former newspaperman, say drily: "Vicar's a regular press bureau . . . with cameramen!"

And that sized it up!

Mario steered clear of Vicar. He was altogether too forward in wanting to be noticed, to be liked, to be pitied. Oh, Mario didn't expect perfection in the friars. He'd learned they were men. They had their good days, their bad days, their pettinesses, their narrownesses, and some he thought sailed pretty close before the winds of conscience, but all in all they were dedicated, sincere, religious. Mario sensed that the really pious moments in their lives were private and not paraded ostentatiously. Mario could not persuade himself that such was the case with Vicar. Everything with him was worn like a badge. And that he should be second in command disturbed Mario.

For instance, Mario never asked Friar Vicar how he was. He used to when he was first working with Brother Benigno . . . and he would get back from Vicar: "Oh, you know, kiddo . . . you take what's dished out . . . why complain . . . ," and then a shadow would pass across his face: "Why talk about it . . . ?"

The Vicar's use of slang, as if it were a mark of his being just another guy, an ordinary Joe. Nothing special about Vicar, just one of the boys. He'd meet you any way he had to. All things to all men and women.

He'd skip no opportunity of emphasizing his common touch. He insisted you like him. It was not a part of the man that he could rest comfortably and sense you didn't like him.

Mario got to understand Vicar had some deep need to be liked. And because Vicar felt Mario was not enthusiastic about him, Vicar tried even harder to recruit his approval.

Vicar was deputy pastor and superior, and treasurer. He was the one who disbursed the funds and collected them at the end of the day's services. They were kept in a cupboard in the sacristy in a special velvet-lined wicker basket, and represented all the offerings from all of the services. Vicar went through a regular ritual. He'd pull out his great ring of keys, find the right one, unlock the cupboard, take out the basket, and weigh it in his hands. "Too heavy, means a light take. Mostly copper and silver, very few bills."

This show would be put on exclusively for Mario's benefit. Nobody else was in the sacristy. It was an overture. He wanted Mario to respond. But why? What could it matter that Mario was not one of his band of admirers? For Heaven's sake, he had the whole parish eating out of his hand!

Then, the next tactic: "Jinks, you put in a long day, kiddo. What a help you are to Brother Benigno. I don't know how he'd manage without you. We certainly appreciate everything you do. It can't be all a bed of roses for you at your age. I'll bet plenty of times you wish you were out on the block playin' with the other guys . . . huh? Well, we all got to carry our load, huh . . . but don't think we don't appreciate what you're doing . . ."

It was marvelous how he slipped from the personal singular pronoun to the institutional plural. He stroked you both ways with his broad brush.

Mario was very bothered by the amount of time he spent mulling over this business of Father Vicar. Perhaps it was a kind of punctiliousness, a fussy, picky, scrupulousness designed to prevent him from coming straight out and admitting he thought Vicar was a downright hypocrite. Yes, it was that which gnawed at him. That, and a sense of standing out from the rest of Vicar's multitude of admirers; and the real barb: Brother Benigno seemed not to object to Vicar. Yes, it was this most of all that troubled Mario. Because Benigno was the most down-to-earth, commonsensical man Mario'd ever met, and just and honest, and a sure judge of hypocrisy. So really what was it about Vicar? And why should Mario be so disturbed about the matter?

Father Vicar was the boss when Father Athenasius, the superior, had to be absent. He was the most easygoing guy in the world at such times. Ordinarily a friar got an afternoon off each week. Now, since they had a vow of poverty, they had no money, and they were given two dollars by the father superior. But when Vicar took over in place of Athenasius, he'd slip his hand into his tunic and pull out a carefully folded bill, you could hear it crinkle, it was so crisp and new. Mario'd once caught sight of the denomination, ten bucks! Wow. A fortune in those days. Catch Athenasius throwing money away like that.

When Vicar was temporarily in charge he'd act like a Tammany politician handing out largesse. He'd float around the friary urging the friars to get out and see a ball game or go to a movie or take a boat ride. What was he campaigning for? Was it that he wanted to curry favor, so that one day he'd make superior? It couldn't be, you couldn't buy that through handing out favors, all appointments were made by the friar provincial in Wisconsin. Vicar was absolutely baffling.

He'd even come into the second sacristy, where Mario and Benigno were working. Vicar would make a pitch to Benigno: "Ah, Brother, you work too hard. You never take any time off. You should get around, see how the city's changing. Take Mario with you. We'll manage to get by for an afternoon." Vicar'd start puffing on a cigarette and peer at Benigno through the smoke.

"No, Vicar . . . thank you all the same."

"Okay, Brother. You're the boss. But, jinks, I'd like to see you go out and have a good time. Nothin' sinful in that." Vicar'd snatch a couple more puffs. "I could get you a coupla tickets to the Polo Grounds. Giants are in town. Just happens I know somebody . . ."

Vicar always knew somebody, somewhere. And it was true; Mario recognized that as a fact. If you had trouble with the cops, Vicar knew somebody who could help; if it was a matter for relief or a job or a license of some kind, Vicar knew somebody . . . if a sinking parishioner needed real brandy or real whiskey in those days of Prohibition, Vicar could get the real stuff . . .

The evidence of proven worth, the sheer weight of it, should have brought Mario to his feet cheering. How could Mario even hint to himself about hypocrisy in connection with Vicar?

Actually, Vicar never asked for anything for himself. His shoes were a disgrace, all wrinkled and creased, scuffed at the toes. His suit of civvies shone from age and wear, his black fedora had a greenish look to it from its long years of use, and his overcoat, that was shabby enough to qualify for retirement. And this personal disdain for his appearance was in the teeth of what Mario had seen time and time again, when those wealthy ladies would pass Vicar money, money he always accepted humbly, looking sheepish as he tucked it away in his tunic.

Did Vicar keep the money, hoard it? Not for a minute did Mario believe that. No, Vicar was not a violator of his vow of poverty. He was the softest touch in the parish. He had a regular reputation as almoner.

Take Rudy Ox for example. He was a fight promoter with a wife and six kids, and a succession of boxers with glass jaws. How did Rudy keep his family alive with his record of failure? Vicar. Yes, Father Vicar believed in Rudy and his promotion of the manly art.

Take Charlie Kohlenbach or as he used to be known professionally, J. Framley Worth. Charlie was a broken-down ham, never a headliner. He lived alone in his furnished room on Twenty-seventh Street with his battered makeup box and his memories. He had palsy and was as poor as a church mouse. What had once been his theatrical wardrobe now served as bits and pieces of his everyday wear. It was nothing to spy Charlie in a pair of tattersall pants and a cutaway coat on his way to St. Ansgar's. He'd spend hours in the church, in the same pew, every day. He was a lonely, friendless, old has-been (perhaps never-been). Vicar befriended him. Every week Charlie got a stipend. Vicar would occasionally make up work for Charlie to do so he'd maintain his self-respect. Charlie would have sacrificed his life for Vicar. He worshiped the very ground Vicar walked on.

Charlie would stop Mario, tears in his eyes, his palsied tremor making his rosary beads clatter. "Someday, someday, Mario, I'll do something for Friar Vicar . . . someday . . . someday . . ."

That day came unexpectedly soon during Holy Week, a particularly trying time for Brother Benigno and Mario. There are a variety of services, each of which makes demands upon the sacristan. Benigno had had a cold but pushed himself as always; by the evening of Maundy Tuesday the doctor had to be called to the friary. Benigno was ordered to stay in bed. Of course no doctor could order Benigno, he was going to get up; after all, next day was Good Friday. But the doctor knew his patient: he got Friar Athenasius, the superior, to order Benigno to remain in his cell. There was no arguing in that case. Benigno submitted, grumbling of course, but he submitted — after giving Mario the most painstaking instructions about the Good Friday tableau.

A crucifix was arranged on the steps that came down from the sanctuary directly before the open gates of the communion rail. The crucifix was placed on a diagonal, and it was almost life-sized in proportions, the corpus of Christ slightly smaller. During the day the faithful would approach the cross and pray before it, some of the more fanatic (nuts, Benigno called them) would have to kiss the wounds of Christ (Benigno would call that mushing the statue up). This ceremony had been of long custom and the corpus of Christ was showing bare plaster and holes here and there. Benigno had meant to have it replaced but . . .

Father Vicar came into the second sacristy to talk about its condition to Mario.

"Hey, kiddo, that crucifix is pretty ratty. Have you taken a real look at it? I don't think Benigno would let it go the way it is if he was around."

No denying it, the corpus had taken a beating, especially the stigmata.

"See what I mean . . . looks like it's been chewed at, huh, kiddo."

While they were examining the crucifix, J. Framley Worth, never losing a chance to be close to his idol, came from his pew and joined them. Friar Vicar asked him: "Pretty beat up, huh, Charlie. Not a very reverent-looking object with that plaster showing through."

J. Framley Worth was half beside himself; not only his hands shook, his whole body shook in anticipation. The day had arrived when he could show some small measure of his gratitude to Vicar.

"Don't worry, Father Vicar. I know exactly what to do. I'll fix it up so it'll be beautiful."

"You're a pip, Charlie. I knew I could depend on you. Okay, kiddo, Charlie'll take care of it."

And Charlie did. The former trouper rushed back to his furnished room, grabbed his makeup box, and returned to St. Ansgar's. He touched up the corpus. Mario was filled with admiration; how Charlie with those palsied hands could so skillfully apply greasepaint to those disfigured red spots! What a wonderful job of restoration! Why, the wounds of the fallen Christ positively glistened, as if just inflicted. Vicar was delighted, delighted.

"Oh, Charlie, I can see now why you were in the theater. It's the cat's meow! Terrific! Okay, kiddo, huh? Oh, Benigno would thank you if he was on his feet, Charlie. What an improvement. Benigno'll be overjoyed."

Perhaps. But it would have been short-lived. Benigno would have known something, something of very great importance, something born of experience: never dismiss the antics of the nuts.

Old Alois Dieskau, a real, genuine charter member of the nut club, and a particular target of Benigno's ire, a man forever kissing, rubbing, talking to statues, went through his usual shenanigans, and came up with blood on his lips and hands. Blood!

Before anybody knew it, St. Ansgar's was overrun by hordes of people, coming to see the miracle of the bleeding Christ. *The Graphic*, *The Sun*, *The Journal*, and other papers sent droves of reporters to cover the supernatural occurrence.

Brother Benigno rose from his sickbed in sheer fury. Nothing could keep him down. "Mario . . . Mario. How could you leave them do it? You know the nuts is out . . . out by hundreds on Good Friday. By jingo, it teach me a lesson. I don't get bronchitis never again during Holy Week."

Father Vicar got the merry ha-has from the other friars but Charlie Kohlenbach was crushed, desolated, what had he done to his idol? But Vicar comforted Charlie: "Listen, it wasn't your fault. Hey, what you did was tremendous. All that happened, Charlie, was simply to prove how much faith, yes, how much faith people have. They want to believe."

And as time passed Benigno came to laugh over the incident, his eyes would crinkle up: "I wish I could have see Old Alois when the paint comes off on him . . . Ja, I would have like to see the look on his face . . . that have been something."

Vicar was undismayed. He was, to say the least, resilient.

◆

A parish house stood across the backyard from the friary. Hans the sexton and his family occupied the top floor. Professor Wolfram used the second floor for practicing on his grand piano and rehearsing the choir, but the ground floor was a huge and empty room with a splendid maple floor. It was the floor which triggered Vicar's inspiration: why not make it into a club for young people and hold dances there? Vicar sold Father Athenasius on the scheme, explaining the teenagers of the parish needed activities, activities sponsored under the auspices of St. Ansgar's church. Besides it might attract other youngsters to the parish. Of course once he got the go-ahead, Vicar knew the right sources to tap for a Victrola, records, decorations, coffee urns, regular supplies of buns, cakes, sandwiches, ice cream. And apart from himself as presiding spirit he appointed Charlie Kohlenbach as official record tender and permanent chaperone.

The St. Ansgar's Social and Athletic Society or, as the neighborhood had it, the S.A.S.A.S., became a dazzling success. Young people attended in droves and that ground floor throbbed to the rhythms of the big bands, carefully programmed by J. Framley Worth. It became so popular, so well attended, the Dutchie parents would come themselves to watch the dancers; they'd bring sandwiches and cakes and pies and other goodies. On Saturday night you could hear the wa-wahs of the trombones and the blare of trumpets for blocks around, and if you passed by on the sidewalk you could see the colorful lights all ablaze, with dozens of young men and women circling about. It was a personal triumph for Friar Vicar, one which enhanced his already exalted position in the neighborhood. Indeed, it brought him fresh adulation from those who came to the S.A.S.A.S. from other parts of the city, who did not belong to the parish. Charlie Kohlenbach was so enthusiastic over the success of the club he said to Father Vicar: "It's like the mission field, you know, Father. You bring in all these young kids who'd otherwise be out on the streets . . . getting into . . . well, who knows what kind of . . . ?"

It was many months later when certain distinct signs of trouble surfaced. A number of Dutchie girls discovered they were pregnant.

Now, these were "nice" Dutchie girls, not your tramps or pushovers. Mario served as altar boy at a number of very discreet and private wedding ceremonies which took place in the inner chapel, away from curious eyes. The bride usually decked out in her best, unable to conceal the bulge of her stomach, and the groom looking dazed, and somehow unprepared. Yes, there were a number of these hush-hush marriages and a number of christenings that followed. Friar Vicar married them and Friar Vicar baptized their babies. And then somehow, mysteriously, an order was flashed. The S.A.S.A.S. was dissolved, the maple floor was waxed no more.

Again Charlie Kohlenbach suffered because his idol had been brought low. "You know, Father. No monkey business took place here. No mushing up . . . no corner playing . . . nothing like that here. What a shame to close the club down. It was a great thing . . . maybe it was too successful, huh, Father? Maybe we could reopen with safeguards, huh?"

What happened did get to Vicar. Mario could see he was affected. He smoked more for one thing. And he didn't seem quite so outgoing. Once Mario heard him allude to the debacle by saying: "At least the girls weren't abandoned. I followed through on that. And they're happy now."

But Vicar had pulled in his horns. The other friars rode him pretty hard about the breakup of the S.A.S.A.S. Oddly enough the parishioners sought him out as much as ever, long lines at his confessional every Saturday. It wasn't a loss in popularity; perhaps he was even more popular than ever. Still Vicar appeared more thoughtful, less spontaneous, as if he'd been checked, a sudden frost. Mario wondered about the change, wondered if it was a change, or just something he imagined.

But Benigno noticed it as well.

They were preparing calla lilies, yellow ones, for a fancy wedding to take place that afternoon. Vicar would officiate.

He stopped by the second sacristy where Benigno and Mario were working. Vicar just watched them and smoked. And after a few puffs squashed the cigarette, and turned and left. This was not the Vicar of old.

"Vicar is a funny fella, Mario."

And then thoughtfully, Benigno said: "He give you the shirt off his back. Ja, he give you whatever he have . . . and sometimes what he ain't got . . ."

Mario waited, he felt at last he was going to get some solid understanding of what made Vicar tick.

Benigno stepped back to look at his arrangement of the lilies. "Vicar have to be liked. Ja, he have to make sure you like him."

"But why, Brother? Everybody's crazy about him . . ."

"No . . . no, that not mean nothing to Vicar. He got to know every day that you like him." Benigno looked deep into Mario's eyes. "Like you was once afraid of death . . . Vicar afraid of somebody not like him . . ."

Mario tried to understand.

"All right, I tell you. Vicar's father curse him. Ja, his father tell him he ain't no son of his. He cut him out of his life. He never want to see his face again."

"Wow . . . how come?"

"On account of he want to be a friar . . . ja . . . ja . . . how you like to be told at twelve year or thirteen year old . . . your father never want to see you again . . . he curse you . . ."

"Because he was going to be a friar? Wasn't he proud?"

"Ah, other mothers and fathers be proud but not Old Johann. He have a coal and ice business. Johann work hard when he comes from other side. He gets the good business. And Vicar be his only son, all the rest is girls. And Johann he very close with money, he look to the dollar, and he very hard man. So . . . Vicar he will take over the business . . . and then when Vicar say he joining the friars . . . ach, du liebe . . . Johann come here and he raise the roof . . . he yell at me . . . he stamp his foot. He gonna punch somebody in the nose . . . I tell him to go home and fly a kite . . .

"Can you imagine that young boy, like you are now, having his father curse him . . . it is very exactly like St. Francis as his father the Old Bernardone, who have a big cloth business . . . he have his son St. Francis haul up before the court, and he disown him in public. Ja, with all them people around, because St. Francis is going to become a religious, he disown him. That be something to take. St. Francis strip himself naked, give those clothes back to his father, saying those belong to him . . ."

Benigno caught the look of wonder in Mario's eyes.

"Vicar don't pull off his clothes but he join the order. He stick to his guns. But he don't see his father never again. But you see, Vicar pay a price. We all pay a price. Like Vicar never be sure about that curse his father put on him. He never be sure inside. So he need everybody to like him. He got no family. He try to make family out of all the people . . . he got to be liked. What have happen to him with his father only three of us in the order knows about . . . Vicar never tell anyone about it . . ." Benigno lifted up the vase and passed it to Mario.

"This is his home, his family, that why he worry so about being transferred. Vicar is funny fella, so are you, so am I, funny fellas. You got to take everything into consideration to understand people. Things ain't always what they looks like . . . Mario . . . no, they not."

After that Mario began to ask Friar Vicar how he was. And the Vicar's look, that look of resignation, as if his undisclosed but fatal affliction was upon him, didn't trouble Mario any longer. He'd learned something about things not always being the way they seemed.

8

Paddy Hilliard's Derby

There it was, bobbing, between a Greek tramp and a Panamanian banana boat, odd company for Paddy Hilliard's derby. It rose and fell with the heave of the river, brim downward, as if Paddy himself were still wearing it while he walked just out of sight beneath the surface. One of the kids with an expert cast of his hand line hooked it and gingerly worked it toward the pier.

The derby was so distinctive, so the trademark of a man, that its owner's name rose to the lips at once, Paddy Hilliard! It was brown and round and it swelled at the place it met the unyielding brim, all in all a most unique hat that ordinarily rode on the top of Paddy himself. Paddy was a man of such upright carriage, such stately gait, that you knew at once that he was a lion, a very king among Stanley Streeters. Paddy was a man of few words, significant looks, florid face, and a political mover. He was a bachelor in his fifties, dressed always in a blue serge suit, stiff collar, polka-dot tie, high shoes of a noticeable yellow color, and a mien of enormous dignity — certainly not the type of man whose brown derby would float between a Greek and Panamanian freighter.

Mario had heard the news by the time he'd left school and arrived at St. Ansgar's for his daily stint.

"Terrible . . . what a terrible thing to happen to that man," said Brother Benigno.

"Maybe it just blew off his head, Brother?"

"Ach, never. Not the way Mr. Hilliard clamped it on his head. When he put on that derby, it be there to stay, I don't care what kind of wind is blowing!" Benigno said thoughtfully: "No, he must have suffer some kind of attack. Some of them Greek sailors have see him standing there one minute and the next he be gone . . . swallowed up. That water is very tricky at that place. It sweep you right under the piles, you bang your head and that be it. No, he must have got dizzy, lose his balance . . . it show you that you never know."

Brother Benigno was taking it badly. There had been a bond between him and Mr. Hilliard.

"You don't know how hard it was to get anything accomplished before Mr. Hilliard come into Stanley Street, Mario. You could never get anything done by City Hall. But when he come to live here, why, he can get the doors to open where they have been shut before. It be some loss for us . . . for me."

Mr. Hilliard had been Tammany Hall's liaison with the West Side. Without his intervention a Dutchie hadn't a chance. It was Mr. Hilliard whom Benigno went to when he needed a few cops to take care of traffic outside the church for a special wedding or funeral that brought out a lot of people. Just a word to Mr. Hilliard and Captain Bernard Malloy dispatched a squad of New York's finest.

"Who you think bring Mrs. Keating to the church? Where you think them beautiful flowers come from every Sunday? Mrs. Keating. Mr. Hilliard bring her to St. Ansgar's, he introduce her."

Mrs. Keating had been a Follies girl, a friend of some high-up official in the city government. She was a regular communicant at St. Ansgar's. She used to go to St. Patrick's up on Fifth Avenue but Mr. Hilliard had brought her to St. Ansgar's. She had an open purse. She was an ornament there. What other woman could slip a twenty-dollar bill to Brother Benigno just at the right time? She was Benigno's ace in the hole when he needed something desperately for the crèche or the Altar Boy Society. Nobody ever whispered about her, questioned her relationship with Big Jock who had a wife and nine kids up in the Murray Hill section. No, no, nothing so tawdry was ever brought up about her past.

"She have made the repair of the organ possible. Fifteen hundred dollars! I don't know what she do now that Mr. Hilliard be gone." Benigno sighed. "It be a one hundred percent loss for us."

The quietus was put on the whole matter of Mr. Hilliard's tragic fate when Bertha Hassler showed up in a pew dressed in dusty mourning. That proved beyond a shadow of doubt that Mr. Hilliard had indeed passed over. Bertha Hassler would never have given up if there had been a ghost of a chance of Mr. Hilliard's survival. After all, she had lost four husbands in twenty years. (Kosh Stoltz, that ladies' man, his cigar tilted, said of Bertha: "All her husbands died in childbirth.") Mr. Hilliard had been her roomer, occupying a "suite" chopped out of her eight-room, third-floor flat at 541. No, if Bertha appeared in her black raiment, it meant only one thing, Paddy Hilliard had passed over. And it also meant that at long last the neighborhood knew for a fact that Paddy had been her intended, why else the weeds?

Mario saw her ponderous bulk humped over a pew, her beads dangling, her face veiled, obviously praying for the soul of her late-departed roomer. There'd be no more jokes about the way she kept those eight rooms warm anymore. No innuendos about the greased hinges on the door that separated Mr. Hilliard's "suite" from hers. No more speculation about her age and childbearing capacities. Mario accepted the grim fact of Mr. Hilliard's death, even though his body was held in the muddy clutches of the river bottom.

It amazed Mario that she could take on as she did, clutching Brother Benigno's hand: "It was to be after the feast of the Annunciation, Brother Benigno. We'd planned it that way. When Patrick left the house that morning he was whistling."

Astonishing that such a crusty woman could have the feelings of a maiden bereft of her young lover.

"Whistling as he went down the stairs . . . I watched him go down the street . . ."

Mario could picture the stately Mr. Hilliard, his brown derby clapped on his head, his hands in his pockets, his yellow high shoes gleaming, ambling along the sidewalk, waving and chatting, making his rounds as the neighborhood representative of Tammany Hall. He must have had business down on the docks that morning. And then suddenly stricken he had plunged fatally from the pier . . . just his hat, like a wreath, to mark his passing.

Brother Benigno dressed in his civvies, told Mario to take care of the five fifteen novena service. He was going over to see his friend Captain Bernard Malloy to get firsthand information on the tragedy. The precinct house was just one block east.

Mario was fixing up after the service when Benigno returned. The old man fiddled with the stud of his Roman collar with the slash in the front (it denoted that he was a brother and not a priest). He removed the collar, sat down at his desk. Mario brought him a glass of sacramental wine. "Thank you, Mario," he said, wiping his beard. "They going to send divers down there to see if they can get his body. They got them big lights, like the kind they got in the railroad yards so they can work at night. Captain Malloy say that they will find poor Mr. Hilliard." Benigno had a way of lifting up his eyes when he wasn't convinced about something.

"You don't think so, huh, Brother?"

"Won't be the first time that the river have suck a body clear out to Staten Island or maybe Sandy Hook . . . maybe it never be found."

It was inspiring to see how everyone worked together, police, rum-runners, the fire department, and the neighborhood as bystanders, in the effort to snag Mr. Hilliard's body.

Mario stood with his father on the heavy planking of the pier watching the operation, hearing the gasp of the pumps supplying air to the divers, seeing the pearls of escaping air from their hoses rise to the surface.

"Brother Benigno says they may never find him, Poppa."

"He could be right."

"But he has to come up sometime, huh?"

"Yeah. But who knows where or when . . . or how?"

Ah, the "how" stirred up all kinds of gruesome images of the bloated cadaver of poor Mr. Hilliard, his mustache coated with algae, his sightless eyes blind to the rusty hulls, his ears deaf to the impa-tient tugboat whistles. Mario wasn't the only one who nursed such ghoulish expectations. None of the kids would go swimming there, and the fishermen were conspicuously absent. Nobody wanted to take a chance on making the accidental discovery.

The search was kept up for two straight weeks; Tammany Hall was loyal to its henchmen in those days. But it was futile. Oh, they found one very battered high shoe but that just confirmed what had happened. Brother Benigno told Mario that Captain Donovan said they had found a lot of stuff wedged between the piles — a case of nearly intact Scotch that had been dumped by a rumrunner when he was being chased by a Coast Guard cutter was divvied up among the salvagers — and even more stuff on the muddy bottom, but there was no trace of the mortal remains of Patrick Leonard Hilliard.

Mrs. Hassler was heartbroken. Mrs. Keating was emotional, too. And each of these close friends of the departed went separately to Brother Benigno about saying a requiem mass for Mr. Hilliard. Brother Benigno went to Father Athenasius. Friar Athenasius was a most accommodating pastor but there were difficulties. "There's no body, Brother."

"But we should do something, Father. He was a very good friend to St. Ansgar's."

Friar Athenasius conferred with the august Friar Nicodemus. It was he who suggested the memorial service. Nobody would be committed that way. The bereaved ladies were satisfied, the neighborhood was satisfied, and so was Tammany Hall.

A solemn requiem was scheduled. Mario stayed home from school that day. Captain Malloy himself appeared with two dozen policemen. The first pew was occupied by Mrs. Hassler, the second by Mrs. Keating. And both sides of the center aisle were filled up by men from City Hall. Three priests in black vestments, two thuribles, the full choir, and the high keenings of those volatile Irishmen — most unlike a Dutchie funeral. And in this case it was astonishing since Mr. Hilliard was not present in the flesh, merely represented by a catafalque. But even if he had been there, the ceremony could not have been more affecting.

Mrs. Keating had gone so far as to employ Samuessen, the official undertaker, to provide a hearse and coaches. That took money but she was not niggardly. After all, it was not so different from an orthodox funeral. Wasn't the body unimportant? It was the soul that counted. This was Samuessen's plea. And no one argued with that position. And so Paddy Hilliard was laid to rest in a manner of speaking, honored to the end.

The bell had just stopped tolling, the organ quieted, and Benigno and Mario were removing the black trappings from the high altar. Benigno whispered: "I don't know what we do now." Mario caught the implication. The quiet power that lodged inside Mr. Hilliard was no longer available to St. Ansgar's. No more Altar Boy Society outings to Indian Point in July. Mr. Hilliard had pulled strings and the Dayline officials had made room on the speedy *Peter Stuyvesant* to accommodate those sixty or so altar boys without charge! After all, St. Ansgar's was Dutchie and Tammany Hall was Irish. Yes, St. Fergus's would be looked out for, St. Brigid's, St. Brendan's, but not that German parish. No, without Mr. Hilliard there to grease the way to City Hall, St. Ansgar's would be forced to depend only on the strength and resourcefulness of Brother Benigno. And the old man had a further fear, the defection of Mrs. Keating now that Mr. Hilliard was gone. It was true; she did vanish.

Mrs. Hassler on the other hand remained; she was Dutchie through and through, her people coming from Passau, and her various husbands all having been named, respectively, Schnaltzee, Traunstein, Muldorfer, and Hassler. But she had nothing to remember Mr. Hilliard by. No photograph, no sketch, merely his brown derby, which she set next to the statue of the Blessed Mother in her front room. For a man of his importance it was remarkable how bone-clean his "suite" was. No letters, bankbooks, no cash. He had lived a most austere life, ascetic in its simplicity. It might have seemed that he had never lived. But no matter, Mrs. Hassler mourned him. She had masses said for the repose of his soul. She could luxuriate in her grief because she had collected life insurance on four spouses.

One night while standing around the gutter fire, Mario saw the widow Hassler, a shawl on her head, step out on the sidewalk to bring in her garbage cans; she was the janitor of 541. "Taking bread out of some other poor slob's mouth. What she need that job for with all the money she's got?" That had been a neighborhood gripe of the past.

Kosh Stoltz, his cigar tilted, stared at her. He said to the band of guys ringing the fire: "Christ, can you imagine anybody wanting to get at her? Four husbands she's wore out." There was a calculating glint in his eyes. "She's got a temper like a file. Old Paddy was lucky that she only got his derby and not him." And though the fire threw a lot of heat, Kosh suddenly shivered.

But no event, however prominent, enjoyed a long life on Stanley Street; everyday existence was too urgent. So Paddy Hilliard was forgotten, wiped out by other deaths, marriages, struggles. Mrs. Hassler looked out of her back window and screamed at the kids who used to climb the fences from 541 to 543. She threatened to get the cops if the kids' mothers didn't stop their mischief at 541. Yes, Mrs. Hassler had become embittered and crabby. She thought nothing of siccing the cops on the guys who shot craps under the lamppost. Kosh said: "Jesus, would you believe an old bat like that could be so horny?"

One of the guys snapped: "Watch out, Kosh, she'll gobble you up." And inside of three months Mrs. Hassler's grief was ignored, the neighborhood once again thought her a disagreeable old woman who hated children.

July came and Brother Benigno knew that there would be no outing for his boys to Indian Point. It made him very unhappy. He knew what the day meant to all of those boys, a day on the river, eating hot dogs, looking at the moving parts of that big Dayliner in the engine room. The kids of Stanley Street rarely got out of the neighborhood. He was sitting in the second sacristy smoking one of his Bengal Tigers, brooding away. Mario said: "Why don't you try and see somebody at Tammany Hall, Brother? I mean, they got to remember Mr. Hilliard."

Benigno stirred: "You give me an idea, Mario. I go see Captain

Malloy at the station house. I explain the problem. See, I don't know none of them mucky-mucks' names. When I go to their door and say that I am Benigno Zoller I am lost right away, Zoller ain't O'Grady or Boyle . . . but you give me an idea . . . I go over to see the captain."

Benigno went and came back and reported to Mario. "He tell me he's going to try and find out who be the one to see."

A few days later Benigno greeted Mario with a flash of tickets. "I get a whole block of tickets, Mario. They come through the mail to me. I go over and try to thank Captain Malloy for getting them. He says he have nothing to do with it, he have not time to get in touch with anybody."

"Maybe he doesn't want it to get out, Brother."

"Ja, that could be the explanation. Otherwise he have every Tom, Dick, and Harry after him to get something."

So the Altar Boy Society had its outing, and a great day it was, too. What with the river breezes, the potato races, the hot dogs, and the swimming in clear water, all those Dutchie kids had a high old time. Benigno said when it was over: "Well, Mr. Hilliard have helped after all. You were right, Mario. They must still remember him downtown." And Brother Benigno, who had gotten a sunburn from sitting on the upper deck of the Dayliner, peeled some skin from his nose. "Funny thing that his body never turn up . . . funny."

A year passed, and on the anniversary of that day when the brown derby hat bobbed between the Greek and Panamanian freighters there was a memorial mass celebrated for Patrick Leonard Hilliard. All the altar boys turned out. They had a stake in the service; it was a new year, a new outing.

A whole batch of flowers had arrived at the church. Expensive flowers, too. Not just gladioli but yellow calla lilies that cost four dollars a dozen, and several sprays of bleeding hearts. Benigno looked at the cards inside the cartons, scratched his beard with one of the cards. "You know who they be from? Mrs. Keating . . . you remember her? She send these."

Ah, it woke up memories. Mrs. Hassler sat in the front pew. She had sent a couple of pots of begonias that she had raised on her fire escape, she was careful with her money. And you could say what you want, contrasting her mean floral tribute with the opulence of Mrs. Keating's, still, Mrs. Hassler was there in the church weeping softly during the mass.

The sight of her reopened grief affected the Dutchies. Tears went a long way toward softening attitudes on Stanley Street. They forgave the widow for her nastiness toward the kids. They gathered around her on the sidewalk in front of the church after the service. They reminisced about the late Mr. Hilliard. Yes, it was a nice moment, and Mrs. Hassler sobbed.

She went to Brother Benigno: "I want to pay for a brass tablet to be put up in the rear of the church . . . will it cost much?"

"I see what it come to, Bertha, and I let you know."

A brass plate was put up next to the grotto of the Miraculous Medal. So Paddy Hilliard was remembered by St. Ansgar's in style. And nobody could call the widow Hassler cheap anymore. That plate and installation cost twenty-five dollars.

Christmas was coming. This meant practicing for the younger altar boys. Mario played the part of the priest, and the novice servers were put through the routines, Brother Benigno observing and correcting where necessary.

But there were two boys missing, two of the smallest and youngest. Benigno made inquiries: "Where be the Fanowitz twins?"

Nobody knew. And then they showed up. Benigno was very gruff. "Where you been, huh? Put on your cassocks and surplices. Schnell." The twins, scared, got togged up in a jiffy and the practice went on.

When it was all over the Fanowitz twins, seven years of age, quiet as mice, towheaded, with eyes like rabbits, grabbed Mario.

"Where were you guys? Brother Benigno was mad."

They said, jumping over one another's words: "We haff see der Geist." They never heard anything but Bavarian spoken at home.

Mario looked from Shonnie to Bastien, nothing to identify one from the other. "You saw what?"

"Der Geist."

Mario knew that they were notorious wanderers, floating all over the city like sightseers.

Shonnie or maybe it was Bastien drew himself up stiffly, put a finger beneath his nose to indicate a mustache, and tramped importantly up and down the second sacristy. The gait was unique. "Mr. Hilliard?"

"Ja . . . oh, ja." They nodded their heads so hard that their straight white hair fell down over their eyes.

"He's dead . . ."

In unison: "Ja, chust the same, we see his ghost . . . up on Fifty-ninth Street . . ."

"Ah, come on, you guys . . ."

"Oh, ja, Mario . . . we see him . . . he even got on a terby . . . a schwarz black terby . . ."

Both of those kids got whipped by Julia Fanowitz that night, not for the outrageous tale they told but because they had strayed all the way up to the southern border of Central Park.

Mario was of two minds about it. For one thing, the inhabitants of Stanley Street were always seeing the dead. It was a conviction with them that you saw the dead when you were in need of prayer. But why should the shade of Mr. Hilliard materialize before that pair of little Fanowitz twins? It didn't make any sense.

It was a very delicate matter and Mario was cautious in his approach to Brother Benigno. "Brother, once you said that it was funny Mr. Hilliard's body was never found."

"Ach, the river and the tide . . . who knows what have happen to it?"

"No doubt that he's dead, huh, Brother?"

Benigno gave him his full attention. "Why you ask that, Mario?" Mario told him what the Fanowitz twins had reported.

"Ach, those two schizzers. They don't even have the sense to come in out of the rain. They can't even be here on time . . . that's nonsense. If he not be dead why he not show up . . . why he pull this trick? Ach, Mario, look at all the things that brings up . . . why should he do it . . . huh? A man like Mr. Hilliard . . ."

Yes, Brother Benigno was right. Look at all the questions it raised. Mario put it out of his mind.

Each year a mass of memorial was said for the soul of Mr. Hilliard. And as long as she lived Mrs. Hassler sat in the front pew and wept. When she died, the brown derby hat which was kept on her front room table was auctioned off along with her other personal belongings. The brass plate is still in place at the rear of St. Ansgar's church.

♣9♣

Friar Blaise

Stories were handed down by word of mouth from one generation to the next and stood as gospels of parish marvels. Friars who'd left the scene decades before still figured in Dutchie conversations, kept alive by oral report; Stanley Street had very little to do with books or reading. Written accounts meant only one thing: bills.

Lots of times Mario felt he'd been born too late, those earlier days seemed charged with wonder, a period of most miraculous happenings. It seemed a pity to him that none of the accounts had been put down on paper. But Mario had Brother Benigno, he was a living repository of the past, and Mario would tap his memory.

"Friar Longinus Schaeffer? Ja, I know him very well, when he was living. What you want to know about him?"

"Was he strong like Samson, Brother?"

Benigno crinkled up his eyes: "I never see the Samson fella but Longinus he was one powerful fella. Once I see him lift a horse right off his four legs. He have scrunch himself under the horse's belly and slowly he raise up the horse. You should have see the look on that horse's face."

Mario was fascinated by these reminiscences. He never got enough of them, and once he got Brother Benigno started he'd ply him with question after question.

"What about Friar Eleutherius and the Krauss girl?"

"Ah, that story! Well, I tell you. It have to do with Tutti Krauss's little girl Mitzi who have accidentally fall into the river and go under the water. They fish out the poor little schizzer and they say she is drownded! They stretch her out in Buhlander's drugstore and they put the sheet over her. Her mother Tutti keeps screaming out: 'Mitzi,

Mitzi . . .' The water from the river keeps running off the child's clothes. It is no doubt a terribly awful moment. Well, anyhow Friar Eleutherius he come running to give the last rites. He say 'Take off the sheet from the little child.' Everybody standing around could see the little girl's face all white and still. Tutti, the mother, is taking on like she is a crazy woman. Eleutherius say to her softly: 'Tutti, you stop crying.' He gets down on his hands and knees, he's so big a fella he cover the little thing with his habit. He say: 'The child is alive.' By jingo neddies, them words is like lightning have struck. He lift up little Mitzi, he hold her close in his arms and she twitch and she sneeze because his beard tickle her nose. Pretty soon she stir and say: 'Father . . . Father, you be squeezin' me to death!'"

The whole scene spread before Mario's eyes, the puddles of river water on the floor, the faces white with anxiety and dread, the smell of the drugstore, the wild cries of the mother. Mario said: "It was a miracle, huh, Brother. Friar Eleutherius brought her back to life."

Benigno shook his head. "No, Mario. No miracle. They have been too quick to say she is dead. They raise such a hullabaloo they don't check enough. Everybody got it in his mind they have seen the miracle performed. Eleutherius tell me himself when he have bend over the little girl he had catch the heartbeat, so he knows she is alive. He tell that to the people but they got it in their heads that he have brought her back from the dead. So forevermore the story pass along that Friar Eleutherius have the power to restore life."

Benigno watched Mario's large brown eyes. He threw his arms up in disgust.

"You see, Mario, no point trying to make the people sensible about it. Once they get it in their thick kopfs they have seen another Lazarus lift from the grave, you got no way of making them see it ain't so." Benigno mused. "It is a miracle. They don't want to look at anything else. They don't remember nothing else. Never do you hear mention of how Tutti Krauss, the mother, that dunderhead, let her little girl fool around down by the docks, go walking on the pier like she's an acrobat. No, no, that part slip away, only the miracle part gets held on to."

Benigno studied Mario's face.

"There is something to learn here though, Mario. People picks out from what have happen only what they want to have happen, not what have happen at all. So you cannot always put your trust in these stories that have got passed along. That's why the church investigate the miracles with a fine-tooth comb. By jingo neddies, the church knows about people."

Mario stared solemnly at Benigno, so solemnly that Benigno began to tease him.

"You wait, someday they will have stories about me. Ja, all kinds of stories, and you will be around to be the witness and you will tell them they be ganz verrücht. You will tell them the facts, the truth. Benigno Zoller was a grouchy old man who can't control his temper." Benigno chuckled . . . and then laughed. "Most likely they won't listen to you. You'll have to argue with them. They be bull-headed, they hold on to what they want to believe and that be the whole thing. Fact don't mean nothing when the feelings come up!"

Mario was impressed by Benigno's argument, his debunking of the legends. Still, maybe because he, too, was a Dutchie, he wished he'd been there on the ground floor when one of those parish legends got started. It never occurred to him he might not recognize such an event because he was involved in it, a witness of it.

Professor Wolfram had a double hernia!

Hans the sexton scratched his head. "How that can happen, Mario. Here I haf to lift the heavy ash cans, the heavy ladders, carry the heavy loads and I don't get no rupture. The most Wolfram have to lift is the fingers and the feet to make the organ go. And all the time he sit on the bench while he do this and he get a rupture! He must push and pull too hard. I watch him the way he move the body when he play, in and out, side to side. It must push his bauch that it bust open. Ja, that must haf happen. To make the music is hard work, that I never know. So now the doctors have to take the knife and fix up the bauch like it was before. Oh, Mario, it is a very funny business . . . you have heard they sending a friar in to take Wolfram's place?"

No, Mario hadn't heard. But Hans knew everything that went on.

"He haf the perfect name for the chob. You know what his name is, huh? It be Friar Plays. Ja, Plays. Ja, that almost be a joke, Mario!"

Mario said to Brother Benigno: "Friar Plays is coming to take Professor Wolfram's place, Brother?"

Benigno laughed so hard he had to wipe his eyes. "Where you pick that Plays up, Mario?"

"Hans told me."

"Ach, that noodlehead! The friar's name is Blaise."

"Blaise! Where's he coming from, Brother?"

"From the monastery in Wisconsin, the motherhouse."

Ah, the motherhouse, St. Joseph's Monastery in Wisconsin, a place Mario often puzzled over.

In the following days he picked up odd bits and pieces of conversation concerning Friar Blaise, merely fragments. Blaise had been at the motherhouse for six years. Blaise was an only child. His people were rich. His mother was a pill! Blaise was a very great organist. He'd won many prizes in competitions. And then, tantalizingly, he heard this snatch: "I wonder if Blaise is cured?"

Mario had learned through experience to respect the friars' grapevine. They knew most of the things to be known about their brethren. They'd all come out of that motherhouse in Wisconsin at one time or another, and consequently one or the other had been a classmate of this, that, or the other friar. They had the lowdown on each other.

The fragments about Blaise kept Mario's imagination going overtime. Why was Blaise kept at the motherhouse for six years? The motherhouse was a place which seemed to serve many purposes. Not only were the candidates for the order educated there. No, it became a hospice for ailing friars, a retirement berth for the elderly religious, a retraining ground for returned missionary friars . . . and it was the spot where friars who had gotten into some kind of trouble were "shipped," a kind of rustification. This was a rather closely held bit of information.

Benigno once said matter-of-factly to Mario: "Friars be men. They get into trouble, too. When they do they got to pay for it like everybody else. They get sent back to St. Joseph's until they get their feet back on the ground again. They have to stay there until they do!"

Wow! What had Blaise done to be kept at the motherhouse for six years! Mario was well primed for the new organist's arrival.

And then one afternoon as he worked in the sanctuary, he was startled by the sudden, mighty chords from the organ. He'd never heard sounds made by Professor Wolfram like that. From the sanctuary he could look toward the rear, toward the organ loft. He could see a brown-habited figure at the keyboard, his back to Mario. St. Ansgar's was throbbing with a great tumult, storm music, a tempest was raging.

Hans leaned over the communion rail and beckoned to Mario in the sanctuary.

"My Gott, Mario. If he plays like that all the time, we haf to get the earmuffs . . . he gonna bust the organ and get the rupture, too . . . I never hear such playing . . ." Hans winced as if in pain.

Mario found Brother Benigno and the superior, Friar Athenasius, talking quietly together in German. They were in the second sacristy. It must have been a very serious matter they'd been discussing. Mario only understood bits of it. Something about Blaise not saying mass in the church . . . saying it in the choir. When Athenasius passed him on his way out, the superior's face was grave, a most unusual thing in Mario's experience; the superior always had a joke for Mario.

Mario emptied his scrub pail and filled it with clean water. He said tentatively: "Friar Blaise has come, huh, Brother?"

There was no response. Mario looked over his shoulder. Benigno was standing on his toes, looking out the small window in the sacristy door, looking toward the rear, toward the organ loft.

And then: "Mario, tomorrow morning I like you to serve mass for Friar Blaise in the choir."

There was something preoccupied in Benigno's manner, and his gray eyes seemed troubled.

Mario was surprised at Blaise's appearance. What a contrast between the way he looked and the way he played the organ. There was nothing mighty about the friar at all, no powerful build, no booming voice, no imposing presence. Blaise was slight, fair, with high cheekbones and a feathery blond beard. He kept his eyes lowered. And he wore the tonsure — not too many young friars affected that anymore. Mario gave him a careful going-over as he waited in his surplice while Benigno helped the priest vest for mass. There was not a word spoken during the robing.

And then with Mario leading the way, they went into the choir and began the mass. Mario had to strain to hear the priest's preparatory prayers. But Mario by now was used to all kinds of individual mannerisms shown by priests in their saying of the mass. One thing struck Mario as being out of the ordinary: Friar Blaise seemed . . . tense? Or uncertain? Something seemed checked about him. His movements at the altar were spasmodic, he never looked up, his prayers were mumbled and halting, his cheekbones glinted in the candlelight, and his Adam's apple bobbed up and down a lot.

At the lavabo, when Mario passed the priest the napkin to dry his hands, Mario's fingers happened to graze the priest's wrist. The wrist jerked back as if Mario had burned him. And Mario saw the sweat breaking out on the priest's brow. It was very upsetting.

When the mass was over, Mario busied himself around the sacristy while Benigno assisted Blaise taking off the vestments. Nothing was said. And Benigno seemed very careful in his movements, as if he was afraid to disturb the priest by any untoward motion. Mario had never witnessed anything like it. Yes, it was very upsetting!

There seemed to be some unspoken compact between Benigno and Mario: neither mentioned the subject of Friar Blaise even though it hardly seemed possible the matter could be avoided.

Every morning Mario served at Friar Blaise's mass said in the choir, and every morning the same strained air of whatever-it-was pervaded the service. Mario might just as well not have been there for all the notice the friar gave him. Not a single word ever passed between them and Mario made very sure he never touched the priest's wrist again. Mario sometimes wondered if the priest was blind since his eyes were always closed. Blaise was a source of endless study for Mario. He reminded Mario of those pictures he'd seen of hermits in the desert: anchorites, half starved, gaunt, emaciated, utterly isolated.

One thing was for sure, Blaise certainly perspired. After mass, Benigno would have to air out Blaise's alb by the window. It was very strange that so spare a man, a man just skin and bones, could sweat like a fat man. But again, though this was such an obvious and peculiar circumstance, neither Benigno nor Mario talked about it. And no one else seemed to talk about Blaise, though he certainly was different, and everybody was aware of it!

And then by chance Mario overheard a conversation. He was in the kitchen having a mug of coffee and a hunk of the crusty bread. He was seated at one end of the long trestle table, looking out the windows into the friary garden. Just outside he heard the soft voice of the superior talking to someone. Mario soon identified whom Athenasius was talking to by the scent of snuff; only one friar used snuff, the Very Reverend Doctor Nicodemus, that erudite friar.

"He don't seem changed at all. He starts already," Athenasius said fretfully.

And then the soothing, reassuring tones of Nicodemus: "Be patient. He has a heavy cross to bear. You have to give him time to get used to parish duties. Slow, Father, slow. We have to be very understanding. After all, he's been kept in the motherhouse for six years. He is very ängstlich . . . und skrupelos."

Mario understood the first word, *ängstlich*, Blaise certainly was shy, but the other word he'd never heard before.

Friar Athenasius said: "I try to be patient. I thought he would have improved. I keep waiting for him to start . . . at night."

"Ach, Athenasius. Give him a chance. After all, he is a very great organist . . . like the Anton Bruckner . . . very great!"

Athenasius was anything but a stern man, Mario knew, but he sounded stern when he said: "Oh, many times, Father, I have question myself. I should have cast the black ball."

Nicodemus said tranquilly: "Ach, no, Father. You did right. Blaise is young. He will conquer this."

Mario bided his time. They were at the flower market off Sixth Avenue shopping for the specials offered for the season. It was a bustling place, carts and trucks unloading their freight of shrubs, plants, trees, huge cartons of flowers, ferns, bales of moss; the sidewalk strewn with leaves, stems, petals, men shouting and running about.

"What's the black ball, Brother?"

Benigno was startled. Perhaps he hadn't heard right with all the noise. "What was that, Mario?"

"What's the black ball?"

"Why you ask?"

Mario told him what he had overheard.

Benigno considered for a moment, debating how to handle the situation. "Come on, this is no place to talk. We go have a cup of coffee . . ."

They sat in a cafeteria. Benigno explained: "Now, I tell you. When a fella have finished his studies to be a priest or brother and before he makes his solemn profession, all of his masters — the teachers or the people who have guide him for all the years he have been in seminary — meet and talk over the fella. They decide once and for all if the fella is to be ordained. How they do this?" Benigno stirred in a great heap of sugar into his coffee.

"On the table is a basket with wooden balls in it, some of them white, some black. A velvet bag is passed from master to master, and each master picks out one of the balls from the basket and puts it in the velvet bag. Nobody can see which color ball the master have put in the bag, because the vote is secret. Then when they all have done this, the bag is emptied on the table. If all the balls be white the fella he is okay, *but* if there be one black ball, alles ist kaput."

Mario's face showed so much. He understood now what it was Father Athenasius said so sternly. He should have voted against Friar Blaise being ordained! But Benigno knew Mario and he brought him up sharply, saying: "I have been in the order a very long great time and in all that time I have know only of five black balls cast. Yeah, in sixty-some years only five black balls — and do you know why? Because it don't come to that. They watch you like a cat watch a mouse when you in the seminary. They know everything about you. They don't want you with them if you ain't going to be right, you see. So they have the tests all the time, they catch a fella before it come to the vote . . . so it is very, very seldom the black ball is cast . . . you understand, huh, Mario? Come on, we got flowers to buy!"

All those flowers, the dazzle of color and the intoxicating fragrances, and that crowded market. Mario seemed asleep. Benigno said to him, gently, as if waking him up: "Mario, whatever you be thinking about Friar Blaise, I want you to remember something about him." Benigno paused to let his words sink in. He watched Mario's face: "God have put a very heavy hand on him."

Mario saw in Benigno's gray eyes a profound sadness. Yes, after this Mario would do everything in his power to help Friar Blaise.

But the parish soon developed its own ideas about Friar Blaise. Perhaps it was due to the way he played the organ. It was to them, as one old-timer said, "movement-y music," the kind which set the parishioners twitching with restlessness, made their ears ache. They couldn't daydream with such music. No "Oh, Promise Me" at weddings, no Chopin Funeral March at funerals, no Brahms Lullaby at christenings. Why did he make the organ sound as if it were working off a curse?

And why was he so standoffish? Blaise would charge along the aisle, his hands tucked inside the sleeves of his habit, looking neither to the right or left; brushing by people, as if he couldn't stand the sight of them. And the fixed expression on his face. Mario had seen it. Was it disgust?

Hans the sexton said: "I never catch sight of a friar like that guy before. He got a grollen" — a grudge — "against the whole world. By golly when he come along the aisle, you get outa his way, otherwise he knock you down. You say hello to him, it go right over his head. What the devil kinda friar he is?"

But it was the choir which was really up in arms. They were a powerful group and very vocal. Milly Brenwasser was their spokesman. She had a velvety contralto but her speaking voice was not so agreeable, and she was opinionated. Professor Wolfram had buckled in to her. She was accustomed to being deferred to. After all, everybody knew she was wasting her talents sitting at a switchboard for the New York Telephone Company when just up the avenue was the Metropolitan Opera House!

Milly swooped down on Benigno and Mario as they cleaned out the holy water stoups at the rear of the church. She had blood in her eye: "How long will it go on, Brother? He's destroying the choir!"

Benigno said, extra placidly: "Why, what's the matter, Milly?"

"You don't know, Brother? You can't hear? My God, the way he plays. He never consults with me. He won't look at me."

Benigno was very German and very old when it suited him: "Oh, ja, that's his loss, Milly, that he don't talk with you. Oh, ja."

"He has no idea how to treat singers. We're not blocks of wood. He's ruining our voices. And the music he picks for services . . . I tell you, Brother, in a few weeks St. Ansgar's will have no choir!"

She watched Mario and Benigno, made sure they understood the direness of her prediction, and then ducked out the rear doors.

They sopped out the dirty water. Benigno made no remark, but Mario knew he was troubled. Milly was a prima donna, but she had a reasonable grievance.

The parish made up its mind. Friar Blaise's sin was that of pride and superiority! He was as proud as Lucifer! And the Dutchies lost no opportunity in telling Mario what God had done to Lucifer.

Pride. Excessive pride. Was that the heavy hand laid on Blaise by God? Mario pondered it as he waited in the sacristy watching Benigno helping Blaise to vest. Mario saw the ribbons of sweat on the young friar's forehead, his gaunt face with those high cheekbones, the passage of his Adam's apple like some rigid bit of machinery. He was suffering an ordeal. Was that pride? And how tenderly Benigno draped the alb over his shoulders, and chasuble, as if the lightest touch against Blaise's skin was torment. And the swelling of the priest's jawbone into a knot. Pain. He was in pain. From what? Pride?

And then Mario overheard Benigno murmur: "Are you all right, Father?"

Blaise leaned his head against the ledge of the robing table, breathing heavily, swallowing, passing his tongue over his dry lips. In an instant it flashed through Mario's mind. He knew what it was. He knew why the slightest touch made Blaise wince. He had been flagellating himself! Yes, scourging himself. Every friar had a scourge, a wicked-looking spider-shaped whip used to mortify the flesh. Pride?

Blaise straightened up. Benigno nodded toward Mario, and they started into the chapel. Suddenly Mario was thrown forward. Blaise must have stumbled, the chalice crashed to the floor, the paten rolling like a wheel over the tiles, the communion wafer fetched by the stalls. Mario had a double vision of what was taking place: the priest struggling to get to his feet, his eyes wide open, haunted with fear, Benigno bending over him, whispering, trying to help him; the spasms of pain racking the priest's face. Mario saw in his mind's eye that back, crisscrossed with the stripes made by the scourge. At last Blaise stood, rocking on his feet, Benigno steadying him, leading him back into the sacristy.

In a daze Mario picked up the chalice, the paten, the unconsecrated wafer, the burse. Mario examined the chalice; it was dented. He felt he was caught up in a slow-motion proceeding. Everything came dully, and with an echo: the slap, slap of Benigno's bare soles against his sandals, the closing of the door from the sacristy into the friary, the receding scrape of feet going up the stairs, and the strong, sour reek of sweat coming from the vestments tumbled on the vesting table. Pride?

Hans twirled a finger in circles at his temple and nodded: "You could tell he wasn't one hundred percent in the belfry. Nobody who plays the organ like the way he plays it. Ganz verrücht. He so stuck up, he haf to break down. You know, he have been running in the hallways of the friary every night. Ja, Mario, running, in the hallways . . ." Hans's dull brown eyes stared into Mario's eyes. "Like the devil wus chasin' him. You see what happen, he chust break apart."

And Milly: "It was plain to see. The man wasn't all there. Nobody would have treated the choir the way he did had he been all there."

The parish knew! "Lucifer have get his fall!"

Friar Athenasius the superior announced to Brother Benigno: "We have hired a temporary organist. He be here until Professor Wolfram comes back."

It was quiet in the second sacristy, just the rain hitting the windows. Mario asked Brother Benigno:

"Where is Friar Blaise, Brother?"

"In the infirmary."

"He's sick?"

Benigno didn't quite know how to handle that. "Ja, in a way."

"Is he very sick, Brother?"

Benigno did not meet Mario's eyes, he said gruffly: "Ja, he is very sick."

Mario pushed his luck: "What heavy hand did God lay on him, Brother?"

Benigno growled: "Mario . . . you got . . ."

Mario pressed harder: "Pride, huh, Brother?"

It was the simplicity which disarmed Benigno.

"Friar Blaise is scrupulous."

Mario wrinkled his brow. His mind flew back to what he'd overheard when he was in the kitchen. "Skrupelos." Yes, Father Athenasius had said the same word, but in German.

Benigno regarded the boy seriously: "You don't know what it is. That is the heavy hand God have laid on Blaise. Here, I show you what it means."

There was a pot of narcissi growing in a bed of pebbles. Benigno picked out a very small pebble and showed it to Mario.

"Take off one of your shoes, Mario."

Mario unlaced the shoe and took it off.

"Now pull off your stocking." Benigno picked up Mario's shoe and dropped the small stone into it. "Okay, now put on the shoe, lace it up, and walk."

Mario walked the length of the second sacristy. He didn't know what to expect. For a time he felt nothing, and then gradually as the pebble worked its way along the inside of his shoe, he awoke to the bite of its sharp edges. At first it was merely uncomfortable and then painful; he began to favor his foot, limp, shake the foot, trying to dislodge the stone from his flesh. And then he stopped walking, lifted his foot to ease the discomfort and he still felt the sharp bite, the memory of the pain. It had entered his consciousness.

"That's all, Mario. It hurt you, huh? Suppose you have that small stone in your conscience where it keep biting you, cutting you, always stinging you. That's what it mean to be scrupulous. The stone inside of Friar Blaise, inside his conscience, keep saying to him he is sinning, always sinning, constantly sinning. That's why he never look at anybody, he's scared he be sinning. He never talks to nobody, he's scared of sinning. When he touch anything, when he say the mass, he's scared he's sinning. He's so filled with guilt for what he think he be sinning he can't sleep at night, he run half the night to Friar Nicodemus, so the friar will hear his confession. He can't eat, he can't sleep, poor fella, he brought down like a man hunting himself."

Mario had removed the pebble from his shoe and was pressing his fingers against the sharp edges.

"It be a very old and terrible sickness, Mario. Monks and priests and nuns can suffer from it. It goes a long time back. The conscience gets too fine . . . too finicky. Martin Luther suffer from it when he is a monk. They get no peace. They filled all the time with doubt and guilt. It drive a person crazy, everything they do is sinning. They have to run morning, noon, and night to confession. It is a terrible, awful sickness, Mario."

Benigno's words hung in the air.

After a while Mario asked: "How's it happen?"

Benigno spread his hands: "I don't know how it happen. But all religious know about it. They know it can destroy a person."

"Why don't they know they're not sinning?"

"Their confessor tell them that but they don't pay no attention. It get inside of them. Would you have believe me if I told you when you walked with that stone in your shoe if I said it was all in your head, you wasn't hurting? And your foot now, how it feels? Can you remember the pain?

"Can you imagine how it be if you have a pebble in your conscience? Even St. Francis can't help one of the brethren who is scrupulous. Friar Tomasso. St. Francis try everything with him. He stay up with him all night. He tie him up with the ropes. He tell him it not be possible for him to be sinning. But the friar he say he sinning in his mind, sinning with his eyes, his ears, his lips. He say he have to leave the order. St. Francis beg him on his knees. He say: 'Tomasso, little sheep of Christ, stay, God will give you peace.' But Tomasso he run away."

"What happened to him?"

Benigno dodged the question. Tomasso had hanged himself. "He disappeared forever."

Mario tied his shoelace. "Will Friar Blaise disappear?"

"Oh, no, they not put him out of the order. They take care of him. He be sent back to the motherhouse. He be a professed priest. He be taken care of. You see, Mario, Blaise have suffer with this for a long time . . ."

"Maybe he'll run away like Friar Tomasso?"

Benigno's face flushed. The thought of Blaise committing suicide haunted him.

"He don't have to run away. He can ask to be relieved from his vows. He can do that, poor tortured fella."

Mario stared at the rain running down the windows. Yes, Mario had gotten his wish, he'd been in on the ground floor of a legend. It sprang up around Friar Blaise and his short stay at St. Ansgar's. The legend bore no relation to the facts. It was just as Brother Benigno said, people hold on to what they want to believe and that's the whole thing. For St. Ansgar's Friar Blaise, like Lucifer, had fallen!

♦10♦

The Brown Bike

Friar Benigno would have been the first to admit that he was no longer as positive about most things as he used to be. He'd learned it didn't pay, even if you happened to be right. He would have described this development as broad-mindedness because things were not always as they seemed!

Mario recognized Benigno's attitude as altogether at odds with a fundamental Dutchie canon: they were always right! And the more they were proven wrong, the more vehement they became. Immediate judgment and unyielding opinion were basic in the arsenal of Stanley Street's outlook. Add hastiness to the mixture and you had the key to much of the collective misinformation, misperception, prejudice, and downright ignorance transmitted from father to son, mother to daughter (not that their two cents mattered very much).

Mario himself was a Dutchie and a born-and-bred native of Stanley Street so he was not entirely free from the stain, but working with Friar Benigno had to some extent counterbalanced the tendency. Still, Mario was too quick to judge, to nickname, to support secondhand, cockeyed opinions. His saving grace consisted in his being quiet by nature, and being only fifteen years old at the time. But Mario many times was torn, Benigno tolerant, Stanley Street opinionated. Of course Benigno lived a life in which time was largely defeated; his view was eternal. Stanley Street on the other hand sensed time had to be defeated, life was so swift.

For instance, one opinion demonstrating Mario's Stanley Street begetting: there were very few good-looking girls on Stanley Street! At fifteen it was a subject of most pressing and thrilling immediacy (a subject he did not discuss with Brother Benigno). The girls on the block simply did not measure up to Mario's standard. He was a great reader and as a result his standards were exceedingly high: Jack London, Sir Walter Scott, and Edgar Rice Burroughs.

Take those girls and really look at them. This one had good legs, that one attractive hair, another one lovely eyes, still another swell teeth, and yet another a "build," but no single female on the block incorporated all these features in her person. The Josies, Mitzis, Tillies, Johannas, Friedas, Teresas simply failed to pass his critical standards. These were the Dutchie girls. If Mario broadened his survey to include Italian and Irish girls, well, that complicated matters. With an Irish girl, there was always family, and a terrible lack of organization and discipline, too risky altogether; and the Italian girls? Ah, they at the outset seemed captivating, much in the way of promise, but, but, in a few years how that promise grew into bulk. So Mario struggled with his Dutchiness on one hand and his exposure to Brother Benigno on the other.

Now, other guys on the block didn't have Mario's divided outlook; they seemed above being picky. He'd watch them and their strutting, their courting antics. They were so arrogant and self-sufficient, flapping their wings, baring their talons, making wild, reckless flights, raking each passing female with predatory stares. Yes, but Mario had seen these highfliers plucked of their feathers, their wings clipped, their talons sandpapered, with jesses on their shanks, and in a very few years a bursting nest of young Dutchies.

The girls were something else, tricky, mysterious. They had the gift of blooming brilliantly for short periods, but usually long enough to snare some Dutchie boy. This was true of all girls, whatever their nationality, any one of them could turn on this flow of evanescent attractiveness. Mario thought of Philomena Piccone, now there was a case. All you saw for years was an olive-skinned girl with braided hair and prominent black eyes who had a painful stammer. And then suddenly, magically she flowered, and Artie Blumeyer was caught! Just like that.

And really for that moment, that single rapturous moment, look what followed: Philomena's seven brothers, one with a bigger mouth than the next, always yelling, a mother-in-law whose eyes sliced you like salami, a father-in-law who never took off his hat and who regarded you as if you'd cheated him once and he was going to pay you back. Every Sunday, Artie in his eight-room flat on McDonald Street had to welcome truckloads of dark-skinned relatives who spoke nothing but Italian, and Artie stood out like a mothball in a barrel of olives. His Dutchie contemporaries had a phrase to cover Artie's fate. "In nomine patris, et filii, and twenty-one kids, Amen!"

And with Irish girls pretty much the same drill. Even an eagle like Kosh Stoltz, somebody who'd been around, you couldn't fool him, you couldn't down him in an argument. What he knew he knew even when he didn't! Kosh smoked El Producto cigars. El Productos, fifteen cents each! He had been to whorehouses! He shared this arcane education with the other Dutchie boys, usually around the gutter fire at night. He had the most revealing insights about Chinese, Burmese, and other exotic women. Kosh of all the Dutchie fellas was knowing about women and their secret ways. But what good did his sophistication do him? Molly Sullivan came into flower and Kosh pitched forward as if he'd been felled like an ox. Molly took care of his educated tastes. And it wasn't long before Kosh stopped smoking El Productos and switched to Rocky Fords at two for a nickel.

The Dutchie girls had the zing of their competitors but they also had staying power. They'd hold back and hold back until a guy was so driven by desperation he'd fall right into the trap, it would snap closed, and his father-in-law would get him a job in the same place he worked. And from that time forward, the Dutchie boy had a jailer, one who picked him up each morning and returned him each evening to his waiting Heidi or Helga or Mitzi! No straying with Dutchie wives!

Mario was very much the witness in this matter of girls and boys. He devoted a great deal of careful time and observation to the ins and outs of this serious contest that went on all the time. In time he had a lot of opinions.

Girls were by nature canny. Dutchie girls were not daring. Italian girls were inviting. Irish girls sparkling. Italian girls protected, Irish girls daring, Dutchie girls clannish. Yes, they banded together and hunted in packs! For example, the Dutchie girls had a clique which they called the Coffee Ann Club.

Sixteen or eighteen of them would take over two tables at the back of Baumer's bakery (he also served coffee, buns, cakes, and pies, along with his retail baked goods), shove them together, and hold court on a Friday night. Over coffee, buns, cake, cream pie, or stollen, they'd laugh, whisper, conspire, dissect every eligible guy in the neighborhood. It was strategy over the coffee mugs. Territories were mapped out, victims assigned. Mario wouldn't want to go to the bakery on Friday night with the Coffee Ann Club in session. It was too embarrassing.

Oh, the tactics which came out of those Friday-night meetings. You never knew where they'd surface. Mario would recognize them when they showed. For instance, on Sunday, at the ball field, at an inning change, a Dutchie girl would very casually and artlessly pick up one of the Dutchie player's gloves and hold it for him until he was ready to go back on the field. She'd hand it to him, a look in her eyes, and the dope would go gaga. And then she'd cheer him on, yell encouragement when he was at bat. And pretty soon a perfectly good second baseman, who perhaps aspired to play big-league ball, would be changed into a guy who wore a shirt and tie and suit, and who instead of showing up for practice would be discovered walking along the docks with a Dutchie girl on his arm and a cuckoo look in his eyes.

The Dutchie girls were clannish, determined, and they used their heads. As a group they had a terrific batting average. Very few marriageable girls on Stanley Street became spinsters. Ironically, one whose future seemed questionable, who seemed unlikely to find her boy, was none other than Aggie Baumer, the baker's daughter. Aggie naturally was a stellar member of the Coffee Ann Club. She was treated just like the rest even though the coffee and cake were on the house for her. Aggie giggled and whispered and laughed with her contemporaries but underneath she was anything but satisfied with herself. She was a perfect advertisement for her father's excellent products. Aggie was fat. Moreover, she suffered an additional handicap. She had completed high school, an achievement and a disability at the same time on Stanley Street. It meant Aggie was fundamentally a loner among the other girls, giggle as she would. What with her abundance, and her learning, she put off the Dutchie boys. They steered clear of her, except for Mario, and he was out of the running because of his age.

Aggie and Mario had a great deal in common. They were both readers. She'd stop Mario on his way to St. Ansgar's and ask him if he'd read the latest best seller or caught Lowell Thomas's last broadcast about the salt tax in India. Mario had no fears about Aggie as far as being a designing woman, oh, no; but with his Stanley Street jumping-to-conclusion bent he knew Aggie would never land a fella. Any girl who knew when to use a full colon and when the nominative case was always used following a *to be* verb was doomed to spinsterhood. But Aggie was a nice girl.

Rudy Baumer, her father, was concerned about his daughter. He hadn't approved of her graduating from high school. He'd rather she'd come behind the counter of the bakery. But she was pigheaded.

Baumer had gold-rimmed teeth, and a smile. And Baumer was a drinker. Not a drunk, a drinker. His tipple was flavoring extracts. His wife was anti-booze, and Baumer was a dutiful husband. Never whiskey, never brandy, gin, no, none of those spirits, but Baumer had large bills for almond, vanilla, orange, lemon, lime, cinnamon, clove, and other alcoholic-based extracts, nearly all of them potent. When Baumer waited on you he exuded the most marvelous smell you could imagine, but his eyes were nearly always glassy. But

Aggie was a source of worry for Baumer and Mrs. Baumer. Mrs. Baumer was very, very opinionated. Aggie had gotten it into her head she wanted to go to college.

Baumer discussed it with his customers. He was totally opposed to any child of his, especially a girl, going to college. If he had it to do all over again, he would have yanked her out of high school after the second year. Never would he compound his mistake by letting her go on with her education. What for? A girl from Stanley Street? Ridiculous.

"She's a nice, good girl, maybe a little too sure about things . . . so if a nice Dutchie fella . . . ja, just a nice Dutchie fella . . . make all the difference in her . . ."

Baumer would lean over a huge baking tray of freshly made streusel and deftly cut it with his flat knife into twenty-cent squares. "Just a nice fella . . ."

He sought out Brother Benigno. He wanted to know what he should do.

"Nothing," said Brother Benigno.

Baumer was nonplussed. "Nothing . . . nothing?"

Benigno leaned close, looked into those glassy eyes: "Rudy, don't interfere . . . you only make happen what you don't want to happen. Keep your hands off . . . she's twenty-two!"

"But she need to be a mensch . . . she ain't got no fella . . . and college don't make no mensch outa her . . ."

Yes, Mario agreed with Baumer in this instance. Aggie's chances were slim. Even when he opened up the choices beyond the Dutchie fellows, included the Italians and the Irish, Aggie didn't seem likely to get herself a guy. But then Mario was too Stanley Street. He never even considered Hindu Jim.

"Hindu" Jim was an exotic who'd come to roost in a single back room on the top floor of 535, which he rented by the week from Mrs. Anna-Lisa Schleuter, the widow. Jim was a fascinating person. He was in the country studying textiles. He was tall, of stained skin and broad face, and had dazzlingly white teeth. And he was the owner of a brown bicycle, which he kept in show-window condition. Jim used to carry it over his shoulder up and down the five flights of stairs to his room.

Jim's eyes were so luminous Mario could catch himself reflected in them, and his hair was jet black like coal. He regularly patronized Mrs. Martin's run-down candy store where he regularly bought two cents' worth of Indian nuts, which he would crack between his teeth and carefully spit out the shells. He would share that small bag of nuts with Mario or any other kid who'd cluster around to admire Jim's magnificent bicycle.

Jim was a foreigner of such extraordinary foreignness, he was completely out of the range of Dutchie experience. Italians, the Irish, perhaps even a Puerto Rican, they might somehow admit into their recognition, perhaps; but Jim, ah, he was strictly an import, yes, like the bales of silk which were hoisted from the holds of those stubby freighters tied up along the wharves. He spoke like a foreigner as well. You could hear every word he said; for him consonants were meant to be struck! Mario had the idea Jim's speech resembled that of the Englishmen he'd seen in the movies, even some of the words Jim would let drop, words that were very English: *jolly*, *chap*, *ruddy*, *twig*, *sorry*, and, in moments of stress, *bloody*.

Jim was friendly, open, always smiling, a man whose personality gained him a place for himself, despite his unfortunate beginnings, on Stanley Street. Jim put in long hours in the textile house where he was studying manufacturing techniques and design, down on Varick Street. Mario learned Jim was here on a student visa, and his time in the country was limited; one day he would have to return to his very remote land, a land so strange, the Dutchies couldn't imagine it.

Baumer the baker gave his opinion. He said Jim was more accustomed to elephants walking the street than trucks and cars. Baumer said more. He thought it was a wonder that Jim didn't wear a bandage around his head, like the other Hindus. Mario heard Aggie correct her father: "He isn't a Sikh."

Jim was everlastingly polite. His manners were impeccable; courtesy for him seemed inbred. Anna-Lisa Schleuter, his landlady, said she felt like a regular duchess being around Jim. No matter that his skin had a kind of iodine shade, her lodger was a gentleman, and a most educated man. And wonder of wonders, Stanley Street agreed. And Jim enhanced his position on Stanley Street by his out-and-out admiration of the neighborhood. And Jim's high regard for Stanley Street was never far from his lips.

"It is a superb district! The views, the location, and the advantages afforded even to the most humble. And you the dwellers are so frightfully inventive and resourceful. The energy you reveal, and your cultural mores."

You can imagine the impact such encomiums had upon the Dutchie sense of pride of place. The average Stanley Streeter would stand up to his neck in pleasure hearing Jim's praises. Mario sometimes wondered what Jim's country was like if Stanley Street struck him as being marvelous — for sure, Jim wasn't a hypocrite, his enthusiasm was sincere.

Jim would have his bicycle down on the sidewalk, a wrench in his hand. He'd pass from nut to nut, tightening, adjusting, and talk as he worked.

"Consider this admirable wheel. Through my effort, I generated the dollars to purchase it, in the very short period of three months. Astonishing in every regard both as to the money accumulation and the availability of the vehicle! And I am a visiting student. Most wonderful!"

Once the hot nights came on, Mario would catch sight of Jim sitting cross-legged on the fire escape outside his top-floor room, gazing at the stars, while the strains of Mr. Stoltz's accordion wheezed from two tenements away, and Mrs. Disbrow's parrot squawked on the floor below. Occasionally Jim would glance down into the backyard, where Mario and his buddies were playing cards on the stoop. Jim would wave enthusiastically. He'd point toward the sloping-roofed brick structure which was the outdoor toilet for the tenement. It resembled a square old-fashioned railroad station, with its many doors, each of which was the private cubicle of one of the various families of the tenement. Jim never quite got over this outdoor sanitary accommodation (as he phrased it). He declared it was an advance of a high civilization. To think that each family had its own private cell. It was topping! Again Mario realized Jim was absolutely sincere. Couldn't he catch the very distinct cloacal stench carried on the hot night air? Sometimes that became positively overpowering. But Jim seemed oblivious.

And talk of wonders, Jim never tired of exclaiming over the public baths, municipal, where for three cents you'd be supplied with towel and soap, and you could use all the hot water you'd a mind to. That was for Jim luxury, pure unadulterated luxury, he'd declare.

"Oh, Mario, my lad, you live in an enlightened country. This rivals the Augustan age."

Mario supposed so. But then Jim's experience was limited. There were other sections of the city where cold-water flats were unknown, and outdoor toilets outlawed. When Mario tried to temper Jim's enthusiasm, Jim wouldn't be daunted.

"My dear fella, you simply have no concept of the luxury you are coddled by."

It was certainly a different perspective for Mario. As it would have been for Mario's mother, lifting the great wash basin of cold water onto the range to be heated.

But Jim had the answer for that, too.

"Running water inside, inside your digs, old chap . . . inside!"

And gas inside the flats. Not electricity like so much of the city but gas.

You couldn't dampen Jim's admiration.

"Gas laid on in every flat! Quite incredible. You know, Mario, old fella, yours is a high civilization. You have creature comforts."

Jim was wantonly enthusiastic about the attainments of the West Side. He even lauded the intellectual level of the Stanley Streeters! It was from Jim that Mario learned that old Mr. Seibenborn, the coal heaver, spoke French. French! Mr. Seibenborn could barely make himself understood in English. But French? But Jim knew. Yes, he'd distinctly heard Mr. Seibenborn say "Tout de l'heure."

Mario tried to catch the old coal-streaked man using French. The nearest he came to understanding what Jim had reported was when he heard Mr. Seibenborn say: "Toodle-oo." But then Mario didn't know French.

There was only one serious imperfection in this paradise on earth for Jim: the West Side winter. Oh, when that knife-sharp wind blew from the North River, rattling windows, penetrating every crack, when the skin became chapped, and fingers numbed, and lines of wash hung stiffly, frozen as codfish, Jim suffered most acutely. Mario would see his athletic body swathed in layer after layer of wrappings so that he looked positively corpulent.

And with his teeth chattering he'd say: "Your winters, old chap, are rigorous, frightful."

And Jim added, blowing on his hands: "St. Agnes Eve, ah, bitter chill it was. The owl for all his feathers was a-cold. The hare limped tremblingly through the frozen grass. And silent was the flock in woolly fold."

"What?" asked Mario.

"Keats, old chap . . . Keats . . . c-c-c-cold."

Is it any wonder, given this most unusual resident, sooner or later, Aggie Baumer would discover him to be a kindred spirit?

The first symptoms of the discovery came from Jim's great sense of honesty. Aggie had been behind the counter when Jim bought a nickel's worth of molasses cookies. Aggie had given him six instead of five of the big, flat, brown cookies.

"You have miscounted, surely." Jim passed back one cookie.

Aggie's face turned red. But girls are resourceful. Without missing a beat she said: "We have them on special today."

"How perfectly splendid!"

Jim gave Mario two of the cookies.

♦

Every Sunday rain or shine Jim would bring down his "wheel" and go for a spin along the waterfront. Jim was a free spirit, the wind tossing his rather long black hair, his graceful body swaying, he would pedal along joyfully. Occasionally he'd come to a stop to look at a liner tugging at its hawsers as the tide changed or watch them unloading a freighter (double-time pay) with a perishable cargo. Or Jim would lean over the string-piece and stare down at the murky water lapping against the piles.

He'd exclaim: "This is the gateway to the West. Samarkand." And then he'd vault onto his bike, and off he'd go on his handsome machine.

Mario was astonished to discover another rider making the same circuit one Sunday. On a red-striped bike! Aggie Baumer! Oh, Baumer raised the roof. Whoever heard of a grown woman taking up bicycle riding, huh? But Aggie seemed more purposeful, suddenly. She reminded her father of two facts. One, he had refused his permission for her to go to college, and, secondly, flavoring extracts contained large amounts of alcohol, and in high school chemistry she had learned that alcohol destroyed brain cells! Baumer backed off.

It wasn't very long before Stanley Street had a fresh piece of gossip. Mind you, they liked Jim, but Aggie was a Dutchie girl. Certainly some Dutchie girls had strayed and married into Irish or Italian families, but Jim . . . say what you will, it was a big lump to swallow.

Baumer brooded behind the counter, deep in the bowels of the earth where his ovens were located. Yes, Baumer brooded. When might Jim appear with that bandage around his head, perhaps an earring in his earlobe? Mrs. Baumer let him know he was Aggie's father, he should do something before it was too late. And Aggie was huffy!

Mario took to going down to the waterfront of a Sunday afternoon. He'd perch himself next to the huge bollards and stare out over the big, dirty river, smell the effluent of sewer and water-carried debris. Jim and Aggie would pedal up and sit next to him. It was all very innocent, Mario concluded. He was a witness. They talked of poetry and literature, about the enormous population of India and the British "yoke." Yes, there was no concealed lovemaking, not a single note of it in their whole exchange.

But who would believe in so innocent a relationship, a friendship between an educated man and a girl hungering for companionship, a friendship cemented by bicycles and bright minds. Perhaps if anybody could have persuaded the Dutchies to accept the situation for what it was, it would have been the unfailingly polite, courteous Jim, but that was just Jim — Aggie tipped the scales. Yes, it was Aggie who was responsible. She went on a diet. That unnatural, extreme step, antithetical to every principal of Dutchie outlook, put the fat in the fire.

Even the members of the Coffee Ann Club turned on Aggie. The diet was too much. They could understand the use of tactics, but dieting was underhanded and turning your back on the bounty of God. Baumer put his foot down. No more bicycle! Mrs. Baumer ordered Aggie to take a regular trick behind the bakery counter. Yes, Aggie wouldn't be strong enough to resist sampling those wonderful tortes, the whipped cream fruit pies, the napoleons, and the luscious prune tarts. Aggie would soon come to her senses. But Aggie proved to be a tower of strength. She continued with her diet, lost weight at an alarming clip. For the first time in anybody's memory, they discovered Aggie had a neck. She shrank from a size twenty to twelve in a matter of months. And when Mario's mother sent him to the bakery on an errand, Mario'd catch Aggie staring at her svelte lines in one of the mirrors on the walls. Though Aggie was under a kind of house arrest, she remained faithful . . . in a symbolic way.

Baumer was a harassed, troubled man. Nowadays he reeked of flavoring extracts, kind of mixed together, not just straight vanilla but a blend. He went to see Brother Benigno. He had tears in his eyes. He said in his soft Bavarian: "What to do, Benigno? I am a father. She is my daughter. What to do?"

Benigno was sympathetic but sensible.

"You tell me you wanted her to be a mensch."

"Yes, but whoever thinks, at this price . . ."

"Rudy, you have tried to drive Aggie. It won't work. She's old enough to do what she wants. Don't you see, you are forcing her . . ."

"Ah, Brother, you want me to throw her into the arms of this . . . this . . . Schwarze . . ."

"Come on, Rudy . . . what you saying . . . don't mix things up . . ."

"Julia, she after me to bust it up . . . she keep pushing me to do something . . ."

Benigno said firmly: "You want me to say what I think you should do . . . ?"

"Ja, ja, of course. Why else I come here?"

"All right, Rudy. Send Aggie to college!"

"What?"

Benigno said sharply: "Send her to college!"

Later, Benigno spoke to Mario about Aggie and Jim. Mario told him how innocent it was. What they talked about, how they spent their time.

"Well, all right for us to see what it is all about, Mario, but who else going to believe it? Besides, Aggie, she ain't been run down by fellas chasing after her . . . but this Jim fella, he's educated . . . ja, you gotta give him some credit . . . he must see what's going on . . . he ain't no dumbbell."

What Benigno said was very perceptive because Jim did tumble to the situation. Mario learned about it firsthand.

Jim and Mario were fishing off the coal pier at the foot of Stanley Street. Lafayettes, those small, scaly, oily fish, were running. Jim said gravely: "Old chap, I fear I am responsible for a deucedly awkward contretemps."

The river splashed against the piles.

"Yes, it is decidedly awkward. I cannot acquit myself of short-sightedness and perhaps worse. All unwitting, I assure you on my honor as a gentleman. Still, perception is everything."

Jim's brow was furrowed, and those luminous eyes sad. "It would be a very poor return for the hospitality and acceptance I have received here to be the source of strife in a family. I'm guilty of a cultural insentience. That is the offense but who will believe it?"

Mario thought he followed the meaning of Jim's remarks. "Oh, I believe you, Jim . . . I do . . ."

Jim put an arm on Mario's shoulder: "Yes, old chap, but you are enlightened beyond your years." Jim sighed and brushed hair away from his face. "I must repair the damage I've occasioned. My friendship with Miss Baumer has made for division. That is deplorable. I must repair that. Do I make myself clear, old chap?"

Mario gave a tug to his drop line.

"Oh, yeah . . . yeah."

"I am desolated by the prospect. It has been one of the most rewarding experiences of my life. I have been awakened to a world I never imagined existed, a standard of living undreamed of. But I cannot return strife for all the goodness showered upon me. I must remove myself, old fella. Yes, I must depart from Stanley Street."

Mario saw the anguish on Jim's face but he also recognized the determination behind Jim's words.

Mrs. Anna-Lisa Schleuter wept. Jim was the most wonderful boarder she'd ever had. She confessed that the darkness of his skin hardly seemed to matter, he seemed like a son to her. She felt Stanley Street had much to answer for. Jim entrusted Mario with one final commission. Would Mario be so considerate as to deliver to Aggie Baumer his brown bicycle? Jim explained that Aggie had been renting the one she rode!

Mario carried out the request. He witnessed Aggie's moment of piercing sorrow. The poor girl lifted up her skirts and sobbed into them. She was heartbroken. She took on so emotionally Mario had to get her parents. He didn't know how to console her. My God, who would have thought Aggie Baumer was capable of such strong feelings? It got so bad Rudy was shooed out of his bakery by Mrs. Baumer to go and search for Jim. But he was gone . . . gone.

Rudy went back to see Brother Benigno. He started in on his emotional schlepp. Benigno thrust out his beard and growled: "Rudy, you make me sick. Go home!"

Finally Rudy followed Brother Benigno's earlier counsel. He went with Aggie while she enrolled at C.C.N.Y. It's doubtful she'll ever find a fellow after her experience with Jim, but she does bike back and forth to college on the brown wheel.

The Coffee Ann Club has kept alive the whole romantic affair. Yes, Aggie Baumer and Jim have become part of the Stanley Street folklore.

And on summer nights, Stoltz accordion playing, Mrs. Disbrow's parrot squawking, the moonlight splashing the outdoor toilet building, Mario looks up to that empty fire escape on the top floor where Jim used to gaze out upon the wonders of Stanley Street.

♦11♦

Friar Venard

Periodically Brother Benigno would embark on what he called a "dop" — a kind of thoughtful, unhurried tour of inspection — around the neighborhood. Mario never knew when Benigno would get the impulse to set off on one of these dops. He'd unexpectedly appear all decked out in his square black suit jacket, his baggy pants, his soft leather shoes; he'd be rubbing his derby with his sleeve.

"Ja, I have to look around, Mario. You keep your eye on things."

Mario knew the pattern, because when Benigno returned from one of these expeditions he'd fill in Mario with where he'd been, what he'd seen, and what his comments were about the trip. Mario also knew these strolls answered some deep need inside the old man, some kind of renewal with his origins plus keeping abreast of the changes taking place on the West Side.

Paddy's Market was Benigno's destination.

Nothing was in greater contrast to the old friar's ordinary surroundings, the quiet, dim solitude of St. Ansgar's, than the teeming, raucous, jostling pandemonium of Paddy's Market, where the sidewalks were crowded with shoppers and the pavements littered with the debris of the goods displayed: fruit skins, vegetable leaves and stems, oyster and clam shells, and the occasional entrails of fish and meat and poultry.

People of every kind and description, talking in tongues Benigno found exciting because he couldn't make head or tail out of what they were saying, pushed along examining the fruits of the earth heaped in pushcarts, stalls, counters, wagons, bins. Once swept into the tide of Paddy's Market, there was no such thing as strolling. No, it was a matter of being carried along. It was this which refreshed

Benigno, this physical rubbing of elbows, having the breath of garlic and sausage, hot dog and sauerkraut, hot chestnuts, sweet potatoes, blown into his face.

Paddy's Market was like a huge bazaar. It extended for blocks along Ninth Avenue, awnings and umbrellas of every stripe and color covered the stands while overhead the open steel and trackage of the Ninth Avenue elevated railroad created an arcade-like suggestion to the entire scene. The structure with its latticework of track and girder broke the sunlight into strange zigzag patterns which splashed the shoppers and stands, and when it rained or snowed, it also splashed the shoppers. And added to the noise and cries of the hawkers and salespeople was the clatter of the wooden railroad cars, passing in rattling succession.

Yes, Benigno took it all in, fascinated by the life, the color, the coarseness. And then, too, he'd be recognized by a cop, or a former altar boy, or a merchant or peddler. He'd be told of this or that occurrence, someone's trouble, someone's success. And before he knew it, both his arms would be extended carrying shopping bags, bulging with largesse.

The climax of the afternoon would come at the moment he'd enter the second sacristy, his derby tilted from the jostling crowds, giving him an unexpectedly rakish look, his face rosy from the wind, and his eyes sparkling. He would say:

"Look, Mario, look what they give me."

The old man would sink wearily into his chair, take off his derby, and wipe his face with a blue work handkerchief.

"Ich bin müde" — I'm tired.

Mario would bring him a glass of the sacramental wine.

"But also it pep me up, the whole thing. Ja, it pep me up. Look at all the stuff they give me." Benigno smiled. "The more I tell them I don't want it, the more they pile on me. So you have plenty of stuff to take home with you, Mario. Look at this chunk of halibut . . ."

Benigno studied Mario's face.

"There's a connection with my dopping and the order . . . St. Francis do the same thing . . . he gets out with the people. St. Francis makes the order to serve the people. We ain't Carthusians or Cistercians or Trappists. We supposed to be in the cities where all the crowds is. To be out with the people." Benigno would take out the bread and wursts and kale and spinach and pomegranates and bananas and sweet potatoes and apples. "This is the food of the people. The things St. Francis love. I go out to make me get knocked around by the people. That's what we are, not sissies, sitting in the common room smoking our cigars and making our faces smell pretty from the shaving lotion . . . no, Mario, we suppose to come to the people, not the people to come to us . . . don't you forget that . . . we suppose to serve them . . ."

Mario bent down to open Benigno's shoelaces.

"Thanks. Ach, that's better. The order be much better off if it have to go out and struggle. St. Francis have no idea in his mind we should be comfortable and have things easy . . . that way very strange . . . things takes place . . . it ain't healthy to cut yourself off . . ."

Was it coincidence? Or was it another example of Benigno's making Mario aware, obliquely, of something about to take place, something he could not come straight out with . . . ? A warning?

Lilac fragrance. Yes, lilac aftershave lotion. This announced to Mario the arrival of a new face, Friar Venard.

Venard was not young; his beard was shot through with gray. He was tall, strongly built, his hair was well groomed, as if he spent time arranging it. He was not at all standoffish; he smiled easily.

Benigno watched Mario's face very carefully as he explained: "This fella can't take the muscatel for the mass. His stomach is weak. You fill the cruet with the chablis for him. Ja, Mario?"

What was so unusual about that, Mario wondered. Other friars couldn't take the sweet, heavy muscatel wine, either. Why was Benigno making such a thing about it — giving him such a watchful look? No, that wasn't what Benigno had on his mind.

Benigno lingered, a sure sign he was trying to make up his mind.

He said, as if taking the first step: "This fella ain't going to be here long, Mario. He have the meeting in the city . . . some kind of meeting, I don't know what it is . . ."

There was something Mario was supposed to get, but it was too guarded; he couldn't figure what it was.

Benigno suddenly went on: "This fella is from the motherhouse. He be one of the teachers there. Ja, he teach something . . . Greek or something like that . . . I don't know . . ."

They stood looking at each other, Mario expecting more, and Benigno not knowing how to supply it. It was disquieting for Mario because he sensed he was being warned! Warned of Friar Venard? Benigno wasn't fond of him? Distrusted him? Knew something about him?

Mario served Friar Venard's masses. The priest was extremely cordial. He had very expressive, almost liquid eyes. Often Mario found the priest staring at him.

"You're going to become one of us, Mario?"

"I don't know, Father."

"Your Latin is splendid. You have an ear for language. I teach Greek and Hebrew at St. Joseph's."

Mario blushed, he felt the heat, and it made him very uncomfortable.

The priest could see the color mantling Mario's cheeks.

"How old are you now, Mario?"

"Fifteen, Father."

"And you come here and work every day before and after school."

"Yes, Father."

"How fortunate Brother Benigno is to have such an assistant. You're in high school?"

"Yes, Father, my second year."

"Smart young man! Pushing right along. Won't be long before you'll have some decisions to make."

Mario felt tongue-tied. He couldn't figure out why. His words got mixed up coming out ". . . I don't . . . know, Father . . ." And Mario knew he was blushing again, and he also knew the priest was regarding him with even greater intensity because of it.

When the mass was done, Mario came into the sacristy with the empty cruets. Benigno had just finished helping Friar Venard disrobe. The priest said as he grabbed his breviary from the table: "Mario has a marvelous Latin pronunciation. Thank you, Mario." And Venard left.

Benigno said, as if his feathers had been ruffled: "You gave him the chablis, Mario?"

"Yes, Brother."

"That's all right then."

Mario waited for Benigno to say more but nothing came. Mario wanted to explain what a funny feeling he got from being around Friar Venard. He felt something . . . something as if he were closing up, pulling himself inside . . . he looked at Benigno . . . the old man thrust out his beard. Yes, he was not in the mood to be talked to . . . or was it, he didn't know how to get into it? Mario turned away and went back to his work.

Mario was putting away taborets, stacking them on the overhead shelves in the second sacristy. He was on a ladder and he smelled the lilac. He knew immediately he was being watched and he felt a sudden closing up inside himself.

"Always busy, aren't you, Mario?"

"Not . . . all the time . . . Father."

"I enjoy coming here. Most of the year I'm stationed way out in the country. I see nothing but fields and trees. It's true I teach but that's lonely, very lonely. So I relish this opportunity to spend a little time at St. Ansgar's; it shakes me up . . . you've never been to our motherhouse, Mario?"

Mario felt trapped, standing on the ladder. "No . . . no, Father."

"You've heard plenty of mention of St. Joseph's, working around here?"

"Yes, Father."

"It's remote." The priest looked up trying to meet Mario's eyes. It was a searching kind of look, as if his eyes were talking to Mario. "Out there, such a conversation as we're having now is not possible, no, not possible." The priest laughed. "But I know every little pig that's born, every calf, every lamb. Yes, that's daily life at St. Joseph's. We grow our own food both for the animals and our own table . . . you're not a country boy, though, Mario."

"Stanley Street, Father."

"Yes. Never could mistake that for the country. A bustling place, people packed together. So much of living takes place on the street, doesn't it, Mario?"

Mario thought he would burst. When would he go?

"That's the way the ancient Greeks lived, on the street, in the marketplace. No need for a newspaper to keep up with the daily happenings when your neighbors can supply you with the latest doings. Privacy must be hard to come by . . ."

Mario was not paying attention to what he was saying, why was he so troubled by the priest? He'd have to move soon, his body was cramping up there on the ladder.

"I was once assigned to a parish. I was once a secular priest. I only became a friar later . . . I had a church in Arizona. Great land of sunlight and desert. I was the pastor and curate, everything rolled into one. I was lonely there, too . . ."

Mario forced it out: "I got to get back to work."

"Go ahead, Mario. Don't mind me . . . maybe I can help you . . ."

Mario felt caught up in something from which he could not disentangle himself. The priest's eyes never left him, there on the ladder. And the extra friendliness. Mario was more profoundly uncomfortable than he'd ever been in his life. A kind of dread had taken hold of him.

"Your neighborhood fascinates me, Mario. Its educative principle is life itself. Nothing recorded, life is squandered with no thought of catching any of the magic of living. No cherishing of beauty, or poetry. What is retained is what is passed by word of mouth, just like the American Indian, everything spoken, no written history. In time nothing will be remembered of the generations who lived here. All that accumulation of life will vanish, buildings will be razed, the piers and waterfront will decay, the culture be dispersed . . . all will have disappeared like a summer's day. Fleeting. It puts one in mind of those nomadic tribes who pass over the horizon with no trace of their having existed."

Mario found himself fascinated, in spite of his dread, by the priest's eloquence, and the picture he painted of the dissolution on Stanley Street. Mario had a teacher who read poetry aloud; Friar Venard used his voice in exactly the same way.

Everything had grown still, except for the clock, and the scrape of Mario's sole on the rungs of the ladder.

"Why do you work here, so young?"

Flustered: "Why . . . do I?"

"You need to help your family with the money you make, is that it?"

"I take it home to my mother."

"Naturally. And I imagine she's happy to get it. Do you ever play with the other kids?"

On and on in that melodious voice, as if to charm Mario with the sound. He'd once seen a vaudeville act where a hypnotist had picked someone out of the audience and put her to sleep right in front of the crowded house. Mario hadn't believed it could be done. Now he felt it was possible. Yes, possible.

"Do you ever get out of Stanley Street, Mario?"

"Sometimes . . ."

"I'd like to take you and show you places, museums, take you to hear concerts, open up your world . . . you're such a bright fellow . . ."

The interruption came with shattering force.

"Mario! Ain't you finished with them taborets yet!" Benigno was furious. "For crying out loud, what you need, a week for a little job like that? Come down, we got work to do."

Mario's legs were so stiff he nearly fell. But he understood something as clearly as if he'd been told it. Benigno was not rebuking him, he was directing his anger at Friar Venard through him.

Venard must have sensed as much for he said contritely: "Please, Brother Benigno. Mea culpa. All my fault. I'm a chatterer. Forgive me. I'm sorry, Mario."

And Mario felt the priest's eyes on him, but he wouldn't look at him. Mario heard the clop of his sandals retreating.

Benigno growled: "How he like it if I walk into his classroom and tell his pupils about some darned thing, huh? Oh, the shoe be on the other foot then . . . a different story . . ."

Something was very wrong and it burdened Mario. He was oppressed by uneasiness — and shame? Why shame? One thing was very evident from this time onward, whenever Friar Venard appeared, Benigno always showed up to be with Mario!

It was raining, pouring rain. The windows of the second sacristy which faced out on the street were steamed up. The single gas jet was lighted; Mario was burning off wax from the candle sconces. Brother Benigno was in the church talking to Hans about a wedding the next day. The twelve fifteen services were over, and a fragrance of incense was wafted from the thuribles, the charcoal embers slowly expiring. And then cutting through the spicy incense odor was a stronger odor, that of lilac.

"Wretched day, Mario. I've just returned from my meeting. It was cut short because of the weather; very few showed up. I suppose by rights I shouldn't be talking to you this way. Brother Benigno was very testy the last time he found me interrupting you at your work. And he was within his rights. I shouldn't disturb you. But I find you so interesting, Mario. I've never met anyone like you before."

The priest smiled and seemed to be waiting. Mario almost burned himself, passing his hand too close to the flaming gas jet. Friar Venard suddenly seemed to catch himself; he turned away and walked toward the steamy windows. He wiped away the film and stared out on the wet sidewalk. He said, the length of the second sacristy between them: "I wonder if you'd take me around the neighborhood before I have to leave. I'd like to learn about Stanley Street from someone who really knows it. I bet you know every nook and corner . . ."

The priest had left the window and walked halfway back toward where Mario worked de-waxing the sconces.

"And you probably know all the stories and tales of the neighborhood. I would enjoy that so very much. Do you suppose you could ever find time to escort me around?"

Mario's breathing was being affected by his tension. It came out dry and tight: "I don't . . . have . . . any . . . time . . . for . . ."

"I'm so interested in you, Mario. I can hardly understand it. I would like to teach you so many things. There's so much more to the world than you'd ever imagine living here on Stanley Street. I would like to see you have the opportunity to grow and learn. What a pity for a boy like you not to have a chance to really develop."

The priest's eyes were moist. It was sentimental. It was sickly, and Mario was afraid and repelled at the same time. He turned up the gas jet higher. The old wax hissed and bubbled as the hot drops fell on the metal catching tray.

"You bring poetry into my mind, Mario." He said it with great tenderness in his voice. "Do you like poetry, Mario?"

Mario shook his head.

The priest was standing near now.

"Poetry speaks to the heart, Mario. What we can't say right out can be said through poetry. You have beautiful eyes, Mario. Has anyone ever told you about your eyes?"

Mario was being wound in coils, like the statue of the man being encircled by the snake. He stammered: "I've . . . got . . . to get done . . . with this . . ."

The priest frowned. "Yes, of course, Brother Benigno will be angry again. I am a bother to you, Mario. You have to set out special wine for my mass, you have me prying into your life, asking you questions, saying things which may embarrass you. But I can't help it. I find you so . . . so interesting. I want to be around you. I want to expose you to beautiful things . . . I want to get you to love poetry . . . have you ever heard of St. John of the Cross, Mario?"

Mario shook his head.

"St. John of the Cross was in the world for a while. Sometimes his life reminds me a little of my own experience. I was in the world for a while, too . . . and I wrote poetry . . . but not like St. John of the Cross. There are all kinds of love, Mario. And St. John wrote this rapturous love poetry. St. John captured for all time the pain, the ravages of love, that aching hunger . . ."

Mario's eyes were wide with fear, so wide that the gas jet was mirrored in them.

The priest's voice became low and intense: *"En una noche oscura con ansias en amores inflamada. Oh, dichosa ventura . . ."* He translated: "On a dark, secret night, starving for love and deep in flame. Oh, happy, lucky flight, I slipped away, my house at last was calm and safe." He looked into Mario's eyes. "Gorgeous . . . you have such dwelling eyes . . . Mario."

In an instant the candle sconce in Mario's hand wavered, Mario's hand was touched by the gas flame. He cried out in pain. It was not the lick of the flame, it was the bursting pain of his inner tumult which loosed the cry.

The priest tried to take the wounded hand, Mario pulled away from him, his face filled with terror.

Venard caught the look, his face seemed to fall in, he turned away as if to consider something privately . . . and when he looked up again, he seemed changed.

Venard's face had become a mask. Slowly, he passed his hand into the open gas flame, and held it there. And then he withdrew it. He swallowed the pain. He gasped: "How stupid of me, how stupid of me." And he looked old, old.

Benigno came rushing in from the sanctuary. "I smell something awful burning . . ." And then he saw Venard's disfigured hand, and Mario standing, his back against the cabinets.

"I was clumsy, Brother Benigno. It's frightened Mario. I'm sorry about it. I was clumsy, Brother, and I burned myself."

"You better let me get you to the doctor . . . get that hand tended . . ."

"No . . . no, I wouldn't think of it. I'll tend it. I shouldn't pester Mario when he's working . . . I shouldn't play with fire." Venard's face was twisted with pain. "Forgive me, Mario."

Benigno put ointment on Mario's hand. It was more blackened than burned. And he asked no questions. But he saw caught in Mario's eyes all the choked-up tangle of feelings, and the old man understood the whole sad story.

"Ja, Mario . . . Ja." And he pulled Mario's head into his tunic and ran his callused hands through his hair.

Several days later Friar Venard, his hand heavily bandaged, departed on the long journey to the motherhouse in Wisconsin.

Mario had very bad dreams for a while.

♦12♦

Friar Roland

The Dutchies like Chicken Little looked about them and bollixed up what they saw.

They lived smack up against a vast freight yard, trains clearing, shunting, switching, marshaling every hour of the day or night, the locomotives like farm animals always in sight. The Dutchies would stand on Tenth Avenue, look north, look south, in either direction the railroad tracks bisected the wide street, and they mistook the vanishing point of those rails for infinity and not for the optical limitation it was.

The same way with the river with its throat and tongue deep in the bay, that North River with its driftwood, debris, bootleg booze, silk stockings (stolen), coconuts, bananas, sugar, dried fish, coffee. They saw those proud vessels with their flags and pennants flying, their mighty steam horns blaring out their arrival and departure, regular oceanic blowhards, and they had the notion that they, the Dutchies, were as entrenched as the princes of puissant Carthage, their sway guaranteed. Alas, neither those panting locomotives nor those salt-stained hulls bore new Dutchie arrivals to these shores.

Oh, many came, many Shanahans, Mulcahys, Leahys, O'Dwyers, Carrolls, Hagertys, Lavatchis, Frangonis, Acquavivas, Tonettis, Sfaros; these were the fresh arrivals on the West Side. Mario was astonished by the invasion, by the breaching of the Dutchie enclave. My God, all those foreigners, and they walked the streets as if they owned them.

Why there was even one colored man, one colored man who shaped up along the Stanley Street docks for a day's work as a longshoreman. One colored man, Herbert Applewhite. That should have said it all to the Dutchies: Applewhite, not Applegartner, Applebaum, Appleholzer. The summit had been reached, the descent of the Dutchies had started.

Brother Benigno was conscious of the change. And perhaps it disturbed him. Mario couldn't quite decide exactly what his own feelings were about the population change. Benigno, though a Dutchie born and bred, would say philosophically: "You got to expect it. Nothing stay the same forever, except God, and we really don't know Him in every way."

Perhaps the Dutchie circulation was sent racing by the arrival of Friar Roland. Maybe his coming really put the finger on their loss of sway and pointed to their ultimate dispersion. Friar Roland was not of Bavarian stock! He had been born Sidney Cromwell. Yes, Sidney Cromwell, his people Limey through and through! Mario wondered if there was some connection with his religious sobriquet and his British heritage. It was almost as if the older friars were admitting their loss of the order's Bavarian bias. Roland! It did not jar the tongue like those accustomed twisters: Venantius, Melchiades, Desidorio, Praxedes, Agapitus. They'd dubbed him Roland. Maybe it even sounded kind of namby-pamby.

Friar Roland was stalwart and handsome with slick black hair, black beard, rosy complexion, and intensely blue eyes. He was furiously energetic. When he strode through the church in his habit, his sandals slapped against his bare soles as if they were applauding, so vigorous was his gait. He was in his twenties; St. Ansgar's was his first parish assignment since leaving the motherhouse. Roland stood out in every way as a foreigner. He could not speak Bavarian!

Roland's father owned his own business (that was something in itself for the Dutchie mind to grapple with). He operated a limousine service. His family lived way out in the country (Fordham Road in the Bronx!), a place with trees, grass, small one-family houses, a place with lawns! His sister was a schoolteacher! A most unpromising background, scarcely the preparation for his labors on Stanley Street.

Roland became very popular among the young women of the parish, his looks of course. You could tell which was his confessional by the composition of the penitents, all young, all female. And when he celebrated Sunday mass, the pews were mainly occupied by new hats, colorful scarves, moist lips, and soprano responses. Yes, Roland soon carved out his own unique sphere of importance. In a way it seemed unfair because these Dutchie female admirers turned up their pretty noses at the Dutchie boys who had not Roland's panache, or even his energetic manner.

Brother Benigno blinked a couple of times when Friar Roland referred to Stanley Street as a domestic mission station, the neighborhood a collection of slum tenements, and the North River as a cesspool. These comments jarred Friar Benigno. It was a matter of perception of course, but what a matter it was!

But Mario liked Friar Roland; he thought him quite a guy. Roland would come into the second sacristy where Mario was working and say: "Come on kid, put 'em up. Come on." He's start to box with Mario, throwing imaginary jabs. "Oop, got you that time, Mario. You left yourself wide open. Keep the chin down."

Or he'd seek Mario out and drag him off to a game of boxball in the friary garden, using one of the big flagstones as the court. Roland was a bug for athletics. He'd go to the neighborhood settlement house where they had a gymnasium in order to play basketball or handball or punch the bag. He was a first-class athlete and when he played, he played to win, he asked for no quarter and gave none. And by rights he should have earned more in the way of acceptance simply because of his prowess in sports but that remark about Stanley Street being a domestic mission station, and those redbrick dwellings tenement slums . . . the Dutchies could not rise above such disparagement. No, the Dutchies considered Roland to be entirely too breezy, not dry behind the ears yet. And *not* a Dutchie.

But Roland did attract the females. Yes, they began to attend St. Ansgar's in droves. Even some of the not-so-young women showed a marked interest in coming to services. Actually some of the women hadn't been very faithful in their church duties, finding excuses for not coming. Even some women who simply didn't come period — so-called lapsed Catholics. Roland even brought back to church someone as rackety as Lizzie Talbot, who was never going to see thirty-five again, and who had three kids, and who was the wife of Blackjack Talbot, an Irish cop.

Lizzie was a full-blooded Dutchie, even though she married an Irish cop. She had been baptized Elizabeth Hedwig Rothe. Some said she had Hunyak blood in her because of her ash-blond hair, her columnar neck, and her mysterious long eyes. But there was nothing Dutchie or Hunyak about her tongue; it was plain foul. Lizzie when she really got cranked up could swear in most languages, and her phrases were of her own coinage and always depended heavily on the scatological.

Yes, Lizzie had been christened at St. Ansgar's, made her communion, and was confirmed there, but once she got married everything went kaput. What could you expect from a local girl marrying an Irishman. And a cop at that.

Blackjack Talbot was a surly-looking guy with high color and he looked as if he always needed a shave, even after he'd just shaved. He was the kind of man who wore a perpetual frown, as if he had a grudge against the world. Besides, he was a drinker. And some of the arguments and fights that took place on the top floor of the corner tenement at 501 Stanley Street were classics of their kind. Everybody agreed they were well matched.

Jack would come home stewed, say something to Lizzie. She'd say something back. He'd yell, she'd scream. He'd curse her out, she'd fling obscenities about his mother, father, Ireland, at him. He'd take a poke out of her, she'd pick up plates and throw them at him. And for the next few days Lizzie would walk around with bruises showing on her face and that columnar neck, and Blackjack would go off for his tour of duty with sticking plaster covering the cuts on his face. Yes, they were well matched.

The neighborhood had all kinds of nicknames for Lizzie (not in her hearing!). Hunyak. Sewer Mouth. Gypsy. Mary Jit. And for the Dutchie women, they referred to her as falsch — false.

Mario understood the relevance of most of the nicknames. Gypsy for instance: every now and again, Lizzie would appear with long earrings, a bright scarf on her head, with those mysterious eyes of hers focused on some faraway object, as if she were reading someone's fortune. The Hunyak slur was obvious because of her physical setup and her look of superiority; only Hunyaks looked superior without reason, according to the Dutchies. As for Sewer Mouth, all you had to do was be half a block away and you could hear her light into the fish peddler: "Don't you try and gyp me with that shitty-looking mackerel, you Ginnie bastard!"

Or if you were down on the sidewalk at the end of the month, rent-collection time on Stanley Street, you'd hear: "Why you cheating, low-down son of a bitch of a landlord. Pay my Goddamned rent on time? And all the time those Goddamned shits of cockroaches and mice and rats all over the place. Why you ought to be railroaded, you bastard." The landlord would come clattering down the stairs, Lizzie flying after him. And she was falsch. No denying it. She'd smile sweetly, talk hoity-toity, and then whirl on you with venom on her tongue. Falsch.

And a most surprising perspective on Lizzie came from a pair of Italian street pavers who, straightening up, stretching their backs, were gobbling up Lizzie with their eyes, and Mario could unscramble their broken English comments: "Jesus-a Christ, I likka to fuck-a that woman."

And the other paver, as if to pass on that judgment, and with a preoccupied expression on his face, said: "Nah . . . nah . . . she bite . . . she bite."

Lizzie arousing romantic feelings? Certainly it was a fresh angle. Mario looked at her more critically. She was what the Dutchie women characterized as a zaftische momma. Certainly it was an entirely new view of Lizzie: as a woman and not an instrument of war. Yes, beneath the not-too-clean housedress, and allowing for her age, perhaps, just perhaps she had this other side to her.

Lizzie had had her kids one after the other. They were small, dirty, and always rooting around in the dust and soil of the sidewalk in front of Lizzie's tenement. They hadn't a handkerchief among them, so their noses were always running, and their little bottoms were not clean. Didn't bother Lizzie; she'd stand near them basking herself in the sunlight, her stockings hanging down, her ash-blond hair sparkling, her hands on her wide hips, her bosom lifted, her eyes squinting in the dazzling light.

Why did she neglect those kids? Why was she such a slob? Why was that top-floor flat of hers such a pigsty? Dirty dishes piled in the sink, unmade beds, floor littered, a smell of sour diapers, clothes thrown every which way. God, it was a disgrace. A Dutchie woman such a slattern! It outraged a fundamental Dutchie ethic, thou shalt be cleanly in all ways. Here she had a husband who had a terrific job. He never had to worry about being knocked off from work. A depression held no terrors for him. He brought home a bang-up salary every two weeks and that was only the small part of his takings; every Dutchie on Stanley Street knew about cops and their freeloading and grafting. Why, Lizzie had to be rolling in dough. And her such a slob! No wonder Blackjack knocked her around. She was falsch. Falsch as a wife, a mother, falsch as a Dutchie, and probably falsch in other ways as well.

Mario's eyes bulged: there was Lizzie in church. Yes, in the center aisle, third row of pews. She was dressed with care, her hair neatly gathered under her coal-scuttle-shaped hat, rosary beads dangling from her hand. Mario forgot himself and stared at her. She must have lost a relative. It was the only thing he could think of.

"Lizzie Talbot was in church today, Momma!"

"And the walls didn't come down?"

And the visit was repeated, and again. She became a regular worshiper! At communion time, the priest lifting the host from the ciborium, Mario holding the plate beneath Lizzie's chin and outstretched tongue, she took communion!

Mario's mother said: "Next thing you know she'll be washing up her kids. That'll be the day."

That happened, too. The three little ones were whisked from the sidewalk in front of 501. No longer happy little gutter sparrows, now neat, starched, and unhappy, they were kept upstairs, or allowed on the fire escape to stare disconsolately down to where they'd once played so happily, so unregarded by their mother. And lines of wash fluttered in the west wind from Lizzie's top-floor back window. New linoleum was on her kitchen floor. The bill collectors could climb the stairs to the top floor and knock at the door without protecting their heads. The pushcart peddlers could hawk their wares without worrying about a dish pail of water being thrown down on them. It was said even Blackjack couldn't figure out what his wife was up to.

Mario could understand: Lizzie had become religious. It happens. Benigno said: "What's so strange? St. Paul, he was going along, everything okay while he's giving the Christians you-know-what, and suddenly the Lord strike him down, get his attention. And St. Paul he know he got to stop them shenanigans. Who know what happen to Lizzie?"

Whatever it was, Lizzie attended mass daily, came to the five fifteen afternoon services, and on Fridays she made the stations of the cross. Moreover, her appearance was affected. She got herself dolled up, not loudly with those earrings and bright scarves, not showy at all. Lizzie dressed quietly, her stockings pulled up taut, her heels not run-down.

Mario's mother said: "I wouldn't go ordering any medals yet. I went to school with her. I know her tricks. She's up to something. The Hunyak! She's as falsch as a three-cent piece!"

Sometimes Mario caught her eye as he worked about the church, she'd smile at him. Perhaps it was the dim light of the late afternoon which played tricks with Mario's sight but it looked to him as if Lizzie had lost weight. He'd stand by the second sacristy door, open it a crack, and spy on Lizzie. Her cheekbones seemed to have swelled, pushed up, making two hollows on the sides of her face! God, she looked Hungarian now. (Why Hungarian? Mario didn't know, it just rose to his lips.)

Mario was feather-dusting the stations of the cross. Lizzie came and stood near him. Mario smelled lily of the valley. It was the wrong season of the year. It was coming from Lizzie.

In a hushed tone, her eyes soft: "Mario, you look like a young friar. Oh, I bet your mother's so proud of you. Is Father Roland inside?"

"Yeah, he is . . ."

"Thanks, Mario."

Mario's mother said to him that evening: "I ran into Lizzie Talbot at Moltke the butcher's. She said she spoke to you in church."

Mario recognized the offhand manner of his mother. It was her way of concealing something she had on her mind. And maybe Lizzie had gotten off that remark about his looking like a young friar, that was a sure way of getting his mother's hair smoothed.

"She had all three of her kids with her. They were clean! They looked like little angels. She invited me up for a cup of tea!"

What had happened to Lizzie being falsch?

Dim light had nothing to do with it. Lizzie was slimming out. It was as if a young girl had been tucked inside of that wide-hipped zaftische momma, and had now stepped out. As one of the older Dutchie boys said as he watched her going into her hallway: "What a tomato . . . what an ass she's got. Look at it."

How subtle it was and how fickle. Lizzie still failed to pass muster among her own. She had to be flawed. Her very improvement was subject to criticism. She was dieting. Yes, dieting! Dieting, in spite of all that mullah her husband brought home regularly. That was sinful. Unnatural not to eat when you could get food. Yes, it was a sin. A little speck — a little fat — keeps the skin shiny. Whoever heard of cutting down on your weight? Wasn't it the other way around, a daily struggle to put food on the table? Wasn't that why the Dutchies uprooted themselves in the Old Country and sailed over to Stanley Street? Oh, Lizzie was a turncoat Dutchie!

Some others, the older Dutchie matrons, whispered Lizzie'd had a miscarriage. That would account for the loss of weight and her sudden religious kick.

Mario's mother said succinctly: "Lizzie's had her troubles."

Mario pondered the matter. Benigno had set it in perspective when he said: "They got to have something to talk about. It keep them away from their own troubles. But you keep your eyes open and your mouth closed and you find out everything after a while."

Friar Roland had latched on to Mario and got him out to the friary garden. He pulled out a ball from his habit pocket. Roland pointed out the joints of the large fieldstone. Those were the foul lines. And then he slapped the ball toward Mario. It started a fierce boxball contest. Roland was a very vociferous player. "That was outside, Mario. Hey, it was outside!"

"Right on the line, Father . . ."

Benigno interrupted the game. "You wanted in the rectory, Friar Roland."

"Damn! We'll pick it up later, Mario."

Mario stood with Benigno, watched Roland shove the ball in his pocket and go inside. He and Benigno were right behind Roland. They saw him swing open the door connecting the friary with the rectory; in its opening, Mario got a glimpse of Lizzie Talbot.

Falsch?

Mario looked at it from a number of angles. A fella like Friar Roland was young. It was his first parish assignment. He was a greenhorn. He didn't have the first idea of what a complicated place Stanley Street was. After all he came from Fordham Road in the Bronx. What did those hicks know about Hungarian women up there? A young priest like Roland could be in over his head before he even knew he was in the water. Mario had heard from the scuttlebutt around the friary just how guileless Roland was. When he was growing up, his brothers sheltered him, protected him. One time a salesman had come to the garage, which was where the family business was operated from. His brothers were mechanics as well as chauffeurs for the limousines. This salesman came peddling rubbers. He asked Roland if he needed any rubbers. Roland looked at him blankly. Rubbers? Why? He wasn't in water. It wasn't raining. His brothers chucked the peddler out on his ear. Talking to Roland about rubbers! Roland who was slated for the priesthood! The friars had a good laugh over that story.

With that kind of innocence a guy like Roland didn't stand a chance on Stanley Street. Sure, he did sit in the confessional, and he did get his earful of the human condition, but that was all on a kind of upper level, in the head. Lizzie Talbot was not in the head. No, Lizzie was a Hunyak. Mario was convinced Roland hadn't the ghost of an idea of the kind of game he'd gotten involved in. He didn't know those foul lines!

Stanley Street wasn't far behind Mario in putting together its own script. They wasted no adjectives. Lizzie Talbot had set her cap for a poor, dumb priest. They had an illicit relationship going. Blackjack Talbot the cop would shoot the priest and Lizzie as well. After all, he was an Irishman. Yes, the situation was fueled by something, rancor, jealousy, life being so grudging on Stanley Street, or, Mario wondered, was it the fact that Lizzie had become radiant; yes, ugly as the situation was in the Dutchie eyes, Lizzie had become radiant.

Mario's mother stood out from her neighbors. Lena was not small. "And them such devout churchgoers! And with such dirty minds and tongues! You'd think they'd be scared of being struck down in their tracks as hypocrites! Here Lizzie finds a priest that brings her back to church, helps her to find some peace after all those years with that Irish son of a bitch she's married to, and right away those Heinie mouths start in. Oh, it's get me so mad . . . mad. What about all those same gossipers who schlep over to see Friar Vicar, huh? What about them?"

It was a confused, disturbing neighborhood concern. One thing was agreed: Lizzie was lovely and it was just a matter of time before Blackjack looked at her and her loveliness registered in his mind — it was generally agreed, Blackjack for years had made it a practice of never looking anybody in the eyes, especially his own wife (he was such a crook!).

Since Mario saw Roland close up every day, he had plenty of opportunity to study the young friar. He couldn't detect anything out of the ordinary about him. If he had a crush on Lizzie, he sure could keep it hidden, and that didn't fit in with his reputation for being guileless. No, Roland was as energetic and open as ever. He went to the gym for his basketball games, boxed with Mario in the second sacristy, argued with the other friars about the Dodgers' chances in the upcoming season. No way he could be falsch . . . Lizzie was falsch?

The rumor had reached Benigno. The old biddies had stopped in the church and wagged their tongues to him.

"I tell them, the noodleheads. I don't know where they get the time to spend on all of their stupid talk. Friar Roland has a job to be the servant of the people. The people who ain't got no trouble he don't need to help. But Lizzie she got trouble. Look what she be married to. He have help her." Benigno glared at Mario.

No doubt about it, no matter how he defended Roland, Benigno was not easy about the ball of rumor that was building up. Mario knew him too well not to be aware of his concern. After all, he had seen other young friars climb over the monastery wall after an older woman.

But it went on. When Roland came down the street whistling merrily, with his free-swinging energetic walk, every Dutchie window went up and the ladies leaned out of those windows. And when Roland paid a "parish" visit to Lizzie's flat, the hallway of 501 filled with neighbors gathered on the ground floor straining their ears. Everybody knew Blackjack was working the eight-to-four tour of duty. And to think those three little kids were upstairs while all of this was going on. The door to Lizzie's flat was propped open with a flatiron so the breeze from the roof could blow through the rooms. Lizzie wore a blue-and-tan dress. She served Roland French coffee cake and tea. All this was known. Documented. And Roland played with the three little kids. Yes, he got down on his hands and knees and played with them on the new kitchen linoleum!

Blackjack must have noticed some details out of the ordinary about his flat. It was picked up. It was clean. His kids didn't smell sour. There was wash on the line. There were curtains in the windows. Lizzie hadn't thrown a plate at him in weeks. And she spoke softly.

Oh, yes, chronically stewed as he was, he'd have to have been totally gassed not to have picked up the change.

The Dutchies kept their eyes on him, expecting some kind of furious development. He'd come down from Ninth Avenue, his high, stiff uniform collar undone, his pistol belt slipped down below his beer belly, his florid face tinged with black stipples of whisker, his nightstick hanging from his shield, and that sullen, Black Irish look in his small eyes, eyes swimming from his intake of homebrew. Ah, yes, Blackjack was watched.

Benigno had an errand for Mario. It was a Saturday. The flower merchant had not sent the baby's breath in the shipment. There was a wedding that afternoon. Mario had to run over to the mart to get the box of gypsophila. Mario ran down the rectory steps, made for Sixth Avenue — the flower market closed early. Mario ran.

Just ahead of him, striding along briskly, was Roland. Mario was by him before he recognized him.

"Don't know your friends?" shouted Roland.

Mario stopped, turned around, and walked back.

"Where you going, to a fire?"

"Got to get to the flower market before it closes . . ."

"Too bad. I'm going to the Polo Grounds. Doubleheader. Fat Freddie Fitz is pitching the first game. You don't know the right people, kid . . . I'll see you . . ."

Mario watched Roland duck into the subway kiosk as he crossed the street. And since Mario was looking behind, he almost ran straight into Lizzie Talbot, all prettied up.

"Hello, Mario . . . I'm on my way to the rectory . . . is Father Roland there this morning?"

"No, Mrs. Talbot."

Oh, it was painful to see the collapse of her joy, as if someone had turned out a light inside of her.

"He's not . . . there?"

"No . . . he's not."

"Where is he?"

"Gone to the Polo Grounds to see a doubleheader."

"Oh . . . oh, I see . . ."

Mario watched her slowly, listlessly turn around and find her way back toward the river.

There it was.

Falsch?

And that was the climax or the end of Lizzie Talbot and her connection with Friar Roland.

All kind of conjecture followed as to what had happened. Perhaps Blackjack got a dose of bad booze. Perhaps he couldn't stand the changed, improved top-floor flat, his clean kids, his docile wife. Perhaps some of the insinuations finally penetrated his boozy brain? Nobody knew for certain. It happened.

All the windows on the top floor of 501 were open. Blackjack was in great form. You could hear him yelling over the noise of the freight yard. You could hear the three kids crying. Hear Lizzie's screams. Pieces of furniture smashed through the air and hit the sidewalk. Blackjack must have been in a towering rage. He tore up the new linoleum, piece by piece, it came hurtling down like slates. It was no wonder one of the Dutchies called the police station.

Lizzie came flying down the stairs, holding her mouth, her ash-blond hair looking as if Blackjack had been trying to tear it out by the roots. Both of her eyes were puffed, she stood at the curb sobbing, blood splattering her new dress. Blackjack stuck his head out from the top-floor flat.

"You come back up here, you Hunyak cunt. You come up, do you hear me? If you don't I'll go over to that Dutchie church of yours and twist that guy's Roman collar around so his tongue'll stick out . . ."

That was hardly likely, Roland being in such excellent physical condition. No, it was an empty threat. Still, Lizzie being falsch (it was said), the threat worked. She slowly mounted the steps toward the top floor and Big Ned Swayne the cop was right behind her, to temper the ire of his fellow cop. It might have made an awful stink for everyone.

Lizzie's life changed abruptly, perhaps not so much changed as reverted. She'd lost two front teeth. Blackjack had knocked them out with his fist. He wouldn't let her go to a dentist to have them replaced. She never smiled, it was her only way of hiding her disfigurement. And he wouldn't let her go to church. If she had to go, he said, she'd go to the Irish church, St. Fergus's. And Lizzie began to run to fat again. Her kids were down on the street happy as three gutter sparrows, their little bottoms soiled. "What a slob she is."

And didn't she have to be falsch? Anybody who could change around so completely had to be falsch!

And Friar Roland? Certainly he'd heard about the domestic explosion. And he did preach a most impassioned sermon on the barbarity of wife beating. Neither Blackjack nor Lizzie was there to hear it but it was said to be a most moving address. But Roland had struck a deadly blow at the Dutchies. They regarded him (except the young women) with hurt eyes. After all, he had called Stanley Street a domestic mission station, their dwellings a collection of slum tenements, and the North River a cesspool.

Next thing anybody knew Friar Roland had been transferred.

"Where's he going, Brother?"

"He have ask to be sent to the mission station in Guam."

"Guam . . . where is that, Brother?"

"I don't know, Mario, far away somewheres."

Yes, far away somewhere. And Lizzie Talbot and Blackjack, they moved far away, too. All the way to Staten Island, way out in the sticks. Apparently a storekeeper lodged a complaint about Blackjack shaking him down. But who knew what was fact or just made up.

Was Lizzie falsch? Mario didn't know. All he remembered after a while was seeing that young girl step out from inside of Lizzie Talbot and shimmer in the noonday light, like the brief bloom of a flower.

13

Brotherly Love

Half the things that had happened to Tommy Hunding could be traced right back to his having been born in a rear house. Mario pondered that explanation, he talked it over with Brother Benigno.

The old man put it this way: "In a rear house you never get straight out into things. You not one way or the other, so where are you?"

That made sense to Mario. You were always one step removed from the street, you never got to life directly, you couldn't plunge into things, you were always caught in the middle. That's the important point about "rear" houses, they're not actually in the rear — they're in the middle, with all their tenants, too! Mario pictured it, he'd seen it often enough looking from his rear top-floor window. You have three tenements running front to back, spanning the width of Stanley Street, squeezed into an area ordinarily meant for two. It was a chiseler's trick, a way for the landlords to make a third more in the way of "gelt." Mario now grasped what was meant when the Dutchies said Tommy Hunding's troubles were largely caused by where he lived. Tommy never enjoyed the privilege of leaving his flat and stepping out onto the sidewalk! No. He had to run down the stairs from his second-floor flat, go through the hallway, bop across the postage-stamp-sized yard, then go up the back stoop of 530, run through its hallway, and only then would he emerge on Stanley Street! No wonder every rear-house occupant was different. How could they help it. It was a matter of outlook, and being in the middle!

And it occurred to Mario, if ever there was a bloke in the middle, it was Thomas Valentine Hunding, age thirty-nine, cruelly bald, and driven like one of those panting horses that used to pull the heavy express wagons. Tommy wore a cap winter or summer to protect his hairless scalp. He was always rushing. When Mario went up the block at six in the morning on his way to St. Ansgar's to serve mass, he'd spy Tommy beating down the block, a bag of rolls in one hand, a bag of buns in the other, he'd be coming from Baumer's bakery, and now he was hurrying back to that rear flat to make breakfast for the kids before he'd have to run to work.

"Morning, Tommy . . ."

And without a hitch in his rushing past: "Swell, Mario, swell. Gonna be a nice day . . . got the kids nice fresh rolls for their breakfast . . ."

Kids? Their breakfast. Boys? Whose? Tommy's? No, they weren't his offspring. They were his brothers, four of them, and probably every single one of them was still in bed! Their breakfast? Oh, sure, Tommy made it for them! He wanted to make sure they had a good nourishing meal inside their bellies before they started their day.

Benigno knew all about it. He'd known Tommy's mother and father, known all about the family.

"You see, Mario. He's the oldest boy. He have made his mother a promise. He look after them kids when she's gone, and by jingo neddies, he certainly live up to it!"

No doubt about that! Tommy was cook, washerwoman, housekeeper, mother and father, and breadwinner.

Tommy had a perpetual look of gratitude in his eyes. He was the only guy on Stanley Street Mario had ever seen with that particular kind of look. What the devil did he have to be grateful for all the time? Mario's mother explained: "His mother kept him on the breast for nineteen months! That's why. None of the other kids ever had that kind of feedin', she was ailin' by then. It gives a kid a terrific start, it sticks to him all his life."

Ah, that was it. "And his brothers didn't come in for that, huh, Ma?"

Mario saw the shadow cross his mother's face.

"Poor soul, she lost her milk after Tommy. The rest of the boys were raised on watered condensed milk!"

Ah, lost her milk! But how did that happen? Simple. There were nine years between Tommy and his next brother. But nine years! How did that happen?

Brother Benigno said: "After Tommy was born his father, Rupert, went to jail first, and then when he comes out he goes on a bat for months at a time. The only reason he ever sober up was because Friar Remigius have knocked him out and when he was out make him take the pledge!"

"Take the pledge, Brother?"

Benigno chuckled.

"You see, Mario, Old Rupert Hunding, he was a fighter when he get a coupla drinks in him. He got his fists in the air, he bounce around on his toes ready to go to war, and he yells: 'Put 'em up. I knock you block off.' Now the Dutchies, they don't want no trouble with him, so they cross the street when he starts his nonsense. You see, Rupert was a big, thick, thick Dutchie, and he scares the people. But Friar Remigius, he is a giant. One time Friar Remigius he have the pyx on him, carry the host to old Mrs. Tanzer who is sick in her bed.

"Now you know how it is when the priest be carrying the host, he be silent, he be trying to get where he got to go, quickly with no fuss. And then this noodlehead Rupert he suddenly show up. Up with his fists, he bounce around in front of Friar Remigius, he stop him in his tracks. So Remigius he cross the street to get out of his way, Rupert goes right after him. He is one nuisance on the block. Well, Remigius, though he is a peaceful man for such a giant, and he's carrying the host don't forget, but, you know, he's taking communion to a sick old woman. What else can he do? He shoot out one fist. It catch Rupert right under the chin. Kerpow. Rupert go down like he was hit by a sledgehammer. Remigius don't stop. He go right on to sick Mrs. Tanzer, gives her the communion, and then he comes back to where Rupert is still stretch out on the sidewalk. And now he don't have to be silent, and he don't have to hurry . . .

"Remigius grab him by the collar and sit him up. He point out to Rupert that he have almost commit the sacrilege. He almost have make a priest carrying the host have an upset. He could get his soul condemned to hell for that. And Remigius keep shaking Rupert while he talk to him, shake him like a dog shake a rat. By golly, Remigius lace into him good and plenty. And he don't stop just by dressing him down on the street. Oh, no, he drag him back to the friary and he sit him down and he really tear into him . . .

"So that's how Rupert Hunding takes the pledge. Ja, he takes it and stick to it . . . if he don't, he got Friar Remigius to face."

And Mario guessed it was after that confrontation that Mrs. Hunding resumed giving birth to the rest of the Hunding family, no fewer than twelve, only four of whom survived, and of course Tommy, the eldest.

"Poor old soul, never had any life at all," said Mario's mother. "No luck at all, except in having her first, her Tommy. When she was dying, she called for Tommy. She told him she was leaving his brothers to his care. And she knew he would not disappoint her."

Mario's mother looked at him, a smile of maternal radiance filling her face.

"You see she knew her Tommy. A mother knows. Yes, she knows. Tommy lived up to the promise. A wonderful son he's been. Our Lord sees that kind of sacrifice. Tommy'll go to Heaven if anybody ever does. He's raised those brothers of his. He took care of his father until that old rip died. He's sacrificed his life for them, and all because he loved his mother so much."

Mario was very affected by his mother's emotion. He thought back on the times when the Hunding brothers played stickball or kick the can or stood around the gutter fire in the winter and how their oldest brother Tommy would stand in front of 530 and yell: "Shonnie . . . Shonnie . . . Emuuuul . . . Emuuuul . . . Frankie . . . time to come home. Supper . . . come on . . . supper . . ."

Tommy washed their shirts, starched and ironed them. They were the neatest kids in school. And on Saturday nights Tommy would fill the big washbasin with cold water, lift it up on the gas range and heat the water, and one by one he'd bathe his brothers. He saw to it that they did their homework, learned their prayers, went to mass, and grew up decently.

Mario's father said it was too bad Tommy had done so much for his brothers. Maybe it wasn't right.

Mario's mother flashed out: "He promised his mother!"

Mario's father suggested: "Tommy has a right to his life, too, Lena."

Bristling: "Yeah, well, who's heard of his losing it? Besides, I never heard Tommy complainin' about his life!"

Mario witnessed it all. And some of it seemed comical, in a way. Tommy's cooking and sewing, and running over to school to see a teacher if one of his brothers was kicking up. Or overhearing Tommy talking to one of the neighboring Dutchie women about his recipe for prune pupfels or his addition of dill seed to the paprika goulash. You sometimes forgot Tommy was a wood turner in the piano factory on Chelsea Street.

But not Brother Benigno, who had an inveterate admiration for the skilled craftsman: "Ja, don't you forget, Mario. Tommy is a A-number-one mechanic. Union. He makes his thirty-six, sixty a week. That is big money!"

Somehow, though, Mario only remembered the apron stained with flour that Tommy wore at home and not the coarse brown overalls of his trade.

One thing was accepted by all the Dutchies: Tommy Hunding deserved their respect. He was a most unselfish, conscientious, decent, kindly man, always ready to oblige. And an outstanding example of brotherly love.

Boy, when the fall holiday season started, Mario would see Tommy, his eyes shining with that grateful look, rushing from Moltke the butcher's, the turkey legs sticking out of the bag, or him beating down the street, a Christmas tree over his shoulder. The boys had to have all of the joys of the season. Yes, his brothers! And on a Sunday, his only day off, Tommy would get up and go to six o'clock mass so that he could be at Krinsky's store to pick up the Sunday papers; this way when his brothers finally tumbled out of bed, they'd find the comics waiting for them. Yes, his brothers!

One by one the brothers grew up and left home, except for Frankie, the number two brother, nine years younger than Tommy, the one who gave Tommy "heartache." Frankie took after his father; he was a drinker, but not a nasty one. He started sneaking drinks by the time he was ten, and by twelve he'd developed tactics to conceal the smell on his breath, either chewed cinnamon bark or peppermint LifeSavers. Mario could always tell when he'd been boozing by the smell which preceded his approach. It was a shame, really, because of all the Hunding boys, Frankie had gotten the good looks. He was tall and straight, and had a head of light, wavy hair. He was a nice guy drunk or sober, nearly always smiling. The girls on the block cast languishing looks his way but Frankie only had eyes for the bottle.

Brother Benigno said it probably was bound to happen that one of the Hunding boys should like the bottle, after all look at the thirst Old Rupert had until he met Friar Remigius's fist. But Benigno held out hope for Frankie; he thought he might outgrow the curse because he was not rampaging and miserable like his father. And Frankie had one God-given talent: he had a glorious tenor voice. Really, St. Fergus's, the Irish church, had its full share of Irish tenors, but St. Ansgar's parish had the nonpareil of tenors. Frankie's voice had the sweet, pure lyrical quality of liquid sunshine. And him a Dutchie!

Mario was there at the end of the six o'clock mass that Sunday when Benigno broached the project to Tommy Hunding.

"You bring your brother Frankie to see me, Tommy. I talk to him. I take him to Professor Wolfram who I have already speak to. Wolfram put him in the choir. You see if that don't straighten Frankie out."

Mario told his mother.

She said: "I hope it works out. Now maybe at long last, Tommy can marry Mary."

◆

Mary Castiglione. Yes, Tommy had been keeping company with her for twelve years! Mary was of Italian extraction and she lived in the next block on McDonald Street. You could see the rear of her father's store from the backyard of 530 Stanley Street. And on a heavy summer's night you could smell the tickling fragrances of sweet basil and tomatoes which grew in Ascanio Castiglione's garden.

Mary was a very quiet, serious girl. She had not much animation in her face, but her black eyes shone. Her looks put Mario in mind of one of those female heads he had seen stamped on a Roman coin one of the friars had shown him. The same heavy, blunt features. Mary was strongly built, sort of hippy.

Her father brushed off talk of an engagement.

"Twelve years! Zaaaah. Never. He's too old! What the hell kind of foreigner you want to mix up wid. No good!"

After all, an Italian boy would have been able to come into the store, wait on a customer, and after a while take over the business. What a happy life!

Ascanio would shout, out of the blue: "Never . . . never . . . I never let you marry that foreigner! You hear me, Mary! Never." And he'd slam his fist into his palm.

Mary did have a mind of her own. She found ways of seeing Tommy. Very boldly, she gave up attending St. Carmine's and switched to St. Ansgar's. There she and Tommy separated by half a dozen pews could stare at each other.

But Tommy with his inherent respect for family was above subterfuge.

"We gotta be on the up-and-up, Mary. I'm going to go over and see your father. Everything's gotta be out in the open!"

Mario and the Dutchie kids sat on the back stoop of 530, staring across the darkness to the lighted rear of the Italian grocery store. Those Jersey mosquitoes were fierce and guys didn't dare slap them for fear old man Castiglione might pull all the shades down while he and Tommy Hunding had their talk.

"Mr. Castiglione, I want to be all square and aboveboard about this. I want to marry your daughter. I love Mary."

"Never!"

"I don't like doing things behind anybody's back. I was always after my brothers about that. Nothing underhanded. Out in the open. I want to marry Mary."

"How long you keep her company?"

"Twelve years. But I made no bones about it. I been tied up. I had family responsibilities, my brothers, you know. But I told Mary about it, all on the up-and-up."

"How old are you?"

"Forty in May . . ."

Mr. Castiglione flicked his fingers together as if he were shaking off a snakebite. "Ahhhhh. Forty? Forty years old? And my Mary already be twenty-nine. Oh, my God. And she have wait for you since she has be seventeen. Santa Maria!"

"Sure, I can see your side of it, Mr. Castiglione. But you gotta look at mine a little. I had the boys to raise. I never fed her false hopes. You can ask her, Mr. Castiglione."

The bark in his voice carried in the darkness: "And when you figger you marry my Mary, huh?"

"Any day now. My brother Frankie is just about ready to set up on his own . . ."

"Any day . . . any day . . . another twelve years . . . and Mary be then forty-one and you be fifty-two . . ."

Some fearful Italian phrase sliced the air.

"No . . . no . . . don't get all upset. Maybe a few months . . . Frankie's really getting ahold of things now . . ."

"Like the bottle . . . or the lamppost?"

The atmosphere in the back of the grocery store was threatening; Mario could feel the tension from where he sat watching. This was the moment, the real knockdown drag-out moment between Ascanio Castiglione and Thomas Valentine Hunding. And then Mario's attention was caught by a shadowy figure who moved into the light behind the back windows of the store. It was Mary; she'd been out there in the darkness awaiting the outcome. Mario had a sense of something Mediterranean about the scene, all the smells of salami, prosciutto, bacalao, hard cheese, peppers, anise, garlic, olive oil, onions, and the acrid rankness of a Di Nobili cigar. All the ingredients of love in ancient Rome or Greece.

"I tell you what, Mr. Hunding. When you getta the day . . . you come back . . . for this minute . . . right now . . . I say never . . . never . . ."

And Mario watched Mr. Castiglione's hand wander to the cleaver he used to chop the stiff sticks of dried cod.

"Never! Twelve years . . . oh, my God!"

What happened next was blurred. Suddenly Tommy Hunding turned, as if he'd heard something, something which seized him, like a whirlpool, it turned him around, Tommy charged out of the store, brushed by Mary, tore through the yard, ran up the stoop right by the Dutchie kids, bounded through the hallway and out onto the sidewalk.

Mario and his companions followed after him. Out on the pavement the Dutchie men and women sat in the summer darkness, the men smoking their long pipes, the women gabbing among themselves, Mr. Stoltz playing his accordion, Big Ned Swayne swinging his nightstick in time to the music . . . and up the block under the lamppost, caught in that pool of yellow light, was Frankie Hunding, his wavy hair in disarray, raising his voice, singing with that melting sweetness:

"It's only a shanty in old shantytown
The roof is so slanty it touches the ground.
It's a tumbledown shack, by an old railroad track,
It's a millionaire's mansion keeps callin' me back . . ."

Frankie was plastered to his eyeballs.

And Tommy . . . in the light he seemed stricken by his brother's relapse.

"Oh, Frankie . . . Frankie . . ."

Frankie was so ossified he wouldn't let go of his hold around the lamppost. Big Ned the cop would have given him a hand but a kind of natural delicacy prevented him, lest it be thought he was pinching him. Instead, looming from the dark street came the sturdy figure of Mary Castiglione. So she on one side, and Tommy on the other, and Frankie hanging between them still fluting away, they made their way down the block to the rear house at 530.

Brother Benigno was troubled when Mario told him. "It got to be a sickness with Frankie. Ja, I have seen it before. A sickness from the alcohol. You can't believe he's sick when you hear him sing. I never hear such a voice in my whole life . . . and let me tell you, Mario, some friars I have heard can sing like the birds . . . but I never hear no one to match Frankie. And he have not have a drink in two months . . . never once in that time have I smelled the peppermint or the cinnamon coming from his lips."

But it was Professor Wolfram, the renowned organist, graduate of the Salzburg Academy, who was most cut up over Frankie's breaking out.

"I tell you, Mario, that fella have a throat lined with golden velvet. For years I have dream of a tenor voice like his. You know the Caruso. And here he comes to the choir . . . thanks to the Brother Benigno . . . for once I think now I can do some of the great Bruckner masses." Naturally Bruckner, another Dutchie! "Ah, I tell you, Mario . . ."

Frankie suffered not so much a relapse as a collapse. Just like his father before him he was on a bat for weeks. His falling off the wagon was so acute that Tommy almost lost his job at the piano factory, he had to lose so much time. Only the intervention of the union saved it. But job, marriage plans, everything had to give way to family. It came first with Tommy. And curiously, Mary Castiglione seemed to share Tommy's view. She was brave. She was devoted. No matter what the backbiters whispered, she stood by her fiancé. It was Mary who finally came to nurse Frankie so Tommy could go to work and bring home a paycheck every Saturday.

Her father was furious. He made scenes. He'd stand in the tiny yard between the front tenement and the rear house and let go with a volley of abuse in Italian. What he must have been calling his daughter and the Hundings!

"My God, that girl has what it takes," Mario's mother said emotionally. "Tommy Hunding's a lucky man to have Mary and it's time he had someone in his corner. God knows he hasn't had much of a life with those bums for brothers . . . !"

Mario thought perhaps it was the presence of Mary, or maybe the burning away of the craving, or maybe it was just getting sick of being under everybody's eyes, that brought Frankie around at last. Tommy bought him a new suit. Tommy had that shining look of gratitude in his eyes, especially when his glance fell on Mary.

"After all, he's young" — aged thirty-one — "the brother next to me, and my mother left him in my charge. Blood is thicker than water."

Tommy and Mary walked Frankie over to St. Ansgar's, delivered him to Professor Wolfram, who lost no time in obtaining the score of the Bruckner Mass Number 3 (The Great). Ah, Frankie could sing like an angel, even though he could not sight-read a score . . . but with such a natural tenor . . . ach, Himmel!

Tommy and Mary would stroll along the docks while Frankie was at the rehearsal. Tommy never tired of telling Mary how much he appreciated what she had done, and at what a cost, look at the way her father treated her . . . never talking to her, never acknowledging her as his daughter!

Mary's face never showed much but she must have been touched by Tommy's devotion and praise. In any case, she became even more diligent in regard to Frankie. She took to shepherding him around. She guarded him as if he were a sacred trust. And Frankie stayed dry! And he sang, oh, how he sang. Weddings, funerals, Te Deums, masses, Magnificats. Wolfram boasted about him. People came from all over the West Side to hear him. It was rumored that Edward Johnson of the Met stole down one Sunday to hear Frankie Hunding sing the Mozart Jubilate. Wolfram was teaching him to read music.

Benigno said to Mario: "Keep you fingers crossed."

Mario understood. After all Benigno had said it was a sickness . . . everybody knew about the way sickness strikes!

When Mario left St. Ansgar's at night he'd see Mary waiting by the spearlike iron railing in front of the church.

"Hello, Mario. Going home?"

"Yeah. Waiting for the choir to break up?"

"Yeah, waiting for Frankie."

And pretty soon Frankie would emerge from the church, that handsome face glowing. Professor Wolfram would plant himself at the top of the steps, light a cigarette as if he deserved a smoke after such a successful rehearsal. Mary would slip her arm under Frankie's and together they'd stroll along to Bergner's ice cream parlor for a soda, Mario trailing behind them. And when Mario came down the block on his way to his home, he'd see Tommy waiting in front of 530.

And anxiously: "Mario, you seen Frankie, huh?"

"Yeah, Tommy, him and Mary's at Bergner's . . . I was right behind them . . ."

The lines would fall away from Tommy's face and his eyes would beam with gratitude.

"Thanks, Mario. I can't help but worry, you know . . . it's a habit with me . . ." And then brightly: "They probably stopped to buy me a pint of maple walnut ice cream . . ."

Yes, Mario was affected by it. What a tremendous and powerful thing was brotherly love. And what a wonderful man Tommy Hunding was. Mario said that to his mother.

"You betcha life!"

Ascanio Castiglione did not relent. He would not give his blessing to the union of Tommy Hunding with his daughter. It wasn't necessary.

Mary married Frankie Hunding!

The switch in brothers took your breath away.

But if Tommy was broken up over it, nobody ever knew it from looking at him.

◆

Mario served at the solemn nuptial mass. Frankie made a handsome groom and Mary could not keep her eyes from him. And they knelt, hands clasped, eyes closed as they took communion together. The only thing that was missing (so said Professor Wolfram) was Frankie's beautiful voice singing.

That night Tommy Hunding, to celebrate the marriage, threw a block party. Everyone was invited, even the Italians and the Irish. All pretty much mingling, pretty much. The Italians sipping wine, the Irish drinking anything, and the Dutchies tippling homebrew. And one of the bootleggers threw in a case of good stuff for the cops who had sophisticated palates. Mr. Stoltz squeezed his accordion, Mr. Castiglione played his fiddle, and the dancing started. The Dutchies began to yutz — a kind of inferior yodel — and the Italians sang, and the Irish drank . . . it was a grand affair and no one seemed happier than Tommy Hunding.

Brother Benigno had a glass of wine as he looked thoughtfully at the groom taking small sips of wine from his spouse's glass.

Mario caught the bemused look on the old friar's face. He said: "Really something, huh, Brother."

"Ja, that's true . . . it is really something, Mario . . ."

Mario had a sense something was left unsaid.

When the party broke up, which was very late, Frankie was stewed and singing at the top of his golden lungs: "I'm dancing with tears in my eyes . . . for the girl in my arms wasn't you . . . dancing with somebody else . . . for the girl . . ."

Poignant . . . poignant for Mario to watch Mary and Tommy hoist the bridegroom up and carry him back to the rear house at 530.

It was funny how things worked out. Mary grew fat with her first child. Frankie was drinking. Tommy was working doing the breadwinning. Tommy was cooking, washing, ironing. Mary came down with her labor, Tommy took her to New York Hospital in a cab — Frankie was too drunk to do it.

There was an ebb and flow to it.

Friar Benigno said more than once, and philosophically: "These things, they're hard to understand . . . very hard."

Mario kind of understood what Benigno was getting at. Mary loved her Frankie with a passion. Yes, with a passion (Italian woman!). And you better not run Frankie down in her presence. And chances were, Tommy appreciated her utter infatuation with his sodden brother, more than if she loved him herself.

In any event there were babies galore. Old man Castiglione came round. Especially after the second boy was baptized Ascanio Hunding. And the flat in the rear house at 530 simply couldn't accommodate the tribe any longer, so Tommy rented the entire second floor of a two-story house in Woodside. And they moved and all lived together with more space. Tommy pushed baby carriages, washed diapers, got up in the night with croupy kids, and turned his wood. It was as if time had flowed backward and Tommy was bringing up a family all over again .

Every now and again Tommy would return to Stanley Street to renew old ties. He'd be all smiles and filled with the doings of his nieces and nephews, how many teeth they'd cut, their bouts with childhood ailments. And how happy Frankie and Mary were together. And Tommy would always nip around to Ascanio Castiglione's grocery store for a chat and an update on the news about young Ascanio Hunding.

But there were those who'd never become reconciled to what had happened.

Mario's mother for one.

"I don't see what got into Mary . . . I don't see it at all, she was so sensible."

And Professor Wolfram: "That voice. It haunt me . . . all that boozing, it gonna darken it . . . ach, Himmel . . ."

Brother Benigno on the other hand pointed out to Mario the look in Tommy's eyes.

Yes. It was gratitude . . . sheer gratitude.

•14•

Lily Deihle

Brother Benigno had an uncanny ability to sort out from among the everyday sounds of the church that single note which seemed unfamiliar. He'd stand beneath the choir loft at the rear of the church, eyes intent, beard cocked, body slightly hunched, his bald head covered with his skullcap, as still as a statue. He'd say that that spot was his seashell.

"You know how you pick up the shell on the beach and you holds to you ear and you can hear the sea in it. Sometimes even when you ain't at the beach and you hold up the shell and listen, you can hear the water. This place, under the choir loft, this be my seashell."

As often as Mario stood with Benigno at his listening post, imitating outwardly everything the old man did, straining to hear, he could not plumb the pattern of sound and come up with anything amiss. All he learned was silence was anything but the absence of sound, and the capacity to hear improved with use.

Most times these listening waits would end up by Benigno saying more to himself than to Mario: "Ah . . . ja! All right. Well, that be that." Benigno was satisfied, he'd identified the sound which titted his hearing.

Once, Mario had been with him on one of these aural research expeditions, and Benigno made a startling discovery. Something was flawed in the great St. Bernard bell, that mightiest of the cluster in the steeple. Sure enough, when the workman came and investigated, they found a zigzag in the breeching clamp. How could Benigno have detected that? The bell hadn't been ringing. It was motionless in the bell tower and Benigno was on the ground, in the rear of the church, several hundred feet away.

Benigno dismissed this ability as being anything out of the ordinary. As a matter of fact he'd kid with Mario about it.

"It is a very true thing. I am a great man, only I don't know it, and neither do anybody else."

Benigno didn't want Mario to become too serious about what he observed in his company. He'd go out of his way to pour cold water on his supposed perceptiveness.

"Hey, Mario." It was in the first sacristy. Benigno looked at Mario intently. They were examining vestments, searching for those in need of mending. "Psst. Come here, Mario. I have make a very great discovery. Another one of my very most important ones!"

Mario's eyes widened. "Yes, Brother?"

"Come closer. Stand next to me." Benigno passed the flat of his hand over his skullcap and moved it so it touched Mario's hair. "You have grown. You be as tall as me. You have shot up. Now ain't that a discovery?"

Benigno laughed, and put a hand on Mario's shoulder. "Yes, you have grown, Mario."

In a moment, they settled down to their task of going through vestments carefully. Mario found the tear in the lining of one of the copes.

"You take it with you, ja. When you go home. Drop at Lily's house. Show her the lining. She know what to do."

Mario carefully folded the damaged cope. "Will Lily ever go back, Brother?"

The beard was thrust out, Benigno's eyes glinted, and then abruptly the old man stepped into the full-length cupboard out of sight. Mario heard him moving the chasubles and copes around on the hanger bar. Mario realized what was happening. Benigno was struggling with his temper. It was a tactic Benigno had for trying to control his fierce temper. He was the first one to admit, old as he was, his temper was young and fierce. At such times the only thing he could do was to "duck." This was exactly what he was doing now.

Mario had put the question to him without thinking. He should not have forgotten Benigno's feelings about Old Johann Deihle and the way he'd interfered in his daughter's life. Benigno got all steamed up about the matter. What right had anyone to throw his weight around when it involved someone's soul! It was all right to step into the lives of your kids as a parent but there were limits. One of those limits was everyone had a divine spark. And no parent, no matter who, had the right to go beyond a certain boundary. Old Johann was Lily's father but God was her spiritual Father, greater (hard to believe to hear Johann talk) than Johann Deihle.

Benigno came out of the cupboard, he was too calm. Too calm, Mario knew.

"Ah, that fella. That Johann. I would not like to be in his shoes. Someday . . . you wait . . . someday. I would not like to have on my conscience what he have done to that poor girl. He take on like a crazy man. Ja, like a crazy man. He crazy all right. Crazy like a fox. You know, he get in touch with the mother superior, only through his doctor. Ja, through the doctor, he get the doctor to say he's dying. He got to have his daughter out of the convent. A very slow dying. He have been dying as long as I know him. It was a disgrace . . . and if he had some shame inside, he'd be ashamed."

"They send her out of the convent, huh?"

"Ach, they can't do that. She was a professed nun. She was in the order for life. No, no, that wasn't what he done. Old Johann is too tricky for that. He make the snowballs and somebody else can throw them. You see he know Lily's conscience is very tender. And he know when the mother superior let on to Lily about her father dying, it get inside of Lily and begin work on her. And that what happen. Lily get to feeling guilty, she can't stop herself from thinking she have done wrong by leaving her father . . . the upshot is she ask to be relieve of her vows and she go home."

Benigno was holding tight, but Mario could see his fist come up, and he shook it. "That old devil!"

He glared at Mario. "Lily make me mad! She should know her father; she knows he's an actor and a selfish man. I tell you what kind of man he is. During the Great War in 1914 Johann Deihle becomes overnight John Dale. Ja, that show you the kind of man he is. That's him in a nutshell. And he don't change the name because he is patriotic, oh, no, Johann change the name because he think having a Dutchie name hurt his insurance business.

"I don't like to get into it, Mario. It get me upset. I could tell you some things about that fella . . . I have lock horns with him once. Boy, I almost throw him down his own stairs, he get me so mad . . ." Benigno took to breathing out in great gusts of air. Another of his tactics to defuse his temper.

"You see, years ago, Lily come to me. She tells me she wants to be a nun. I get Friar Nicodemus to talk with her. He get in touch with a mother superior he knows . . . and we get the ball rolling. Well, Johann he raise Cain. Lily ask me to come to her house. So I go. Johann, he think he can insult me, scare me. He puff himself up like a balloon, big shot.

"'Where you get off buttin' your nose in my business? This is my daughter and what I say goes. And you keep your nose out of it!'

"I am trying very hard to keep everything on the level . . . I know this is a chance for me to wrestle down my temper . . . but it ain't no use . . . my temper get up. 'Who you talking to . . . you think you got one of your flunkies, you crazy man. That girl be twenty-four. She's grown woman. She got her rights. She don't fight for herself. You got her so scared. You walk all over her. Somebody got to stick up for her. I'm the one.'

"You see, Mario, Lily is the kind of girl who don't talk up for herself. She take everything inside. She feels guilty. She think she have to do what he say. She come over here and talk to me. She get up her steam while she's here but soon as she gets home with him . . . she fall apart. But I don't fall apart. I know Johann is a bully. He have hounded his son. Ja, the boy run away. By jingo neddies, he go somewhere very far away, Michigan, someplace like that. Nobody ever hear from him again. And Mrs. Deihle, it be like she have been stepped on and squash. I tell him, I ain't scared of him. I tell him there is something very Prussian . . . ja hoch Deutsch, about him, even if he have change his name to John Dale!

"I have go too far . . . that I should not have said, Mario. Soon as it get out of my mouth, I say, Joseph Zoller, you have go too far. Johann's face turn white, white like a sheet, and he slam the door in my face." Benigno shook his head. "Ja, I come back here and I know the fat is in the fire!

"In the days I am talking about we have Friar Agobardus for superior. He call me to his cell. He's an old man. He pull on his beard. He don't like what he about to do, I can see. You see he have known me from the novitiate . . . a very long time before. He talk to me in Bayerische: 'Joe, it ain't your fight. You step out of your place. You can pray for her. That be the way you help her. You can't take God's job from him. You got to sometimes stand back and just wait with faith . . . that be very hard for you, Joe . . . you always want to do . . . suppose, Joe, you have give the Johann a heart attack, huh, Joe. What then, huh?'

"Ah, Mario, I am getting a bawling out . . . and I have it coming to me. You see, that temper of mine. It is my cross and it also be my weakness . . . because the Johann is foxy like I say. He know" — Benigno's beard went up — "I can throw him down his own stairs . . . but he also know he can have a heart attack . . . in that way, he hold on to his daughter and get me in touch at the same time . . ."

Benigno's fingers felt the raised stitching on a chasuble. He said sadly: "That have put Lily right where he want her. She stick around with the old man. And I tell you something else. He don't take it easy because he have won. Not Johann. He got some more tricks up his sleeve. Now you would not think a father'd set out to ruin his daughter, huh?"

No, Mario never thought such a thing.

Benigno's face was filled with disgust. "I tell you what he do. He sic Whoopie Seltzer on Lily. Yah, he sic that good-for-nothing bum on Lily. You know what I am getting at?"

Oh, yes, Mario knew exactly. The story had become part of the Stanley Street legend. It was the kind of tale which was repeated winter after winter, as the boys stood around the gutter fire at night.

It was one of those episodes which quickened the imagination of growing boys and licked at their dawning sexuality. After all, anything which even hinted at women being hunted down by ravening men (on Stanley Street, of all places) was bound to keep generations of Dutchie boys enthralled.

The story was quite straightforward. The kids were around the fire, their shadows thrown by its blaze against the brick walls of the tenements. Old Johann came out on his low stoop, crossed the street, his silvery hair carefully combed, his well-cut business suit, his wing collar accentuating his stringy neck, his long nose and watery eyes. He beckoned to Whoopie Seltzer. Old Johann always acted as if he were King Tut, that's why he beckoned, expecting Whoopie to jump immediately. Whoopie did. The two of them walked along the street together. After a while Whoopie came back to the fire, his peak cap shoved back on his head, a shit-eating grin on his face.

"What's King Tut want, Whoop?"

"Talk to me . . . yeah, talk to me."

Whoopie was not much of a conversationalist. He was not much of anything . . . but he was plenty of that.

"Private, huh, Whoop?"

"Yeah, private." Whoopie grinned and lighted a cigarette.

Mario had heard the story so many times he almost believed he'd been there as a witness. But the end, the seduction part had always remained shadowy.

"I tell you that poor girl she is like a lamb with a wolf after her. One of the boys have tell me about Old Johann talking to Whoopie . . . one of my altar boys . . . ja, I find out all about it. And after Friar Agobardus talk to me my hands is tied. So I put on my thinking cap. I find a way. Years before, Whoopie have been an altar boy. Okay, now I know how to put the kibosh on the plan to ruin Lily. I get his mother Julie to have him come to see me. And I go right for him . . ."

The ferocity of the old man's tone made Mario jump.

"'I warn you, Whoopie Seltzer. If anything happen to Lily Deihle, a girl who want to be a nun, your soul it will burn in hell. And you will be know as Judas Seltzer, for you have betray a girl for a few lousy dollars. Yes, you got every right to take you self to hell, Whoopie, but you ain't got no right to take nobody with you.'

"That take the wind out of his sails all right. I get in touch with my old friend Captain Malloy in the station house . . . he have his boys keep track of Whoopie . . . and Lily she escape what she never knows about . . . I have outfox Old Johann but I ain't gloating . . . nah . . ." And Benigno added thoughtfully: "After all he was an insurance broker . . . they're tricky!"

"How did she finally manage to leave?"

"She run away from home. Somehow the story about what her father try to cook up with Whoopie get back to her. You can imagine what that do to a pure girl. Her own father who should protect her . . . and with such a schizzer as Whoopie! Ja, the story get back to her . . . and she run . . . and she run to the Poor Clares . . ."

"And her father?"

"Ach, that guy. He takes on like a madman. But she's twenty-four years old. He has to grind his teeth. And he knows that if he can get Whoopie to do his dirty work for him, somebody else can get Whoopie to tell who puts him up to the dirty work. Yes, Johann, he gets kind of stuck by his own foxing . . . for a while . . ."

Benigno looked at Mario thoughtfully. "But finally, you see, he get his way. Lily have to leave the convent. She can't turn her back on her father. Ja, maybe I learn a lesson. Maybe I should have pay more attention to Friar Agobardus. I get myself mixed up in something I should not have. My temper it don't improve. And what is the whole upshot? Old Johann he have his daughter home like a slave. That's the truth, Mario. You see, I ain't so very able at that . . . but I tell you this . . . *Somebody* else is able . . . and *He* see it all. And no Prussian, hoch Deutsch like Johann Deihle even though he call himself John Dale can outfox *Him*."

Mario carried the cope over his arm, the way you'd carry a suit home from the dry cleaners. The Dales — or Deihles — owned and occupied an entire house at 536, a brownstone with a low stoop which had an iron railing around it. The front door was massive, and paneled, and there was a brass bellpull, and a small brass plate let into the jamb: JOHN DALE, INSURANCE. Yes, the Dales were pretty rich. Theirs was one of the old houses formerly occupied by one of the prominent families in the area, in the pre-Dutchie days. Yes the Deihles were loaded and Johann was hated and distrusted. He'd made his money selling term insurance to the Dutchies in the early days, before he'd branched out into the more lucrative insurance fields. It was quite a house. It had running hot water. It had indoor toilets, three of them. And a bathtub with shower! That said it all!

Mario did not look forward to these occasional errands, leaving altar linens and vestments to be mended. The mechanics alone bothered him. You'd have to shove the bellpull several times, then step off the stoop and stand in the street, bend your head backward, and look up to the fourth floor. You'd wait for one of the windows to be opened. Old Mrs. Deihle would shove her head out of the window and glare down. She couldn't hear too well. "What you want? We don't want it."

That certainly said worlds about the quality of life in that magnificent dwelling. Not "who is it" but "what do you want!"

Mario would yell: "I got something from Brother Benigno . . ."

"What?"

Mario would shout at the top of his lungs: *"Brother Benigno."*

Her head would be withdrawn, the window closed, and Mario would debate within himself if Mrs. Deihle had taken in what he'd called up to her. Sometimes she did and others . . . Always while Mario waited, his imagination would be after him, an ordeal, "concupiscence" (St. Augustine) would dominate his mind. Again it was because of the grip of Stanley Street and its vast store of knowledge, knowledge which came down in a straight line from generation to generation of Dutchies. Hugo Holzheimer, once a seaman, now an oracle, said: "Ex-nuns have very soft skin, skin like honey, and they smell sweet like a cow's breath. And they're better than Chinese girls, I can tell you! I had one in Portugal. I'm tellin' you once you light the fire inside of 'em, you can damned well kill yourself tryin' to keep feedin' it. Phew,

I'm tellin' you, nothin' like an ex-nun for fun and games . . ." And Hugo would glance hungrily across toward the brownstone. This was exactly the kind of torment Mario went through each time he was carrying sacred garments to the Deihle house.

But Mario stared steadily at the stout mahogany door, trying to make his mind as wooden as the door was. He concentrated on the brass doorknob, the bright brass hinges, the recessed panels, the curved molding of the doorjamb . . . it was no use, his mind would fill with dirty thoughts and he would hear Hugo's talk in his ears. "Nuns . . . I'm tellin' you . . ."

The front-door bolt was pulled, the lock clicked, it opened, and a smell of lemon oil rushed into his face. And there was Lily, a shawl on her head (Mario tried to force his mind into thinking it a coif), the ornate gas chandelier casting her face in shadow. Mario stood on the threshold. That house was a looming house. Everything loomed, ornate stair rail, staircase, stairwell, the various flights.

"Come in, Mario. It's so cold outside. Your hands must be frozen. Don't you have any gloves?"

It was whispered. Lily always whispered, as if someone were dead in the house. Maybe it was convent training, maybe she was afraid of being overheard? There was a rumor that Old Johann, though he was bedridden, had a habit of hanging over the banister rail and eavesdropping.

Mario's throat was very dry and he had a hard time getting his words out.

"Brother Benigno said you'd know what to do with the cope," he whispered.

He didn't look at her but his eyes had taken her in. Lily had to be forty, and her skin was soft and unwrinkled, just a few freckles on her nose, and she had a pillow of a bosom, a large stern, but pipestem legs. One of her eyes seemed fixed. Mario found that one eye most disturbing, disturbing because excitement coursed through him because of it. One eye, fixed, but with such mysterious promise. Mario again tried to bring his mind back, tried to visualize her in her nun's garb. He failed; no way could he mistake her middy blouse and pleated navy skirt for a nun's outfit (though Lily thought she got as close to it as her father would allow).

"Let me see, Mario," she whispered, reaching for the cope. Her hand touched Mario in the exchange of the heavy vestment. It acted on him like a signal, time to go. He turned toward the door.

"Mario . . ."

"Yes, Lily . . ."

Her hazel eyes were drawing him into her, especially that one wild eye.

"Let me see your hands . . . ," she whispered.

Mesmerized, Mario put out his hands.

"Oh," and she whispered it with pain. "They're all chapped . . . they're like ice . . ." She placed them against her bosom to warm them.

Suddenly, behind them, in that looming house, there was a sharp snap of wood. Lily dropped Mario's hands as if she'd been burned and whirled to stare at the stairs. He saw her tremble. She was scared to death. The darkness of the stairway? Old Johann hanging over the banister listening? Or conscience, yes, conscience stopping what she'd been doing.

Lily turned; the color came back into her unlined face. She brought out a small snap purse. She pulled out a dollar and another one and another. "You get yourself a good pair of gloves, with a wool lining." She shoved the bills into one of his lumberjacket pockets.

"I got gloves, Lily . . ."

"Sssssshh. You buy a pair at Krinsky's. Next time you come I want to see them."

Mesmerized. He was. He watched her lips as she whispered. Such soft, full lips, hardly moving because of her quiet speech.

"How's Brother Benigno?"

Mario took a slow step backward, unobtrusively. "He's good." His throat was very dry, it might crack if he had to go on whispering. But the step he took was matched by her step forward, so it was a standoff. And the intensity of her watching him, as if she were starved, and couldn't bear to have him go and leave her in that looming house.

"How's your mother, Mario?"

"Good. Good." Another step backward toward the door, another step forward to maintain the ratio.

Her eyes were all over him, that one fixed eye doing something on its own, while the other just toted him up.

"You're going to become a friar, Mario?"

Such intensity. The gas chandelier threw a shadow on the hallway ceiling, looked like a crown. And the hallway was so warm, the Deihles had that most miraculous improvement, steam heat. Lily moved her body closer.

"Oh, Mario, you'll make such a lovely friar. You have such beautiful eyes . . . so pure!"

It came like an explosion! Mario and Lily both jumped: *"Lily. Lily. What in the name of Jesus Christ is keeping you, huh?"*

Old Johann's trumpet blast echoed in the hallway.

"Nothing, Daddy." Yes, how affected that Daddy was, only someone so King-Tut-ish as Old Johann would insist on being called Daddy and not just plain Poppa. "Mario was just going."

"Hurry up then!"

And then everything seemed to hang fire, breathing, sound, time. Somehow Mario got his hand around the doorknob. But something was present in the atmosphere of that brownstone, something chemical, some free-floating dynamite, something. Lily gave him a desperate look and threw her arms around him. She kissed him on both cheeks, kissed his eyes. Mario had been dreading it. She'd pounced on him, she whispered: "You lovely boy."

And of itself whatever it was that lurked in that place went off inside of Mario's body, he threw his arms around Lily, nuzzled his head into her breasts. It was so unexpected and violent, her shawl fell from her head. Her head was cropped, cropped like a Prussian officer's head. Lily began to cry . . . quietly . . . quietly . . . as if it were all internal . . .

"Lily. Jesus Christ. Do I have to get up from my sickbed" — the liar — *"and come down there? What's going on?"*

Now Lily's sobs could be heard. "Nothing's going on, Daddy. I just bumped my knee against . . . the stair rail . . ."

Mario's heart was thumping wildly. He never closed the front door. His instinct was to run and he did. He ran and the keen wind from the river stung his cheeks. He never stopped until he reached his own doorway. Once inside, he dropped back against the wall and caught his breath. What had happened back there? Oh, yes, he knew. His cheeks burned not only from the river but with shame. What had he done?

For weeks Mario patiently sifted the details of the encounter. What had really happened? Was Lily starved for affection, maternal in nature? Or was she the figure described by Hugo Holzheimer, the rampant nun? One time, Mario thought her love was chaste and another . . . that it was concupiscence. Mario couldn't decide. One thing, he never told Brother Benigno about the incident. And for another, whenever Benigno wanted him to drop off something to be mended, Mario draped whatever it was on the wrought-iron stoop railing, rang the bell, and then left. No more going inside that looming house.

It was not so many weeks after. Benigno showed up in the second sacristy, dressed in his square-cut black suit jacket, his baggy pants, and soft leather shoes.

"Old Johann is dead! Ja, he have got the pneumonia and it carry him off."

"Johann?"

"That's what I said. But come to think of it . . . I don't know. Maybe they put down John Dale on his gravestone. I don't know. You raise a good point, Mario. But he's dead."

"Pneumonia, huh, Brother?"

"Ja. How you can be in the bed all the time and get pneumonia . . . I don't know."

Mario thought he knew how: by standing in a drafty hallway

eavesdropping on your daughter. Yes, it could have been just that. How complicated it all was.

"But it's a blessing, now Lily can go back to the Poor Clares. Well, I go down and pay my respects."

Everyone was astounded by the event. Lily did not resume her vows, did not return to the Poor Clares and the life of the convent. No. When Old Johann's estate was settled up, Lily inherited a pot of money. She sold the old brownstone for a good profit, packed up the furniture and her mother, and moved way out into the country: Jamaica, Long Island. And perhaps even more unexpected, even extraordinary, Lily married. Yes, she married. A truck driver. And had a baby! At forty! And another baby!

The second sacristy was unusually quiet, the ticking of the wall clock seemed almost loud. Benigno was seated at his desk, his cigar had gone out in his hand, and he was looking out the window. At last he turned to Mario who was sorting candles.

"How you figger it out, huh, Mario? By jingo neddies. How you figger it, huh?"

"What, Brother?"

"That Lily Deihle? She have now two babies . . . and the husband." Benigno shook his head.

Mario became very absorbed in his work.

"Well, wherever Old Johann is . . . I bet he is having a good laugh over it . . . Ja, he is having a good laugh over it. He have got his way. He have keep his daughter from being a nun. Ja, he have got his way."

Mario saw Benigno's jawbone harden. And he wanted to fill in Brother Benigno but he suppressed the urge. Yes, he might have told his dear old friend some particulars. Old Johann might be a maligned man . . . and Hugo Holzheimer a very knowledgeable one. But Mario kept it all to himself.

♦15♦

Friar Guardianus

Raphael Samuessen, the official undertaker, was anything but a crêpe hanger. Short gray cropped hair, pasty-faced, always vested, trousers worn high (cemeteries being notoriously muddy), he was a jolly, good-natured man, except when professionally engaged.

Every Sunday he'd pull out of the garage two of his funeral coaches and run a shuttle from the church doors to the tenements down the block, driving the Dutchie women home after they attended mass. There was no hint of a promissory note about this Sunday practice, either. No, Samuessen just thought the ladies deserved being squired home in style after their long week of toil.

But the good-natured undertaker's mood changed. The Dutchie women, their men, their children, everybody in the parish, their collective mood changed. Gloom — solemn, requiem, black gloom — filled the hearts of all the St. Ansgarites. It was the time of the quadrennial Meeting of Chapter, that four-year convocation held in faraway Wisconsin which determined the fate of "their" friars, who would be shipped and who would be spared. Would Benigno go? Would Vicar go? What terrible forebodings!

Samuessen tried to wear a bold front, after all he had plenty of practice, being an undertaker. He'd say: "They dasn't send away Friar Benigno. They dasn't. He's the heart of St. Ansgar's."

Wisconsin? Where was that? For a Stanley Streeter, Wisconsin might just as well have been the moon. But what lightning bolts came from there: friars suddenly packed up and moved out to distant places, and new ones shoved into St. Ansgar's. And all of this without a by-your-leave. Oh, it was a dislocating experience.

Mario found himself just as anxious as everyone else. He couldn't conceive of a world without Brother Benigno, and yet it might come to pass; the old man could get his walking papers. And Mario realized, from Benigno's air of Franciscan resignation, that he was prepared for the worst, too; after all it was a fact of a friar's life, this four-year raffle.

Every time Benigno came into the second sacristy, Mario would try to read from his face and manner whether any decisions had come from that distant convocation. And then one early evening, Mario heard the rapid clap-clap of Benigno's sandals. Mario saw his beard thrust forward, heard his heavy breathing. Mario said fearfully: "It's over, Brother?"

"Ja, Mario, it's over." Benigno sat wearily in his chair. "Everybody gets his walking papers but Nicodemus, Vicar, and me."

Mario dropped his scrub brush in relief. And then he realized the sweeping nature of the changes, fourteen out of seventeen friars would be transferred to be replaced by fourteen new beards.

Benigno said doubtfully: "Friar Athenasius go . . . we get a new superior . . ."

Kindly, long-bearded Athenasius. Athenasius with his chronic anxiety over the church roof. No more special Sunday collections to ensure that St. Ansgar's roof would remain in good repair!

"I going to miss him. Friar Athenasius have been here eighteen years. Ja, I going to miss him. You see, Mario, he is old like me. It ain't so easy for us to get changed at our age."

Benigno seemed very sad and troubled.

"Who'll take his place, Brother?"

"Friar Guardianus."

"Oh . . . do you know him, Brother?"

"Ja, naturally, I know him. Every friar in our province know every other friar. He is young. He be in his forties . . ."

Didn't seem young to Mario but then Benigno in his eighties didn't seem old to Mario, he was always Benigno.

"And he is a Roman scholar."

"What's that mean, Brother?"

"It means he is one very smart fella to get a call to Rome to study. It is a very great honor. It means one day he could be a bishop or some great position."

Mario knew Benigno so well. He could tell how upset he was by the change but whether it was due to Friar Guardianus's appointment or the loss of his old friend Athenasius — or was it something else, was it a sense that he would have to prove himself with a new superior?

Mario came to where Benigno was sitting. He said quietly: "You're still here, Brother."

Benigno looked up, saw the relief in Mario's eyes. He touched his hand. "Ja, I be here, to keep after you . . ."

"You worried about Father Guardianus?"

Benigno bristled, because Mario had touched a tender spot, Benigno was worried. "Ach, Mario, that be nonsense. Worried about Friar Guardianus? What I got to be worried about? That I get fired? He be a friar just like me. You talk foolishly, Mario." Then after a pause: "He's a new broom. Who knows how clean he sweeps?"

Indeed!

The transition took place without fanfare. The friars owned nothing. One suitcase held everything for arrival or departure: two habits, a pair of sandals, two pairs of underdrawers, four pairs of socks, toothbrush, comb, scissors, scourge, rosary beads, breviary, perhaps a razor, and perhaps, perhaps a pair of pajamas in case they had to go to the hospital in case of illness. The door opened, the door closed. They boarded or stepped off a train at Grand Central Station. Very low-key, the whole process, and not at all in keeping with the gigantic tremors, uncertainties, and fears of the weeks preceding the accomplished fact.

Friar Guardianus took over as father superior from Friar Athenasius, as Athenasius had taken over from Friar Agobardus, as Agobardus had taken over from Friar Ludger, et cetera. No one dreamed that such an orderly, silky transition ushered in a new era for St. Ansgar's, for it was not a mere off-with-one-superior-and-on-with-another; oh, no. The Dutchie church said good-bye to the nineteenth century, and was about to be blasted into the twentieth.

Brother Benigno was subdued when he made the introduction.

"This is Mario, Father Guardianus. He have been my helper since a little boy."

"At last I meet Mario. How do you do, Mario."

He was short and fat with a bull neck. He wore rimless glasses, he had a thick, curly brown beard, he exuded the fragrance of bay rum, his ears were small and delicate, close to his head; he had a straight, sensitive nose, and he spoke well, exceedingly well, and with energy.

Friar Guardianus inspected everything. Mario saw him poking around outside the church, along the east wall, checking on the buttresses! Hard to imagine. Checking on those massive buttresses! He had an appetite for thoroughness. Mario learned Guardianus had a reverence for the twelfth century, for him it represented a pinnacle of spiritual evolution in all forms: architecture, painting, music, piety.

Guardianus said bluntly that St. Ansgar's was bastardized sausage architecture! Everything about St. Ansgar's came under the new pastor's searching and highly critical eye: the altars, the services, the statues, the choir, the bells, the music, the friary, the vestments, even the way the church faced, yes, even that (as if he could alter that without first razing the structure).

Guardianus was almost surgical in his analysis of the demographics of the parish. That solid Dutchie core had been eroded by the Irish, Italians, Yugoslavs, French, and a first small trickle of Puerto Ricans. Tenements were being condemned, empty lots were appearing, garages, huge warehouses. The waterfront was decaying, the grass coming up between the cobblestones of the roadway, the railroad no longer ran along Tenth Avenue. Friar Guardianus read the signs: Stanley Street was slipping into extremis, and in order to preserve St. Ansgar's, drastic remedies had to be invoked. Perhaps that was why Friar Guardianus had succeeded to his position?

His first act was a body blow to the Dutchies!

Bavarian was no longer to be used as a second language for certain services, nor to be used by the friars. No more slipping into Bavarian to explain to a muzzy Dutchie a fine point of theology! Treachery. Treachery. Guardianus made no bones of the fact of his own lingual fluency. He could speak French, Italian, Spanish, Latin, Greek, and naturally fluent German; after all he'd been born Otto Benzinger. Yes, Otto Benzinger, and he turned on his own! What could the Dutchies expect from such a man? And they made allowances, realizing he'd been born and bred in Great Neck, Long Island. That he'd been a Roman scholar. But to turn apostate to his own people!

Guardianus was like a bull in the china shop of the Dutchies. His sermons were terrible in their ears, his English strewn with Latinized terms, his references highfalutin. How dare he tell them it was the time for rebuilding, a time for reaching out to transients, a time for broadening the base of God's church. How dare he tell them the old ways were dying? He was going to make St. Ansgar's over, enrich it with new blood. Look at the years they'd wasted, letting the church decay.

"You have a major railroad station just over the way. Tens of thousands of people pass through it every day. Why should we not draw from those throngs, why should we not serve their needs? My friends" — taking too much for granted — "we need to open St. Ansgar's to the new day. We need the infusion of these people. It will be a shot in the arm for St. Ansgar's!"

And the echo came back from an old parishioner: "Ja, or a kick in the head?"

No, nothing resembling the loving shepherd about Friar Guardianus, more like a modern general. Restless, energetic, a bold idea man, excellent administrator, and a passionate champion of the Church Magnificent. The twelfth century, that epoch when fervor, zeal raised up mighty cathedrals, abbeys; when prelates like the Abbé Suger bargained in gold and precious jewels to adorn the house of God. Had Guardianus forgotten he was a friar, a follower of the Poverello? Yes, somehow it bypassed the Dutchie mind, how on the one side of his mouth Guardianus moaned over the diminishing revenues of a dying St. Ansgar's and on the other spent money like a drunken sailor.

Even the estimable, elastic Friar Vicar, one of the three survivors of the most recent housecleaning, held his head. The potato-nosed second in command would weigh the collection baskets in the flat of his hand, and a spasm of dismay would cross his face. Not much coming in, and scads going out.

Mario was in a position to witness the process. It was under his very nose. For Friar Guardianus hired and put on payroll a crew of journeymen! Yes, civilians! A carpenter, electrician, plasterer, plumber, and a painter, and two helpers. What was he going to build, another Chartres? But Mario could see that Guardianus was not swayed from his purpose by people holding their heads and moaning. Guardianus was indefatigable. Mario would see him standing in the church, a bemused expression on his face, no doubt planning, calculating. Seven men on the parish payroll! Ach, Himmel!

It came home to Mario, this renaissance of St. Ansgar's, with a terrible poignance. He reminded Brother Benigno it was time to order the cork and moss for the Christmas scene.

Benigno shrugged listlessly. "Who knows if he wants me to put up the Christmas crèche this year?"

Mario read the pain in Benigno's eyes.

There was an undercurrent of pain; many of the old-timers were suffering. A terrible sense of dislocation gripped the parish. One was never sure of anything anymore. And there were very few attempts to explain, to make everyone understand what was going on. As a result even the simplest, most necessary changes were misunderstood, resented, and blown up all out of proportion! The most innocent remarks in this climate were sure to be distorted.

Mario was there, a witness to one of these instances. Friar Guardianus was watching Mario and Benigno working in the second sacristy. The superior was puffing energetically on a Lucky Strike.

"Brother Benigno, you shouldn't work so hard. There's no need for it. We don't want you getting sick."

It was not a criticism, nor a warning. It was not a rebuke. Just the opposite. Mario was there. The father superior was genuinely solicitous. But it was not received that way. Mario saw Benigno withdraw into himself. Mario felt the old man's pain. Even Mario who could see both sides of the situation found his sympathies came down on one side only. Benigno seemed to have been nicked in a vital spot. He spent more and more time in the chapel, huddled in one of the oaken stalls, praying. Mario would watch him, his head lowered, his cowl halfway up over his head, his hands holding his wooden rosary beads, yes, those wooden, brown rosary beads given to him by his mother more than sixty years before . . . a personal possession? Yes, personal because Mario read on the flat wooden cross: JOS. ZOLLER, PASSAU.

The climate, not age, the climate had sapped Benigno's vitality, his pride. He had become old, old, old. His hair fringe was now white, his gray eyes bloodshot, his gait slowed, and he seemed remote. Mario was heartbroken.

The Dutchies picked it up right out of the air. Mario never opened his mouth, and Benigno would have died before making any complaint about treatment. But the Dutchies knew as if they'd been there. "Our" Benigno was being pushed to the side. It served as the reagent to convert the disarray of the Dutchies into a mood of angry rebellion.

Baumer the baker, his eyes misty from alcohol, looped from his tippling the flavoring extracts: "Who that new shit think he is, huh, ja? Leave him try to toss out Benigno and he finds out . . ." Baumer shook his fist in the direction of St. Ansgar's. "I carry it all the way to the pope!"

And Moltke the butcher grumbled and glowered as he cut up the stew meat: "Who is this shit-ass to come to our church and turn everything upside down . . . and attack our Benigno. He throw his weight around, ja. He want a fight. He don't know how tough we can be . . . he want a fight, he get a fight. Ja, he get what he look for!"

It was an ugly situation which developed, fed and twisted by frustration, a sense of ignominy, and a fear of the truth — their day was waning; the Dutchies were a back number.

Friar Guardianus sought out Mario when he was working by himself in the back of the church. It was an off hour, the church dim and the pews virtually empty.

Guardianus was overweight and his breathing was heavy, too many Lucky Strikes and "smashed" potatoes.

"Mario, have I hounded Brother Benigno?"

It came out directly, no frills. That disconcerted Mario.

"Have you heard me say anything about trying to get rid of Brother Benigno?"

Mario's cheeks burned. What would Brother Benigno think of him standing there being talked to by the Father Superior? Talking behind Benigno's back? And the way Guardianus searched his face, as if Mario had been guilty of telling tales out of school . . . it was a most terrible time.

"I'm not after anyone, Mario, least of all Brother Benigno. I love and respect Brother Benigno. He's an inspiration to every friar in our order. We all look up to him."

Mario melted at once.

"He's a wonderful man, Father Guardianus. And the people around here love him, too. And then, you know, they're trying to get used to the new things you've put in . . . the changes . . ."

Guardianus smiled: "Thank you, Mario. My job is to put St. Ansgar's back on its feet. This parish is falling apart. We're not back in the 1880s. I've got to take measures but trying to injure or get rid of Brother Benigno . . . I'd as soon cut off an arm as hurt him . . ."

Mario's spirits lifted. "Oh, yes, Father."

The priest glanced about the quiet, dusky church and gave a great sigh. "But I'd better do something about this talk, though. Can't have a new Great Schism on our hands, can we. Do you know what that was, Mario?"

"When there were two popes, Father?"

A broad smile from Guardianus: "You know, we must sit down and discuss your future. You do credit to the order."

"Father . . ." Mario caught him as he was about to go. "Father, maybe you could mention what you said about Brother Benigno to a couple of people . . . like Samuessen the undertaker, or Mrs. Baumer . . ."

Energetically: "I'll do better than that, I'll preach a sermon on dedication at Sunday's high mass."

Guardianus was as good as his promise. He devoted his sermon to dedication and compared Benigno and his zeal to the zeal of St. Francis.

Perhaps it assuaged some of the concern about Brother Benigno, but it did nothing toward slowing down Friar Guardianus's rehabilitation timetable. The hammering, plastering, painting, wiring continued at a great clip. The rectory was getting a complete face-lift, all the heavy brown woodwork was either painted a warm cream or covered with light birch paneling. It was being brightened up to attract those thousands who used the railroad station.

Guardianus made moves in other ways as well. Mario began hearing with a kind of insistence the word *liturgical*. It popped up in sermons, discussions, chatter. Liturgical. What did it mean? So far as Mario could tell it came down to off with the old, on with the new!

Professor Wolfram summed it up, a troubled frown on his face. He'd gotten orders about the type of music to be played for services. It had to be liturgical.

"Friar Guardianus says to me, 'Professor, no more "Oh, Promise Me" at weddings.' Can you imagine, Mario. And no more 'I Love You Truly.' The choir they's ready to quit. Ach, Himmel, I never think I see the day . . ."

Yes, the Dutchies stopped attending the high masses. They couldn't take Palestrina, Monteverdi, Pergolesi. That wasn't music. You couldn't hum it. Dreary, depressing stuff, written by some damned sour Italians! Liturgical music!

And all of those beautiful embroidered vestments, those splendid, familiar, time-honored chasubles, dalmatics, and copes, all replaced. They were not liturgical! Instead their place was taken by soft, flowing vestments, vestments which covered a priest like a poncho, a tent. They were liturgical. Guardianus even hunted up a little sparrow-like French seamstress whose fingers were familiar with twelfth-century sewing. Guardianus would spend a great deal of time going into what he wanted in the way of vestments with her. Liturgical.

But it was Brother Benigno who suffered the greatest agonies seeing these wholesale changes. Everything that was going on cut his connection with his life at St. Ansgar's. Mario could just stand by and watch the listlessness, the expression of apathy which took hold of Benigno. Mario ached for him. Benigno had seen the shadow. What was and had been was no longer. Everything was in the throes of what had to be. Benigno was suffering the wound of age, and was cut on the sharp edge of change.

Little fragments escaped from him. Comments Mario had never heard him utter before.

"I hope I die on Good Friday." And then lamely, not with the old sparkle, catching himself lest he sound vainglorious and un-friar-like: "Since you got to die anyways, I like it to be on that day."

Or standing in the back of the church, in the center aisle, as he and Mario had hundreds of times over the years, Benigno would take off his glasses and peer toward the high altar and mutter: "I don't know such a lot. I don't know such a lot. I never catch up now."

It was so soft, the plaint, perhaps that's why it cut so deeply into Mario, standing there tall and thin next to the old man in the gloom of the church. What was it anyway? Arches, columns, aisles, statues, railings, trappings, fonts, confessionals, a nave. What was all of this substantiality? Or was it something else the old man mourned, the substantial transmuted into the spirit, the ages of mankind's devotion to something greater than his own puny efforts and inconstancy.

"I am ready . . . I want to steal away . . ."

◆

Mario chose his time. He had to talk to Father Guardianus. He found him on the third floor of the friary. He was staring abstractedly at a half-taken-down wall. Dust was all over the place; some of it had settled on the superior's beard.

"You need me, Mario?"

They went out onto the landing, away from the pounding. Now that Mario had buttonholed him, he didn't know how to open up the matter.

Guardianus helped him: "Something about Brother Benigno?"

"Please, Father, please, ask Brother Benigno when he's going to start on putting up his Christmas scene . . . please, Father . . ."

Guardianus gave Mario a keen glance. Mario dropped his eyes. "Ah, yes, the celebrated St. Ansgar's crèche . . . Yes. Give me a five-minute start, Mario." And off he went, dust and all, clattering energetically down the friary steps.

Mario dawdled away fifteen minutes.

When he returned to the second sacristy, Benigno was standing on a chair in front of the upper cupboards, he had dust on his bald head. He snapped at Mario gruffly: "Where you been? By jingo neddies, I look for you."

Mario smiled. "I was having coffee, Brother."

"Coffee, huh? Well, we got no time for such nonsense, the Father Guardianus he has been here wondering what's wrong with me that I ain't start to work on the Christmas scene . . . so help me down and you get up here. We got to get the things out . . ."

The curtain went up, the side altar was taken out of service, the fountain, the bare hillsides, the shepherds, the ass and the ox, Joseph and Mary, the manger, the straw, the lean-to stable. There Benigno and Mario worked, hidden behind the hanging from the worshipers. Every free moment and sometimes far into the night they worked trying to make up for lost time. Benigno drove himself but Mario recognized that he was happier than he'd been in months.

And then one night, when he'd stolen down by himself from his cell, no doubt he'd forgotten some detail and he was going to take care of it, Friar Benigno suffered a stroke. They found him sprawled on that mock hillside, his throat cruelly injured. In his falling he'd struck the sprinkler pipe, blood spilled over the cork and figures.

Mario was shot through with guilt. If he had not gone to the pastor . . . if he had not set in motion Benigno's driving himself . . . if he had not gone home . . . if . . . if . . . if . . .

Friar Guardianus could see Mario's torment.

"Mario, it wasn't your fault. You're not to blame for Brother Benigno's accident." Guardianus looked at Mario, trying to get beneath the young man's haunted expression. "If all of us had been there, if a doctor had been standing next to him, we couldn't have spared Brother Benigno having his stroke . . . Benigno had a stroke, Mario. A stroke. That's why he fell and opened his throat. It was a stroke."

A stroke! What the Dutchies of Stanley Street called a shock. Father Guardianus's explanation helped to ease some of Mario's feeling of guilt, his accusations against himself. And he tried to stem the bitterness against the father superior. The Dutchies held him responsible for what had befallen Benigno.

"Sure, the Brother Benigno have a shock. All right. He has a shock . . . but it just come on, huh, huh?"

"Don't you tell me nothin', Mario. I can see with my own eyes . . . all this what has happen here to our church . . . and now to the poor Benigno . . . all because of that Father Guardianus . . ."

Mario could no more stem that tide of rancor than he could have prevented Benigno's stroke.

The Dutchies had judged. Guardianus had driven the old man to the brink of his grave!

The corridor was quiet. It was after the five fifteen service Mario had a chance to visit the hospital. One shaded lamp burned by Benigno's bedside. A network of tubes and wires and hoses was connected to Benigno's nose, chest, and arms. His hands were lying on top of the sheet. They were as white as the covering on which they rested. Mario watched Benigno's chest moving, his eyes closed, his beard pressed against the sheet. It was as if Benigno was caught up in a deep solitude. Mario was awed by the gulf between them at that moment. No word, no touch, no thought could link them now. And yet there was something, something which Mario had always associated with Benigno that was present, something which reached out to Mario across the vast separation.

Mario stood at the window, conscious of that impalpable aura of Benigno. Outside he stared at the twilight, the rooftops, and the lines of wash fluttering in the west wind, the charcoal red of the vanished sun smudging the Jersey shoreline.

Mario turned back and approached the bed. Something, something emanated from that sleeping form of Benigno, like the fragrance of a hidden flower. His eye caught the heap of brown wooden beads. He picked them up. He turned over the wooden cross: JOS. ZOLLER, PASSAU. Mario got down on his knees next to the bed, rested his head against the covering, and prayed.

A routine was worked out. The friars pitched in. But it was Mario who assumed most of the duties of being sacristan while Benigno was in the hospital. Father Guardianus was very much in evidence during this time. He'd be in and out of the sacristies, standing in a blue study in the sanctuary. He was particularly attentive to Mario, constantly cheering him up about Brother Benigno.

"The doctors are very encouraged. He's going to recover, Mario."

The high altar seemed to be a fixed object of concentration for the pastor. Mario thought it might be admiration. Certainly all the Dutchies, Mario included, considered that the high altar of St. Ansgar's rivaled any high altar in the world. Benigno once told him it was a faithful reproduction of the high altar standing in a basilica in Passau, Bavaria. It really was a quite wonderful work of art with its spires and arches, its flutings, columns, corbels, finials and pediments, niches and ledges. When it was decorated for a high holy day, it glowed with a medieval resplendence.

◆

Father Guardianus came into the sacristy, lighted a Lucky Strike, and asked Mario: "The high altar, Mario . . ."

Mario didn't wait for him to complete his thought. "Wonderful, huh, Father?"

Guardianus gave him a surprised glance. "I wasn't about to say that. No, it's not quite the way I'd describe it . . . you know, it's not liturgical."

A great cold shaft opened inside of Mario. Not liturgical!

Guardianus puffed away energetically on his cigarette. "It has a certain jumbled charm . . . but it's not liturgical. It's gingerbread . . . crippled rococo."

Mario was speechless.

Guardianus groomed his beard. "I've had some plans drawn up. And this may be the appropriate time to do something about it." The high altar? "So don't be surprised to see some strangers in the sanctuary, Mario."

Perhaps it was providential that Benigno was in the hospital and unable to have visitors except a chosen few. Yes, certainly it was.

The strangers came in. They were followed by a troop of workmen. The high altar, that monument to God, that pride of the Dutchies came down in practically no time. It was as if it had never been. Gone, swept away. The Dutchies were numbed. Senseless.

The sanctuary was layered with dust, tarpaulins covered statues, all masses were celebrated on the side altars, and a portable hoist was set up.

Baumer the baker expressed the stupefaction of the neighborhood. "I don't believe what have happened."

Hans Breibenkonig, the sexton, stopped Mario. "That man is ganz verrücht. Ja, is ganz verrücht. Why he has destroy such a beautiful altar, Mario . . . I tell you, Mario, this kill the Brother Benigno." Hans made circles next to his temple. "Cuckoo . . . the Guardianus is cuckoo . . . verrücht!"

And Wolfram the organist stared dully at Mario, in shock at what had happened. "Ja, Mario, when the Benigno see this . . . it kill him like a knife in the heart."

It was like being in a quarry. The hoist lifting heavy shafts of marble, the workmen chipping and tracking dust all over the place. And then abruptly the feverish activity ceased . . . everything was vacuumed, the tarpaulins rolled and removed. Mario was overwhelmed by what he saw dominating the sanctuary.

A gleaming white marble table, standing like an island on the upraised altar platform, and in the very center, a bronze Romanesque tabernacle. There was no back altar, no niches, no columns, no ledges, no arches, no finials, no ornamentation. Instead there towered up a colossal shaft of gray-black marble. And attached to it a huge cross, whose arms spanned the width of the altar table. Nailed to this cross was the white corpus of Christ.

This was no sentimental meek Christ calmly awaiting death. Oh, no, this was a man writhing in agony, his body broken by his struggles and treatment; his spirit leaving him in a final paroxysm of suffering.

It was an overpowering sight. It stupefied the senses. How could any man be so cruelly brought to death?

The Dutchies were stunned. They didn't need any reminder that man was inhuman to man. Stanley Street was a daily record of that. No, that brutal crucifixion did not bring on their tears or remorse. It had not been raised up for their eyes. It had been put there for the transients, those strangers, invaders. Maybe they needed to have their hearts wrung, their feelings scraped, maybe they needed to learn about brutality. But not the Dutchies.

Professor Wolfram, from his organ loft, would stare a dozen times a day at the appalling sight. He remarked to Mario: "Pretty horrible, Mario. It fill me with Scham und Krankheit!" — shame and sickness.

And when Father Guardianus asked Mario for his opinion of the new high altar, Mario could say nothing.

The superior was not offended. He said with a faraway look in his eyes: "Someday, Mario, you'll feel differently about it."

Someday?

But what about Brother Benigno? That was Mario's concern. What effect would it have upon him?

Benigno knew. Though his visitors were restricted to a chosen few, among whom were Friar Vicar, Friar Nicodemus, and Mario, Benigno knew about the high altar.

He said to Mario in his guttural rasp (his voice box had been permanently injured by his fall): "Mario, get a holt of Mausch, the candle salesman. See if you can get him to take back some of the candles we have in stock. We ain't no use for so many now . . ."

Mario looked into Benigno's gray eyes. Perhaps in their depths he caught a flicker of Benigno's real feelings. After all, the old high altar had been Benigno's trysting place with God for more than sixty years. But Benigno never brought up the matter of the high altar. He was a friar. He had a vow of obedience to observe.

Benigno's acceptance had little effect upon the outraged feelings of the Dutchies. They had no concern with bringing St. Ansgar's into the twentieth century, opening it up to a broader ministry. Their antagonism toward Father Guardianus was inveterate. He could do nothing to appease them. They were waiting, just waiting for their chance to pay him back. Benigno wasn't the one to give them that chance. But it came. And it came as a direct result of the new high altar.

Again Mario was witness to the incident. It was the Fanowitz twins, that pair of undersized, towheaded altar boys. They'd just come in from the sanctuary from serving the ten o'clock high mass.

They waited until Mario had finished helping the three priests with their unrobing.

Shonnie Fanowitz "pssed" to Mario from the steps of the altar boys' room. "Mario?"

Mario bent down and Shonnie (or was it Bastien?) whispered in his ear: "Der Chusis ist nicht in Ordnung sein. Ja, come, we show you . . ."

"Sehen sie, Mario. The Chusis ist putt mitt der spike tru der wisht." Jesus is spiked through the wrists!

What a scandal!

The news spread through the Dutchie world like burning oil. Had it come at last? Had the great, the arrogant Friar Guardianus taken a fall? Christ had been spiked through his wrists and not through the palms of his hands. What an incredible sacrilege. It would stand for all times! Guardianus was indicted! The Dutchies were triumphant. They'd carry the charge to the friar provincial, they'd have Guardianus's head . . . oh, how long, how long they'd waited.

They couldn't wait. They wanted Benigno to share in their revenge.

The old man rasped out: "Forget it. Put it out of your heads!"

Samuessen, always tactful — after all he was the official undertaker to St. Ansgar's — tried to keep the hullabaloo within bounds. He suggested a delegation go see the pastor.

Naturally the furor reached Friar Guardianus's ears. Mario wondered about it, had he been waiting for the outcry?

In his crisp, careful speech, free of emotion, Guardianus mounted to the pulpit the following Sunday and began a dissertation (or was it a Thomian disputation) on the crucifixion. He complimented the members of the parish on their fervor about the crucifixion. "It is worthy of our most intense scrutiny!" Guardianus got down to brass tacks. He got anatomical: "Christ could not have been nailed to the cross through His palms. The weight of His body, His contortions of agony, would have torn the flesh through the spikes. Jesus Christ had to be spiked through the opening of the wrist bones."

Right after the service a group of the most implacable enemies of Friar Guardianus gathered in Moltke the butcher's large meat locker, their breath coming out in clouds because of the chilly temperature.

Baumer the baker, who was half gassed anyway, said: "We throw it back in his face. We don't need no pulpit. He think we going to swallow what he say, just because he say it. Go ahead, Moltke."

The Dutchies moved closer, to see better and also to get the benefit of one another's body warmth; it was cold in there.

Moltke lifted up a quarter of beef, speared on one of the large meat hooks, speared it through the flesh of the shank, and then he stood back. The Dutchies leaned closer. Slowly the weight of the carcass forced the beef quarter to slip downward. Moltke, apron in hand, caught the sliding carcass before it tore through the hook altogether. They were utterly silent. Then Moltke took the quarter, speared it through the gambrel joint, and let it hang. And it hung. The knot of discontents with cold noses and stinging cheeks slowly dispersed. They went home to their Sunday dinners and said not a word about the demonstration, nor did they admit their defeat.

The Dutchies had to wait fifteen years to get back at Friar Guardianus. And when it came, some of the most vociferous among them had passed beyond dispute, and Guardianus himself had long since departed. He'd left St. Ansgar's and been elevated to a bishopric, a very great honor for a friar. He rose to become a most illustrious and progressive prelate. By all rights he should have been extolled as a Dutchie hero, but he never overcame their animosity. When Friar Guardianus Benzinger, Bishop Guardianus, died in a far-off see, the Dutchies exacted their long-delayed revenge.

In the most remote corner of the church, a place where natural light and artificial light did not penetrate, and high up so the tallest person couldn't see, there was a small handkerchief-sized plate fastened on the wall. IN MEMORIAM. FRIAR GUARDIANUS. Nothing more. No R.I.P. No dates. Nothing. A Dutchie freeze.

But Mario remembered him. Yes, he had witnessed how one man — a friar — had lifted up St. Ansgar's, very much the way St. Francis had bolstered up the Lateran, and catapulted it into the twentieth century and survival!

♦16♦

Hans the Sexton

Mario at last put his finger on what nagged him. He had grown anxious about himself. This was not an overnight discovery but something slowly and gradually understood. At the heart of his fear was the crazy notion that somehow he was rented out to others. He was not able to explain it to himself but despite that, he was sure his eyes, his feelings, his mind, his memory were at the disposal of others. It was a cockeyed realization, one that frightened him and made him worry.

He was convinced it was not a spiritual crisis or part of deepening as a person; rather it was a surfacing of a deeply marked vacancy within him, a vacancy of self! He studied those around him, weighed them, they all seemed to live within soundly based self-fullness. In his case, he was empty, and existed merely to be used. He was certain everybody had a self. How could he have been born without one?

Mario was seventeen and a half. He had graduated from high school in June. The parish made much of it. It was a unique achievement since the bulk of the Dutchie youngsters had working papers by the time they were sixteen; the idea of completing high school seemed an irrelevance, if not a bar to early success. So Mario should have crowed when he was handed his diploma. But he didn't. He realized his was not such an achievement; kids elsewhere went to school and completed their education as a matter of course. No, much was made over Mario's graduation because Stanley Street's horizon was so limited and its outlook so narrow.

His mother, his father, the neighbors, the other teenagers slapped him on the back, nudged him in the ribs, shook his hand: "Wow, hey, Mario, you really got it, huh?" Samuessen the undertaker was so impressed by Mario's achievement, he gave him a five-dollar bill!

Father Guardianus on behalf of the order gave him an engraved gold wristwatch! Professor Wolfram began to talk Bruckner, Mahler, and Haydn in deference to his scholarly attainments.

Guardianus pointed out to him that he was now at the ideal threshold for entering the order. The superior held out to him the dazzling prospect of becoming a Roman scholar.

"You have the abilities, Mario."

To be a Roman scholar (like Guardianus himself) opened up the possibilities of high church office ultimately.

And Benigno? He showed a quiet but consuming joy. His eyes filled with tears and he held Mario's hand and kept muttering over and over: "By jingo neddies. By jingo neddies." Benigno had accompanied his mother and father to the graduation ceremony. Mario looked at them from the stage. Benigno in his old black suit, his father, his mother, there they were out there, filled with admiration. What did it mean? Had it happened to someone else? Mario had not taken it in. No, he hadn't. He took in everything surrounding the event except that it had happened to him!

Benigno was seated at his desk in the second sacristy. Mario felt the old man's eyes following him as he worked at the slop sink. He said in the raspy tones of his permanently damaged voice: "Mario, come here. Sit down. We chew the fat."

Mario dried his hands and sat on a candle crate.

"You have grow so tall it make my neck hurt to look up at you. You know, I think and think, trying to figure out how you manage."

"Manage what, Brother?"

"You have work so hard with me, since a little boy, and yet you have go to school and become a scholar. By jingo, that something wonderful to me."

Mario felt those old gray eyes looking deeply into his own. He had a sense Benigno had gotten inside of him, had seen the turmoil, and was trying to reassure him.

Benigno rummaged inside his tunic pocket.

"I never give you anything for your graduation. I got nothing to give, the order own everything . . . except . . . except . . ." His hand came out of the pocket. "I don't do them up in nice paper. Ain't no ribbon on them. My mother and father have give them to me when I am professed. They had them made in Bavaria . . . I give them to you . . . see on the back of the cross: Jos. Zoller, Passau. I give them to you, my Mario." The old man passed him the brown wooden rosary beads, and his eyes never left Mario's. "I . . . have . . . use them many years . . . they have help me a lot when I have been trouble inside . . ." He tapped his chest.

Yes, Benigno knew Mario was going through a hard time. Mario felt the worn beads with his fingers.

"You see always the changes, Mario . . . look around the church . . . everything has been change . . . the altar, the vestments, even the people who come to St. Ansgar's . . . and we change too, Mario . . . sometime we fall behind, we don't know nothing . . . we feel lost . . . but we hang on . . . that's faith . . . faith, Mario . . . but I shouldn't tell you, you a scholar. Who am I to tell you?"

The beads, Benigno, the quiet of the familiar sacristy . . . Mario's spirits lifted for a while.

But change was the order of the day. You couldn't set foot inside of St. Ansgar's without recognizing that. From the towering crucified Christ dominating the sanctuary, overwhelming the sense, to the many strangers who frequented the services. A mighty wave of change had swept over the world of St. Ansgar's and carried everything and everyone with it except the bells in the steeple and the bell ringer, Hans Breibenkonig. Yes, Hans the sexton remained immutably Hans. Before this rock, even Friar Guardianus had not been able to prevail and was stymied.

For all of Guardianus's being able to speak half a dozen languages, he plainly could not speak Hans. Maybe it wasn't a thing of the head at all, perhaps not even of the heart. Hans lived in a world of his own. Mario realized Guardianus had thrown in the sponge when he exploded in frustration, saying: "That simian!"

Hans knew no today, yesterday, tomorrow. All he knew was work.

He never had a day off, never heard of a vacation, never had any existence but working at St. Ansgar's and occupying the top floor of the parish house. His wife, his two daughters, and he himself were indentured to the church. The only curb on Hans in his closed-in life was Friar Benigno. Periodically Benigno would take his knuckles and knock Hans on the head to bring him up short, get his attention.

He'd rasp out: "You can't be only in your undershirt during a wedding, you noodle!"

Hans would shuffle and say contritely: "Ja, Bruder, ja. I watch that."

"You better if you know what's good for you!"

Hans was not all that Neanderthal. He knew who was on his side. It was Benigno who'd gone to bat for him with previous father superiors. Yes, Benigno was the pivot in his life. It had been Benigno who'd written the letter for Hans, the one that got him his wife.

"You see, Mario, he have in his head the notion only a girl from his hometown suit him. I speak now of twenty-some years ago. He have me write to the pastor of the church in his town." Benigno chuckled. "I tell you what he want me to put in the letter. The girl should have good teeth, she have to be strong, a good cook, and she don't talk much!" Benigno gave Mario a *can-you-imagine* look. "And he want me to put in for good measure, she should have a little bit of money. He think he is a prince. But that's how Tantabet comes to America, and is married to Hans."

Poor woman, stepping off the boat into the maelstrom of New York and then catching her first glimpse of her husband-to-be. Mario wondered often if she'd ever recovered from that shock; not the New York part, but Hans's appearance: his receding brow, knobby eye sockets, cropped spiky hair, barrel chest, and rolling gait. Amazing Tantabet didn't go racing back up the gangplank.

Tantabet herself was not at all bad looking, built along sturdy lines, something heavy about her features. She had lovely wine-red hair which she wore braided in a coil about her head, and soft, luminous brown eyes, eyes which betrayed her feelings. She was always good for a tear or two when she heard a hard-luck story.

Everyone liked Tantabet, even Friar Guardianus. He respected her, went out of his way to pay her little attentions. He had a theory about the wives of alcoholics. They were by nature addicted to work, craved great responsibility, and needed to sacrifice themselves. It seemed to Mario that the pastor's theory fitted Tantabet to a T, although he wasn't sure Hans was an alcoholic. No one had ever seen him staggering or stumbling around, or discovered him sleeping off his load in the many hiding places offered by the church. He wasn't a drunk in that sense but then he was never sober, either. Mario knew his favorite drink was Old Overholt, winter and summer. You could pick up Hans's approach without looking; the smell of booze and sweat preceded him.

Brother Benigno had a very different view of Hans and his tippling.

"He have to drink, ja. Who ever have to work so hard as that poor fella? Seven days a week he is on the job. He never have a day off. Nobody think maybe his back hurts, or legs be sore, or his shoulders ache. They look at him like he is some kind of animal. Oh, ja, Mario he's a poor fella who have to drink to keep up with the work. I keep telling the different father superiors if they fire Hans they have to hire four other men. They never find a man to do what he do. Never."

That was Benigno's view of Hans and his ways, and in time Mario came to share that view. Mario came to the conclusion that much of the criticism of Hans came about because of his title, sexton. True, he did perform the duties of a sexton, but ninety percent of his daily activity was serving as a janitor. Yes, a janitor: firing the boilers, lugging up the heavy cans of ashes, scrubbing vast expanses of floor, waxing, polishing pews, maintaining the lights, the mats, the church basement. His was an unending treadmill. Run up from the furnaces and slip into a jacket in order to ring the bells for services, or wash his hands after handling the ashes, in order to help position the coffin for a funeral.

To listen to some of the Dutchies, you'd get the idea Hans had a gravy job. He had eight rooms on the top floor of the parish house, rent-free; lights and gas, free; and steam heat! And an indoor toilet and a tub! Yes, those were the perquisites of an aristocrat on Stanley Street. Hans had no worries about a downturn in the economy, his pay packet came in every week no matter depression or prosperity.

He was considered a favored man by some of the Dutchies — perhaps his only disappointment might be that he had no sons, sons who would have helped him. He had two daughters.

That didn't seem to trouble Hans. He enlisted his daughters' help as if they were boys, and as he used to say with one of his typically oafish grins: "Wait. The ball game ain't over."

Yes, Hans expected his daughters would get for him what nature hadn't; they would bring into the family sons-in-law, fully grown and ready to join the Breibenkonig work brigade. And that's exactly what it was, a work brigade.

Mario used to watch them filing into the church as he locked up on a Friday night. Hans, Tantabet, Minta, and Steffi, carrying buckets, mops, rags, soap, polish, and a waxing machine and buffer. Hans in his kersey pants, red bandanna around his throat, with an undershirt on his upper half and wide, strong suspenders. Tantabet would have an old housedress and apron and wear rubbers over her shoes as her work outfit. And the two girls: Minta was the younger of the pair, a mud-gutter blond, slight, thin, her ears stuck out, pale skin, with her mother's strong nose. Minta suffered from a chronic cold, always snuffling, dabbing at her nose until it became red. Steffi was another type altogether. She had hair like her mother, wine red and attractive, her father's fattish cheeks, and his eyes, small, and one of which seemed forever squinting. But Steffi would catch the male eye because she was zaftische, and her way of walking was to say the least provocative. Minta would have her head swathed in toweling, a sort of turban, while Steffi, who was vain about her hair, and her other endowments, just "was" in a short, tight dress. Actually Steffi used her hair as a kind of prop, it would fall down over her eyes, and she'd make a great show of trying to keep it under control.

She'd titter: "Keeps gettin' in my eyes. Honest to God, I'm gonna have to get it bobbed."

Minta was eighteen and Steffi was twenty. Neither had finished school, nor had they gotten working papers at sixteen; they had just slipped into the workforce, members of the brigade. Sometimes

Mario questioned whether they had a life of their own. They certainly had to work hard and they'd had a long experience at it.

Brother Benigno could remember when Hans and Tantabet would bring the then-little girls into the church on cleanup nights, lay them out in a pew all bundled up, and attend to their scrubbing. "Those girls, they know what work is . . . ja, they have learned very early, since little schizzers."

Mario never paid too much attention to the girls, though he saw them regularly, and always working. Actually, they seemed part of the church, merely more animate. They'd greet one another but that was about it. Some Friday nights the altar linens would require changing and then Mario would be there late, then he'd really get a look at the Breibenkonig technique. They'd quarter the church, each one working his or her own quadrant, and finally meet in the middle aisle. But they were in the church and Mario was in the sanctuary, and that was the size of it.

Several weeks after his graduation, Mario was in the friary kitchen enjoying a post-breakfast mug of coffee and hunk of crusty bread. There was a new cook, Friar Tristram, a tall, thin string bean of a man, with a flaming red beard, short cropped hair, and sad blue eyes. He'd been brought from the motherhouse in Wisconsin to replace Friar Didicus who'd mixed wine corks into the mashed potatoes, mistaking them for mushrooms. Friar Didicus had had a dual job, as cellarer as well as cook. He'd been transferred to Wisconsin. Tristram seemed distant and aloof; he spent all of his free time in the friary garden sitting on a bench and gazing at the sky. He missed the rural setting of the motherhouse, the other friars said.

Mario was seated at the long trestle table in the kitchen. And near him were the journeymen who'd been hired by Friar Guardianus a few years before. They were on their coffee break. They were a tight group, very clannish, keeping themselves to themselves. Mario sensed that they were even more conspiratorial when he was around, since they regarded him as a friar in the making.

Mario chewed the firm bread, sipped his coffee, and the band of workmen were deep in one of their endless discussions. They wore very serious expressions on their faces, and every now and again they'd dart looks toward Friar Tristram in the garden and Mario at his place at the end of the table. Mario knew what they were talking about when they lowered their voices and cast those secretive glances: women . . . women! It seemed incredible to Mario that every one of those workmen had a wife and children and yet their major topic of conversation was women.

One man, carried away by the excitement, said so Mario heard: "Forty by twenty by forty."

The answer came: "I'd like to throw my ruler across it."

Another comment: "It might get snapped off."

"What a great way to wreck a ruler!"

Ah, Mario had misjudged them. They were talking shop.

Then the carpenter, also the sort of foreman, said: "The boss" — their title for the father superior — "says our next job will be the parish house."

Mario heard a funny, clicking sound made by one of the men.

"That should be merry . . . somethin' to keep us going."

"Maybe you'll get your chance to use your ruler . . . then."

Mario rinsed out his mug, ducked his head out of the kitchen, called and thanked Friar Tristram for the coffee. The sad, skinny young man waved his hand languidly, and Mario went about his business forgetting all about the exchange he'd overheard.

The following Friday night Mario worked late. Brother Benigno since his stroke had to take frequent rests. Mario fixed a folding chair for him in the sanctuary and Benigno sat there watching Mario strip the altar linens and change the antependium. Meanwhile the Breibenkonig brigade had commenced their cleanup. Mario could hear Minta snuffling her nose, hear Hans's sozzled humming, and see Steffi and her mother trying to move one of the heavy pediments in order to clean behind it.

Benigno saw it as well. He rasped: "Mario, give them a hand. That be too heavy for them women. Hans is in a world all his own. He don't see."

Mario helped them. Tantabet took his hand, looked into his face, those soft, luminous eyes on him. She whispered: "Ach, Mario, you have graduate. Tsktsktsk . . . you mother must be so stoltz of you. That be something you have done."

And Steffi, chewing gum, smiling, brushed her hair from her eyes. "Pretty nifty, Mario. School's a terrific thing. What you gonna do now, huh?"

The words were perfectly innocent, and yet Mario had the sense he was missing something in terms of meaning. But Steffi was the kind of girl who seemed always to give whatever she said an added twist. And besides, she was forever looking behind you as if she was trying to catch a reflection of herself in any convenient glass or polished surface. Some of the Dutchie guys said she was very stuck on herself. And some of them said she was always on the M-A-K-E. And still others said "pass mal auf" — be careful. "She's looking for a helper for her father . . . a permanent one!"

Friar Tristram had come out into the sanctuary and stood gazing around. Brother Benigno greeted him. "Ah, Tristram, you take a look at St. Ansgar's, ja."

"Yes, Brother Benigno. I don't get much chance being in the kitchen all day."

Benigno followed Tristram's glance at the huge crucifix towering above the altar table.

"It's very different from what it used to be . . ."

Mario returned to his work in the sanctuary. Benigno got up and went inside with Friar Tristram. Mario heard a sudden giggling from Minta and Steffi. What had set that off, he wondered. More giggling and then Hans with a roar: "Den Mund halten, mensches!" — Shut up!

Mario finished in the sanctuary and carried fresh linens to the shrine in the rear of the church. He passed down the side aisle. Steffi was on her hands and knees between the pews scrubbing away. She always wore a very short, tight dress that had a way of working itself up, showing the back of her thighs, and her behind waggled as she worked. Hers was a very round behind. Friar Guardianus had complained to Tantabet about the scantiness of Steffi's cleaning garb. Mario had heard him talk to Friar Vicar about Steffi's callipygian outline. Callipygian? Mario looked it up after he figured out how it was spelled; it meant having shapely buttocks. That's what Guardianus meant about her wearing more covering.

But Steffi brushed off her mother's caution.

"He shouldn't look. I ain't askin' him to come out and watch me work. I gotta do the work. Ain't I got a right to be comfortable . . . he just shouldn't look . . ."

Just as he came by her, he noticed she gave several extra wiggles of her rump. And she startled him by suddenly looking up and catching him staring at her behind. She got to her feet, smiled, and said: "It grabs your back." She stretched it, pushing forward her developed bosom. "Gets you."

Suddenly with blinding clarity, it hit Mario: forty by twenty by forty were Steffi's dimensions! Yes, Steffi's. She was the one being measured by the workmen. Mario quickened his pace down the side aisle, a strange sensation licking inside of him. Was it a self stirring inside of him?

After that, no matter where Mario worked in the church, sooner or later one of the Breibenkonig girls would run into him. He was in the foyer, opening the glassed-in bulletin board, about to make a change in the altar boy schedule, when suddenly there was Minta, sniffing and rubbing her nose. She looked him over boldly.

"You know, Mario, Steffi thinks you got very good looks." And she stood there staring at him, as if to reach her own conclusions about his looks.

Mario felt caught up in a tangle, titillating and intimidating at the same time.

And then there were those obvious "accidental-on-purpose" encounters with Steffi. She had a profoundly unnerving effect upon

Mario. He didn't know where to look when she was around. Steffi filled out her clothes in such an abundant way — ripe, as it were. And her manner was abundant even when what she had to say was completely innocent.

"How's Brother Benigno makin' out, Mario?"

"Okay."

"Yeah? Nice to have him okay, huh?"

"Yes."

She removed a bit of lint from the upper part of his apron. Mario smelled something like cloves coming from her.

"Well, I better beat it. Mama'll be wonderin' where I got to. She's got the funniest ideas about me . . ." Steffi smiled. "I don't wan' her gettin' no ideas about . . . well, my talkin' to you, you know, Mario . . ."

Mario's eyes were glued to Steffi's retreating, undulating figure.

Yes, Mario was under some kind of spell, a type of sorcery under which Steffi was transformed into a creature quite unlike what everyone else saw. Yes, in Mario's eyes, Steffi was ravishing.

Her squint was gone, her fat cheeks slimmed, her resemblance to her father nonexistent. Steffi was a being living on another plane altogether. Mario found excuses for prowling about the church at odd hours throughout the day, hoping always to run into her. He'd have to go to the choir loft or the bell tower, or the church hall in the basement. Mario was haunted by the prospect of seeing Steffi. He'd never been so affected by anything in his whole life as he was by Steffi. He was filled with excitement, joy, sadness, a strange kind of ache, like a hunger. He was dreamy, absent, tongue-tied. He lost weight, simply because food meant nothing to him. Was this real living, this sense of honey on the lips, this throb inside? Was this what was meant by an awakened self? And Mario was very close about all of this, he breathed not a word to anyone, not even Brother Benigno.

It was inevitable. He was passing through the church hall. It was one way to get to the rear of the church during a service without being seen. She might be there!

And she was. Steffi was all dolled up in a blue crêpe dress, her wine-red hair just like her mother's was piled on the top of her head in a very glamorous new style, two red stones dangled on little chains from her ears, and her lips were the orange of a candle flame. She was unfolding chairs.

"Oh, Mario. There's a card party tonight. Momma's shopping, Poppa's snoozing, Minta's starin' out the winda, so you know who gets put into service. Whatcha doin'?"

"I'm going to take up the collection."

"Yeah, huh. Only us two workin' . . ."

Mario seemed automatically to be unfolding chairs, helping her. They moved back and forth from the cloakroom where the chairs were stacked to the hall. She got very close to him when they bent opening the chairs. He was taller than Steffi, but she was older. She suddenly looked at him, a crooked smile on her face. He heard her breathing, smelled the smell of cloves. He suddenly had her in his arms. He was very strong. He pulled her into him, one hand on its own stealing to her breast. She struggled.

"Hey, hey, whatcha doin'? None of that stuff . . . Mario . . . Mario . . ."

She kicked him in the shins. "You gone crazy . . . suppose somebody caught us . . . Mario!" And then in desperation she said: "What about taking up the collection?"

That snapped the grip of his passion. Yes, the collection. He'd erased everything from his mind. The collection, he had to take it up.

Maybe he was crazy. He stood there staring at her, dazed. What had happened to him? Ah, it was painful, like a limb that had gone to sleep, now he was tingling back to his ordinary self. Without a word Mario left her, the smell of clove on his clothes.

Benigno said to him: "Hans's daughter!"

Mario couldn't face those gray eyes. And inside there was a frost. Mario's world had come to smash. Benigno had found out. Mario hung his head.

"You know, Mario?"

Mario nodded. He was not going to add lying to his other faults.

"It happen. But with Minta. By jingo neddies, for me she still seems like the little girl. And of all the noodles to run off with . . . I don't know what got into Tristram . . ."

Minta? Friar Tristram, the cook, the one who always sat in the friary garden looking at the sky? Had it been the sky he was staring at or was it the top-floor windows where Minta sat, staring?

Benigno said: "I feel sorry for them. I hope they know what they have got into . . . especially the Minta . . . she's a silly mensch."

For the first time Mario looked Brother Benigno in the eyes.

"You see, Mario, a friar have his troubles. After all he's a man . . . and a young friar . . . it take a long time for the young friar to learn that the body have a life of its own. Ja, that be a darned tough thing to learn to control."

Yes, Mario could testify to that. He'd learned it in a fierce moment. And he learned, too, that he could never become a friar, not with that raging force inside of him, ready to topple him.

Mario supposed he was relieved to learn that he had a self; he was more than just a being for hire, rented out for use. He supposed so . . .

And Minta and Friar Tristram? It was an ugly situation. Friar Guardianus was up in arms. One of his young friars running off with Minta Breibenkonig! For a time it appeared likely Hans was getting his walking papers, but again Brother Benigno intervened.

Mario smelled the Old Overholt fumes coming from Hans, who stood rubbing his nose.

"What could I do, huh, Mario? What I know about what go on in her head? I don't get nothin' out of it . . . except the misery."

And Tantabet with her soft, luminous, now troubled eyes: "They got three rooms in Brooklyn. Ach, Mario, what a trouble, what a trouble . . ."

And Steffi, giving him very dark looks, declared: "Some people don't know what they're gettin' into . . . they ain't got no control over themself."

Mario agreed wholeheartedly.

EPILOGUE

The Witness

Mario took care that his eyes showed nothing when he saw Benigno trying to genuflect. The friar was no longer able to bend his knees. He had suffered a second and a third stroke. The right side of his face was paralyzed and his already impaired speech was now almost impossible to understand. Benigno was eighty-six years old. For the last two years Mario had taken over the duties of being full-time sacristan.

Still, for all of his infirmities, Benigno insisted upon making a dop around the church a daily event, though such a tour was very slow and often uncertain. He'd feel his way, placing a hand from the back of one pew to the next for support. Very rarely would he use Mario's arm for support, though Mario's arm was always close, just in case.

They'd progress along the aisles, from plinth to plinth, those bases upon which the plaster figures of the saints stood, their eyes locked in a timeless gaze. Benigno would often pause before them, study them, seem to become absorbed in their preoccupations.

"They never got to worry!" Benigno would rasp in those broken tones and catch his breath, anger springing into his eyes. The anger would fade as swiftly as it had appeared, and be succeeded by a blank look.

Sometimes Benigno would seem to be exchanging views with St. Anthony or St. John the Baptist. He'd scowl, tap his cane impatiently against a pew. And then unexpectedly, the left side of his face would lift, Mario would recognize the smile, and see the mocking light in his eyes, as if Benigno was aware of his own irascibility and was making fun of it. Mario knew he was racked with pain, that it was only Benigno's indomitable will which kept him going. But there was that about him now which mystified Mario. Often he'd glance at Benigno only to be startled at the look in those gray eyes, the eyes of a stranger, one who regarded him critically, coldly.

Their stroll about the church was often interrupted by one of the nuts; a whole new generation of them had sprung up over the years, wanting to speak to Brother Benigno. One youngish man, whose compulsion was to make signs of the cross on his lips, his forehead, his cheeks, before his eyes, his heart, as soon as he spied Benigno and Mario, would come rushing up, plant himself in their way, and make his nervous, twitching signs of the cross.

He'd say: "Ah, Friar Benigno, like Jesus making his weary mile." And he'd point to the stations of the cross, mounted on the walls of the side aisles. Mario would watch Benigno's cane begin to twitch in his grasp and Mario would position himself, ready to grab the cane, just in case Benigno's temper got away from him.

Often these eccentrics would waylay Mario in the course of his work, when he was alone, and with a strange light in their eyes they'd talk about Brother Benigno.

"He has his eyes off our world. He has his eyes on eternity. He's no longer with us!"

They'd lean toward Mario, like conspirators, and whisper: "See if you can get me something that belongs to Brother Benigno. Anything will do, just so long as it comes from him."

The demand, that's what it was, would be made with a hissing intensity.

"He's gonna be made a saint someday. Now's the time to get something of his as a relic."

Mario would break away from them, sickened by their air of calculation, their cracked cunning. Benigno canonized, time to get in on the event, time to get in on the ground floor. And it was not only the nuts who were infected; someone as clay-footed as Hans Breibenkonig, the sexton, would scratch his head and say to Mario: "He be slippin' fast . . . it not be long." Then speculatively: "What you think, Mario, he get to be the saint?"

They had Benigno dead, on his way to sainthood, the ghouls, while

Mario hung on desperately to the living Benigno. Mario could not face into what everyone else accepted as an accomplished fact. Mario went about with a kind of numbed helplessness inside.

Friar Guardianus, as the man in charge, had to keep his eye on Benigno. It was his responsibility as superior. Every day he'd visit the second sacristy to touch base with Benigno, as if the old man were still sacristan. As soon as he'd poke his head into the work-room, Benigno would stir about, as if to prove he could still put in a day's work. Benigno's deepest fear was that he might be shipped off to Wisconsin. This fear often made him sound petulant and demanding. Mario knew he didn't mean it when he'd rage in that garbled speech: "How many times I tell you to pick up this place. We ain't in no pigsty . . ." Yes, to prove to Friar Guardianus he was still capable of running the sacristy.

Guardianus understood.

"These are trying days, Mario. I know that. You see, Brother Benigno can't help it. It's part of his condition. Part of age. He has hardening of the arteries. It comes down on him and he doesn't know it and he can't do anything about it. But it falls heaviest on you."

Then Guardianus would pull out his pack of Lucky Strikes, light one, all the while studying Mario's face.

"Tough days, Mario. It's hard right now for you to think beyond the moment, but you have a future, and you should consider it. Really, it's time. You'd make a splendid friar."

Mario's mother had pretty much the same notion: "Why not, Mario? It's a holy life."

Mario's father interposed: "If he's cut out for it!"

"How's he going to find out if he doesn't try?"

"It'll be too late then. It's your life, Mario. You make up your own mind. You're entitled to that."

Not only Benigno was breaking down, it seemed the whole parish, the world, was suffering from hardening of the arteries, in that year of 1941.

Professor Wolfram was resting on the flat rail of the choir loft, his back to the organ, staring out uneasily at the church spread out below. Mario had just given him the new schedule of services.

"Mario, you are a scholar. You believe all this stuff they say about Hitler? It have to be propaganda, ja? After all, Hitler is a Catholic, ja? South German! He's not a Prussian. They got to be making up all this terrible business about his persecuting the Jews, killing them. My God, what terrible things they say he does. Can it be true, Mario?" he asked plaintively.

Then soberly: "I got family in Munich . . . ja, two brothers and a sister in there." Wolfram made a quick turn and hit a note on the organ, it boomed out irritably. "Oh, my God . . . how awful . . . and they take you, too, Mario. Ja, ja, you go to war. You see, they gonna pack you off . . ."

Many of the Dutchie boys he'd grown up with had already been drafted. On a Sunday the pews showed a number of uniforms among the other worshipers. And many young friars had already been permitted to enlist in the chaplain corps. They'd stepped out of their habits, shaved or shortened their beards, and were now officers. Now those voices in the choir, chanting the office, were almost entirely middle-aged or elderly. Yes, the world of 1941 had seeped into the friary.

Friar Cajetan, gray-haired, gray-bearded, his face seamed, looking very old, haunted, had been a flier in the German air force in the Great War. It had been through his experiences in that war that he'd become a friar. It was Cajetan who traditionally conducted the Good Friday service, the three-hour agony of Christ. Formerly people from all over the West Side flocked to St. Ansgar's to hear him preach.

Cajetan would stand upright in the pulpit, his eyes unblinking, his voice emotionless, and he'd declare: "I have slain other men. I have killed. Yes, I have killed." It electrified the congregation. "I have killed in spite of the injunction 'Thou shalt not kill!' But I killed and killed again. And Jesus Christ was slain by men like me."

In years past the altar boys, having heard that Friar Cajetan had been a flying ace, used to pretend they were aviators, spread their arms for wings, with ratatatat imaginary bursts of machine-gun fire. No longer. No more make-believe. This was catch-up time. The world and the friary were caught up together.

Cajetan was not permitted to conduct the Good Friday service now. Friar Guardianus supported the war effort. He cried out against Hitler from the pulpit, Hitler this scourge, this plague, this Antichrist! The Western world, the Judeo-Christian civilization was struggling for its survival! Hitler had to be destroyed! This was not the time for the Friar Cajetans of the order to preach pacifism. Friar Guardianus in his role as father superior denied Friar Cajetan the pulpit. It was an agonizing decision.

It temporarily roused Benigno from his world of gathering shadows.

"What you expect the Friar Guardianus to do? He is the superior and the pastor. He can't let Cajetan say from the pulpit don't fight for your country. Guardianus is responsible for the parish, all the people. And he be responsible to the order too."

Benigno held his head, his eyes filled with anguish.

"And the Friar Cajetan have his conscience, he have his soul to take care of. No, no, it not be an easy thing . . . you can say this is right, this is wrong . . . no, all you should say, thank God I don't have to make no decision about it . . . let the cup pass from me . . ."

Yes, Benigno was roused by the conflict. Even his afflicted speech seemed slightly improved.

But the rift between the father superior and Friar Cajetan could not be improved even slightly. It was a festering wound. Guardianus was determined, robust, filled with nervous energy, Cajetan was quiet, humble, and immovable. At last Friar Nicodemus, the venerable, roly-poly doctor of canon law, was brought in to arbitrate the disagreement.

Each friar knelt: Guardianus the superior, Cajetan the ex-flying-ace, while between them on a low stool sat Nicodemus. It was an official, ecclesiastical hearing.

Several days later Friar Nicodemus handed down his ruling. He found not on the basis of conscience or authority, or the scriptural injunction against killing, but on the simple, indisputable laws of obedience. Friar Cajetan had professed solemn vows of poverty, chastity, and obedience, therefore he was bound to submit to his superior's decision. He was no longer to preach.

Cajetan came into the second sacristy. He was dressed in civvies. He appeared old and ailing. He bent over Benigno seated at his desk. He lifted one of Benigno's hands and kissed it. He said in German: "I go now, Joe."

"Ah, ja . . . it is so, Cajetan. To Wisconsin?"

"Ja, Friar Guardianus have been very understanding. He allow me to go back to the motherhouse." He held Benigno's hand in his own. "We shall not see one another again, Joe."

After he left, Mario watched Benigno sitting and staring out the window. Then the old man got up and shuffled into the choir. Mario saw him, the cowl drawn up on his head, in his stall praying, tears on his face.

Mario was harassed, haunted. He could find no peace. He was desperately unhappy. He had spent eleven years working at St. Ansgar's, eleven years steeped in an atmosphere of reverence, devotion, and prayer, and yet Mario sensed he'd never learned the meaning of prayer, or been quickened into an understanding of its solace. All he could do was look on! Yes, when he came right down to it, what did he know about anything? He knew about light, the way it pattered down from the clerestory, deepening as it fell. He knew about the massive columns, which supported the arches, which in turn bore the weight of the nave. He knew about the symbolism of color, the organ music of Mozart, Schubert, Haydn, wine, water, oil, flame, solitude. But what else did he know?

Those around him expected him to enter the order. His mother, Guardianus, the butcher, the baker, the whole parish, expected him to become a friar. Probably it was Benigno's dearest wish as well, though in all their years together the old man never put pressure on him to take the tonsure and cowl. But then Benigno had scruples about the sacredness of the call. It was a matter strictly between God and the individual. Mario wanted desperately to talk to Brother Benigno, talk to him as he used to, when he was younger, when he was troubled.

Samuessen the undertaker beckoned to Mario. His brow was puckered up in a permanent frown nowadays, no merriment in his eyes; he had three sons in the army.

He said almost cruelly: "You go into the order, Mario? You don't have to go into the army if you do . . . they exempt you. What you going to do, Mario?" Samuessen's eyes seemed to size him up. "My boys don't have to make up their minds. They in the army . . . that's for sure!"

Mario had to talk to Benigno.

They were together in the second sacristy, Benigno at his desk, Mario at the cupboard which held the candles. Mario could feel Benigno staring at him. The smell of the place, a settled blend of burned-out incense, candle wax, starch from the linens, flowers, furniture oil, burnished metal, the aroma of coffee and frying eggs — a friar having his breakfast after saying mass; it was a world, a world he knew.

Benigno made a sound, a croak. It was a summons. Mario approached him. Perhaps Mario was the only one who now could understand what he was saying. "We have a chin."

Yes, a chin, chew the fat, talk. How did the old man caught up in his own thoughts, distant, how did he know Mario needed him more than ever? Mario sat down on a candle crate. He felt a boy again.

Something flickered deep in those old, gray eyes, some fragment of the past. Benigno said indistinctly: "You know why I want you with me when you were a little schizzer?"

Yes, Benigno was rummaging in the past — trying to make final arrangements?

"No, Brother."

Benigno rubbed his hands, trying to keep track of what he felt bound to say.

"It was your eyes. Your eyes. I think to myself that that boy with them eyes . . . he be killed by . . . the world . . . so I want . . . to take you here . . . with me . . ."

Benigno looked at Mario full in the face, as if to part any veil between them.

"Mario . . . Mario . . ." It was a cry. "Sometimes . . . I think I have do you . . . a wrong . . . ja, sometimes, I think I do you a wrong . . . to bring you in here . . . I have take something away from you . . . I . . . I . . ."

Mario watched the cloud come over Benigno's face. He'd lost his train of thought. He looked helplessly at Mario, his forehead wrinkled. Mario nudged Benigno's cane with his foot . . .

"Ah, it come back, ja, we were . . . going for a dop . . . ja . . . ?"

"Yes, Brother, we're going on a dop."

Slowly they shuffled along the aisles. Mario knew he would never again be able to talk to Brother Benigno about his conflict. From statue to stained-glass panels, from the grottoes to the fonts, pausing, inspecting, with the occasional parishioner coming up to Benigno saying something the old man couldn't catch, Mario would have to explain to him, and then translate Benigno's response to the parishioner. And Mario had a hand under Benigno's arm, guiding him, moving him.

Suddenly, guttering, his face red, Benigno brushed away Mario's hand: "Why you got to push me so fast? You going to a fire? You always be in a hurry. What's wrong with you . . . you ain't in no hurry to be a friar!"

Ah, it had come at last!

"You ain't in no hurry about that." Benign had his beard thrust out, his cane raised, his eyes filled with fury. He was trying to catch his breath. "You never be a friar . . . I know that . . . I know it . . ." He clutched the back of a pew. "Why you hang around? I want you to go. You hear me? *I want you to go. Get out!*"

Mario went.

On the avenue, a cop came over to him; Mario was sobbing.

"Bad news, kid? Somebody got killed over there?"

Mario put his hands over his lips to stop them from trembling: "Yes, somebody killed."

The army was no great adjustment for Mario after all his years being with the friars. He was used to following orders, being obedient, being surrounded by uniforms, used to routine. Mario made a good soldier.

He'd gotten a letter from Benigno. It was the first time he'd ever known Benigno to write to anyone. And it was written in the same way as Benigno talked.

"Why have you go away? Something I have say to you? You know I don't know what I am doing. Why you have pay attention to me? I have terrible temper. You come back right away, you hear me, Mario? You please forget whatever it was I say to you . . . forgive me little sheep . . . sometimes, I think I have trouble in my head . . . so you come back . . . I wait for you, my Mario . . . I wait . . ."

Mario wrote back to Benigno. He made no mention of what had happened between them, because it was not really between them, Mario realized; it was Mario's struggle, which had been resolved. He explained to his old friend he could not return. He was in the army. There were no more letters.

Friar Guardianus sent the telegram to the regimental chaplain. He arranged the emergency leave for Mario.

Mario found himself in the same hospital room he'd been in years before, the same view of the rooftops, the wash fluttering on the lines, the western sky. Benigno was in a coma, his head slightly raised in the bed, tubes in his nose, a line strapped to his arm. His breathing was labored, his face rosy, his beard carefully groomed, his white fringe of hair like a slipped tonsure. Mario stood there, staring down at his old friend.

The nun in charge told him it was perfectly possible Benigno might regain consciousness. Mario waited. Sometimes he dozed, sometimes he ate a sandwich provided by the nuns, sometimes he stood at the window looking out. In the distance he could see the steeple of St. Ansgar's, and beyond the flash of light from the river. They let Mario stay, not even shooing him out when the doctor came.

"He's some fighter. He has a strong heart!"

Yes, Mario could testify to both claims for his friend.

It was Maundy Thursday. And there were snowflakes in the air. It was late in the season for snow. The snow came down harder, it would spoil the chance for the Dutchies to parade to church in their new Easter finery. Yes, the snow covered the sidewalks. Baumer's bakery window would be filled with Easter sweets, the bread-dough rabbits, the hot cross buns, the stollen, and the snow would be melted from the pavement in front of Baumer's because the bakery ovens created such heat below the sidewalk.

Night came on. The Tenebrae service would be taking place in the sanctuary at St. Ansgar's, the friar chanting the matins and lauds. And those candles flickering on the triangular stand would be extinguished one after another, until a single candle flamed at the very apex of the stand. It would be the solitary light in the completely blacked-out church.

Benigno's breathing changed. But his eyes remained shut, an expression of remoteness on his face. Mario fell asleep, woke up, fell asleep . . .

The hospital grew quiet, the night deepened, the hours lagged, Mario's eyes opened, he was awake. He gazed at Benigno, on that face he loved so well; he realized it was already too late for words, now he must learn to accept the ache which comes from what is left unsaid. Mario grew stiff from watching, afraid to shift, afraid to look away, and yet it was from the watching, seeing the lift and fall of Benigno's chest, that struggle, that lulled him to sleep.

Suddenly he jerked fully awake, he caught his breath, Benigno's hand was moving. Slowly, like a man trudging a painful mile, that veinous hand toiled across the bed covering; it moved with a purpose. Mario put out his hand, they met. Benigno's hand closed over Mario's, clenching it strongly, and then it rested. In that instant, Benigno died.

Mario searched his face, expecting it to be set in fierceness but it was not. It was calm and dignified. Benigno had finally gained control of his temper. Mario glanced at the luminous hands of his watch. Two minutes past two A.M. Good Friday. Benigno had passed away on Good Friday, as he'd wished.

Somewhere, from way back, the prayer rose to Mario's lips: "Justorum, animae in manu Dei sunt, et non tanget illos tormentum malitiae: visi sunt oculis insipientium mori, illi autem sunt in pace." The souls of the just are in the hands of God, and the torment of malice shall not touch them: in the sight of the unwise they seemed to die, but they are at peace.

Just before Christmas 1944, the Germans mounted a savage counterattack. The casualties were heavy. Mario was among them.

A German medical team scouted the field, picking up the wounded, among them Mario. He had in his hands a wooden set of rosary beads. He was terribly wounded.

Eventually the Allied forces halted the breakthrough, broke German resistance, and swept everything before them.

An American medical team toured the ward of what had been an enemy behind-the-lines hospital in company with one of their captured counterparts and an interpreter. They passed among the casualties, pausing here and there to discuss the cases.

An American major's eye was caught by a pair of brown wooden rosary beads, hanging from a nail over the head of the cot. He reached out and removed them from the nail. He examined the beads, fingered them.

"They've seen a lot of use."

The German doctor, through the interpreter, said: "Yes. They served his use well. He was among the dead. He had them in his hands. It caught my attention. It's a miracle he's alive."

The major turned over the wooden crucifix. He read aloud: "Jos. Zoller, Passau." He looked toward the German.

"He's one of yours."

The interpreter answered for the German.

"If you take the rosary beads for identification, yes. But we don't know. It was all he had on him, that and a heap of bodies. No doubt his parents gave him the beads at his confirmation."

The American major leaned over the cot. "Hmmm. Doesn't make much difference in his state."

Again in translation: "Only to his people," said the German grimly.

Ultimately exchanges took place, and Mario was removed to a hospital in Munich. He was to be there a very long time. Physically he slowly recovered but because of some neurological disorder (it was thought) he seemed unable to comprehend or respond. He was known as "Joe" as he sat by the window of his ward staring at the river.

Later on he was transferred to a rest home.

Various specialists took up his case and gave various diagnoses, prescribed various therapeutic courses, all without the slightest effect upon the patient. He remained silent, eyes abstracted, a man in a labyrinth.

Searches were made among the many families named Zoller in Passau, but none came forward to claim this "Joseph Zoller." In America, Mario's family mourned a son whose remains were never returned.

Nothing seemed to reach Joseph Zoller. Even the most clownish among the patients gave up trying to get a rise out of Joe. As one of them said: "He's not wired up."

He gave no trouble at all. He was the type of patient one easily overlooked. He'd find a window and stare at the sky with the unwavering scrutiny of an astronomer on the trail of a distant galaxy.

The medical staff of the home were doubtful of any improvement in the condition of Joseph Zoller; too many years had passed with no sign of a change.

And then a most astonishing thing occurred.

Every Sunday the ambulatory patients were conducted by van to church. Because of his rosary beads, Joseph Zoller was naturally taken to the Catholic church in the village. For some reason, on that particular Sunday morning the priest came out upon the high altar to celebrate mass without altar boys. He began the mass saying his prayers and giving the responses ordinarily said by the altar boys as well. The small group from the rest home were flabbergasted when they saw Joseph Zoller rise from the pew, walk to the communion rail, open the gate, enter the sanctuary, and begin to serve mass. They heard his Latin: "Quia tu es Deus. Fortitudo mea; quare me repulisti, et quare tristis incedo, dum affligit me inimicus." For thou, oh God, art my strength, why has thou cast me off? And why go I sorrowful whilst the enemy afflicteth me?

"Joseph Zoller" had been reached.

In time Mario stood on Stanley Street. Once again he felt the powerlessness of the sleeper trapped in a dream, the same spell-like suspension of those years after the war. Mario could make nothing from what spread before him. All those contours, those lineaments, those set pieces, taken in by the quick camera work of the eye: redbrick walls, hallways, women leaning out of windows, cobblestones, kids racing along, garbage cans overturned, clothes on wash lines, all vanished. And the smells: coffee roasting, hops steaming, grease, spices, wool soaked by rain, dank alleys; smell, the quickener of memory, gone. No policeman pounding his beat, no Dutchies arguing on the curb, nothing but vacant lots, garages, empty warehouses, and on the waterfront dilapidation everywhere, piers and wharves rotting into ruin. Nothing left but the river. Had Stanley Street been bombed like Dresden?

Slowly Mario made his way eastward. Where was the steeple? The parish house? The sandstone steps? The projecting corbels? Gone! Mario shook his head, as if to rid himself of the clinging traces of sleep. There was the church. Huddled, dwarfed by the surrounding office buildings. It appeared decayed and ancient and out of place.

Shorn. Deracinated. Father Guardianus had used the word many year before; Mario had looked it up. *Deracinate*: to uproot. But who was uprooted, and what?

Inside St. Ansgar's, Mario stared, a hundred thousand sensations striking his consciousness, each one scrambling for recognition. Yes, he stood now as he had stood once with Benigno. Benigno cocking his head, straining to catch the murmurs, those deep currents whispered by the church, like a man holding a shell to his ears to hear the distant sea, Benigno had said. Yes, Mario stood now and strained his hearing: echoes, voices, the chant of yesterday.

He took a seat in a rear pew. The interior had undergone a reduction. That main altar with its crushing cross upon which the broken Christ was spread was reduced, not even life-sized. And that nave which soared was a ceiling with perceptible cracks zigzagging, and the clerestory a gallery of smallish windows.

Mario was asleep, an Alice-in-Wonderland reduction. His eyes slowly roamed the interior, the light shut out, the buildings had cut it off; only the flickering of the candle stands with their few challenges to the darkened church. Yes, Mario sat disconnected. He dangled like a link in a snapped chain. All those voices, the ceremonies, the churning of the bells, the puffs of incense, the thunder of the organ, *Christ Is Risen. Christ Is Risen.*

No, Christ Is Diminished. How torpid he was, dull, every thought coming like a sleepwalker. What had he expected? And what was time? And had the bursting shell in those few days before Christmas blown him out of his senses, caught him between floors?

What had Mario expected? A miracle? Was that it? Was Mario at heart as much of a Dutchie as all that? Had he expected a miracle? Benigno to be there somehow in presence when he entered the church, already in his beatific refulgence? Ah, it was all reduced, and Mario a pygmy. No miracles.

"They make me sick with their talk of miracles. It just be so they don't have to do nothing themselves . . . oh, ja, that what it is. Always let God do it. Ja, someday people ask you about me. And you tell them. Benigno Zoller was no saint. He was a grouchy old man . . . who never learn to control his temper."

An insistent splash of water broke into Mario's musings. He turned to see an old woman, with both her hands in the holy water font, stirring up the water, as if it were tea in need of mixing. And then she lifted her dripping hands and anointed herself. Made the sign of the cross, turned about, and mumbled some incantation.

No miracles. Mario could see Benigno with a knowing look on his face. "You see what I mean, Mario?"

Mario's fingers worked the smooth surfaces of those brown wooden rosary beads, the worn cross. Benigno was there, there as substantially as any materialization. He didn't have to come in an aura; Mario told the beads one by one. Yes, Benigno was there with him, in mind, in spirit, in memory. All that was worthwhile remained. No miracles were necessary, life itself was miraculous, and Mario had now to plunge into life.

That should be the last word. But a piece remains.

Mario's mother, every time she looked at her returned son, was convinced a miracle had occurred.

And Raphael Samuessen, the oldest son of Samuessen, now official undertaker as his father was before him, and as opinionated, made no bones about Mario's return.

He put it this way.

"How come of all those guys killed Mario was saved? Just one of those things, an accident? Oh, no. It was all part of Brother Benigno's doing. He needs Mario to bear witness when they come to investigate his case for sainthood. You mark my words if that isn't the case. Wait. Just wait."

♦ AFTERWORD ♦

My husband, Francis, and I usually worked together on his manuscripts. He got up early in the morning and wrote. I edited, proofread, and corresponded with agents and publishers. Francis worked on the manuscript of *The Witness,* as it was originally known, over a long period of time and eventually rewrote the entire work, finishing the final version in 1985. We both felt that it contained some of his best writing.

As of my husband's death in 1990 we had received no offers of publication, and later I decided to have the novel printed locally at my own expense. My son Erik stepped in with an offer to help and at that point it became a family venture. Erik enlisted the help of his daughter, Christina, who in addition to typing the entire manuscript onto their computer worked with Erik editing and proofreading while consulting my notes. Our object was always to stick with the original wording as much as possible.

After the manuscript had been printed and proofread by a number of family members we began the process of deciding how exactly to publish the book ourselves. Erik decided to make one final attempt to find a commercial publisher and contacted Steerforth Press. The rest is history.

♦

I owe a tremendous debt of gratitude to Erik, who was determined to get *The Witness of St. Ansgar's* before the public. He did not become dragged down by my moments of discouragement or put off by minor worries. In the end it is largely due to Erik's efforts, his initiative and his staying power, that the work has in fact been published.

I am also grateful to Christina, who did such a magnificent job typing and editing the manuscript. From start to finish her work was neat and precise. I must not forget my granddaughter Cora, who had earlier set about reading every work that her grandfather had written: poems, plays, novels, stories, essays, and letters. Her enthusiasm gave a large boost to my morale. Last but not least, my daughter-in-law, Barbara, asked for and then read the very first version of *The Witness of St. Ansgar's.* This act and her positive response encouraged Francis and me at an early stage of the novel's development.

As a family we are thankful to Stephen Morris of The Public Press for his help and encouragement as we looked for a publisher. His expertise was invaluable.

Finally, we wish to thank all at Steerforth Press for everything they have done to make the publication process as easy and uncomplicated as possible. In particular we must single out Roland Pease, whose enthusiasm upon reading the work made our first contact with Steerforth a positive one; our editor, Kristin Sperber, whose skill and sensitivity were very much appreciated; and to Chip Fleischer, the publisher, whose words of praise for this novel and determination to publish it will never be forgotten by a grateful family.

Florence Nielsen
Northfield, Vermont
November 2005